FIVE LITTLE MONKEYS

C. W. Johnston

This is a work of fiction. Names, characters, businesses, places, events, locales, and incidents are either the products of the author's imagination or used in a fictitious manner. Any resemblance to actual persons, living or dead, or actual events is purely coincidental.

Cover design by C. W. Johnston and Michelle Fairbanks
Book design and production by C. W. Johnston, www.cwjohnston.com
Editing by Kate Schomaker
Photograph on cover by Peter Forster (used by permission from *Unsplash*)
ISBN number: 978-1-9991578-1-4

ALSO BY C. W. JOHNSTON

Figment

To Kate, for humoring me.

FIVE

LITTLE

MONKEYS

C. W. Johnston

Five little monkeys jumping on the bed,
One fell down and bumped his head,
Mama called the doctor and the doctor said,
"No more monkeys jumping on the bed!"
Four little monkeys jumping on the bed,
One fell down and bumped his head,
Mama called the doctor and the doctor said,
"No more monkeys jumping on the bed!"
Three little monkeys jumping on the bed,
One fell down and bumped his head,
Mama called the doctor and the doctor said,
"No more monkeys jumping on the bed!"
Two little monkeys jumping on the bed,
One fell down and bumped his head,
Mama called the doctor and the doctor said,
"No more monkeys jumping on the bed!"
One little monkey jumping on the bed,
He fell down and bumped his head,
Mama called the doctor and the doctor said,
"No more monkeys jumping on the bed!"
No little monkeys jumping on the bed,
None fell down and bumped their head,
Papa called the doctor and the doctor said,
"Put those monkeys right to bed!"
—Traditional

Part One

Providence

Five Little Monkeys

Prologue

Everything changed last summer. Not so much with the bang of a starter's pistol, but with a barely noticeable, slovenly seep. It soon had an inevitability about it, like a relentless cancer.

Later, if asked, most would agree it had definitely all started with eight-year-old Becky Green. She was the first to tell someone about the Follower. Everyone laughed at her initially. Even her mom thought she'd "gotten the fever." But looking back, it was definitely Becky that first heard them.

Becky had recently taken to playing hopscotch in the mornings on Birch Street, a couple of blocks from her house. It was simply a strip of tarmac seemingly built for future development; however, there were no houses—only sky-high, thick trees surrounded it on three sides. Birch Street ended at the forest edge, as if city planners had somehow expected Providence to expand into greatness.

For hopscotch it was a perfect spot, and many years ago, some of the local kids had painted a permanent court at the end of the road in bright pink. *POT 10* had been scrawled in green paint inside the end section—the home base. A series of numbers were painted in various rectangles, squares, and triangles down the length of the court, where finally a number 1 stood in the middle of the last rectangle. Some flat stones—*luckies*—were always stacked in a hastily assembled pile beside the first rectangle, all prepped and ready for the next group of kids to arrive.

It was a Sunday morning in early July, and most of Providence was still snuggled in bed enjoying a day away from the tractor, the plow, the engine, or the commute. Sundays were always the quietest days. The Lord's Day was indeed a day of rest—though nary a soul attended Reverend Parker's ten o'clock services anymore. Providence, Washington, was tired in every way.

Becky tiptoed down the stairs. She noticed the twins as she walked by the den; they were fully ensconced in some stupid game on their PlayStation. She didn't bother saying good morning to them; they wouldn't have responded anyway.

Becky gently pushed through the door of the screened-in porch at the back of the two-story house, careful to slowly press it closed behind her. Her dad could be a bit cranky if woken up on a Sunday—*or any day, for that matter*—so she was always diligent in her silence.

Once outside, Becky happily skipped toward the side of her house, finding her shiny red bike with the bundle of white ribbons dangling from the handlebars leaning against the back wall of the garage. She pulled her helmet from the wicker basket and placed it over her head—ensuring her long, carefully braided ponytails were free on either side.

Becky had made plans to meet her best friend, Margaret Cleaves, at the hopscotch court at eight o'clock sharp. Margaret had been her "forever friend" ever since they had met in kindergarten, and they both knew they would eventually end up studying medicine together at *Harvar*, *Ox-fard*, or *Princetonian.*

Throwing the luckies, or *puppies*, as she liked to call them, was one of Becky's weaknesses. She could hop just fine and pick up the stones with ease—faster than most of her friends—but she struggled with the throw, somehow always landing on the lines so she had to miss a turn. It was not yet seven thirty, so she still had time to get some practice in.

Once she reached the end of Birch Street, Becky dismounted, carefully placing her helmet back into the basket, and gently leaned her bike against the trunk of a large cedar tree a few feet away from the court, being extra diligent to not get any scratches on it.

The sun was still behind the trees in the thick forest surrounding Birch Street, and it was cool, but Becky didn't notice. She loved being alone here, away from her disgusting older brothers. She honestly didn't know what planet they came from. They couldn't be more different than her. She liked school, enjoyed dressing up, and cared what people thought of her. Blaine was a snot-faced, foul-smelling, disinterested-in-everything, dimwitted creature; and his fraternal Franken-clone, Bobby, was no better—though he did still have his front teeth. Blaine had lost his attempting a ridiculous jump the first time riding his new BMX bike. *Idiot.*

No, being here away from Blaine and Bobby—*And, by the way, who names all three kids with the same first letter, anyway*, she often thought—her grumpy father, and her overexcitable mother was just fine for Becky. When Margaret eventually arrived, her morning would be complete.

She called herself out on the first attempt. She had tossed the lucky pretty well and even picked it up in a single, swift motion while standing on one leg. It was on her turnaround that she noticed she'd stepped on a line. "Bloomers," she muttered. It was something she'd heard her mother exclaim a thousand times. She didn't know what it meant but knew it expressed frustration.

It was during her second attempt that she first heard it.

Becky immediately stopped, standing on one leg—directly on top of the green number 9—and listened.

Silence.

She shook her head, attempting to recalibrate her focus. *Probably nothing*, she thought. She knew she had an active imagination; she'd been told as much. She then carefully hopped to the next square.

There it is again.

Becky again stopped—frozen like a blue heron on one leg. In her brain, she sifted through the logical list of possibilities: perhaps it was the wind pushing through the thick tree branches above her; or a raven, with its throaty call echoing from deep within the surrounding foliage; or maybe it was a car's engine coughing and sputtering far off in the distance; or even a woodpecker *tap-tapping* on something hard behind her.

But none of those made sense. None of those would keep perfect—albeit, delayed—time with her steps. Almost like something was mimicking her movement.

An echo.

Becky carefully lowered her leg until it touched the ground. She could feel her leg shaking as she put weight on it. She slowly turned around, looking in each direction. The silent forest seemed to be leaning in toward her. All was ghostly still.

Becky's heart began to race. Something wasn't right—she could feel it in her bones, and she knew at that moment that she needed to get home.

Now.

It was only when she took the first step toward her bike that she heard it again.

Five Little Monkeys

Chapter One

"Did you get my text, JP?" Pudgy Murtland yelled out as he skidded to a dusty stop in front of Jermaine. He was clearly animated as he jumped off his bike. Jermaine had been the first to arrive, and he had watched as his buddy furiously pedaled his bike toward him between the verdant rows of corn.

School had only recently dispersed, and once again the clan had miraculously made it through another year. All five boys had survived eighth grade relatively unscathed, and each of them had been handed a graduation certificate on the final day in June (even Lenny, who had needed every ounce of encouragement—and plagiarized homework assignments—that his friends could offer him in order to pass). With the dismal prospect of being the low men on the ladder when they moved to Pulltown Secondary in the fall, best friends Jermaine Prescott, Pudgy Murtland, Duncan Simpson, Lenny Cartwright, and Bernie "Big Balls" Maclaren had every intention of making the most of their summer.

The first few mornings of their holidays had consisted mostly of waking just before noon, followed by the inevitable systematic raiding of each other's fridges. Afternoons were any combination of online gaming, biking around town, or fishing at Swift Current Creek; occasionally they would opt to hide behind a juniper bush—in stealth surveillance mode—staring at the large bedroom window of Mrs. Baldwin. She was the widower who lived on Pine Street and who, rumor had it, never closed her drapes when she changed her clothes. While they'd never corroborated the rumor with any evidence, the thought of missing out *in case it happened* was too tempting not to check in each day. Just in case.

As towns go, Providence, Washington, itself was puny. And isolated. They didn't see it as such growing up, but it was—and still is. There were just over five blocks on either side of Main Street looking east to west; from tip to toe, there were two shops; a tiny, dilapidated Methodist church; a well-stocked hardware store; a grocery store called Langmaid's, and a lonely service station and repair garage. Providence was little more than an insignificant dot between Musgrove and Pulltown—both slightly bigger dots on the main road heading west out of Chandler, five miles south of the Canadian border.

The North Fork Nooksack River (or, as Lenny Cartwright called it, *My Sack River*) crossed Canyon Creek a few miles outside of town. Each spring, Providence was on flood watch as the melt from the mighty glaciers of the Great Divide poured down the valley on their annual western migration toward the Pacific Ocean. In 1989, "the Great Rise" did hit, almost wiping out the entire region. But Providence folks have always been resilient, and they stood together as a community—sandbagging, digging, and pumping their way back to life.

Providence was a place where you created your own entertainment. While the internet had definitely changed life, the culture had always been an outdoorsy one. Social media was only a part-time obsession in Providence, due in part because of its earthy history, but in all probability, primarily due to the frustratingly unreliable cellular and internet service.

During the school year, their parents allowed the five boys to spend Saturday nights playing their go-to games, though they could never really agree on one. "*COD* is God!" Bernie would proclaim. "*Fortnite*, any night," Pudgy would inevitably reply. Lenny didn't care, as long as it involved shooting something. It was the only time of the week that their parents allowed it to happen with any regularity—and even then, only for two hours. Ironically, much of their online gaming time was spent chatting over their headsets, planning their next adventures. By default, for generations, the woods, hills, and creeks surrounding their town had been the virtual playground of the kids of Providence.

There was a picture of Providence hanging at Langmaid's Grocery. It was taken years ago from a helicopter. From above, the tiny town appeared completely surrounded—almost engulfed—by the dense cedar forest. Other than the main road leading in and out of town, it looked like an island. "Looks like we're floating on a raft in a sea of trees," Pudgy once observed poetically as he stood at the counter buying his usual haul of gum, licorice, and sci-fi comics (Pudgy was old-school in so many ways, and the clan loved him for it). For all the kids in Providence, this was what made Providence and the surrounding area a heaven on earth. Its seemingly endless forest made for limitless opportunities.

By the first week of July, summer had taken on its own timeless rhythm. Their days were filled with adventures, and only when it was too dark to see anything did they then reluctantly return to their respective homes and crawl into bed, happily exhausted from the exploits of the day.

As usual, the clan had agreed to meet at Base Camp, Lenny's name for Farmer Granger's abandoned shed at the far end of his cornfield. Over the years it had become their official headquarters. It was their safe place. A place where they'd all examined, in awe, the various positions of the Kama Sutra Duncan had showed them on his phone; where they had vaped on their first e-cigarette, measured each other's peckers, practiced their moves for the sixth grade Christmas dance; and where they had all watched Lenny bravely putting his own dislocated shoulder back into place after a bike jump gone wrong. Base Camp was their refuge and whence all adventures began.

"Did you hear me? Did you get my text?" Pudgy's real name was Oscar, but no one ever called him that. To Jermaine, and everyone else who knew him, he was Pudgy, and he would even introduce himself as such.

Pudgy wasn't fat, but he was jiggly, and he moved the awkward way overweight kids do. When he ran, his knees appeared to knock together, and he seemed to always have one hand tucked behind his back, yanking up the shorts that were typically hanging halfway down his ample butt. Everyone who knew him thought Pudgy was honest, insightful, and deeply kind.

Jermaine shook his head and waited until Pudgy was directly beside him. "Outta juice," he replied, holding his phone out toward Pudgy. It was dead from spending the morning watching mindless TikTok videos.

"Ugh. Typical," Pudgy replied, plopping down beside Jermaine, attempting to catch his breath.

It was obvious to Jermaine that something was bothering his friend. "What's going on, Pudgy?"

"You ain't gonna believe what I just heard happened."

"What?"

"Becky Green. It's batshit crazy."

"What happened to her?"

Pudgy caught a glimpse of the other boys approaching on their bikes. "Hold on, wait until they're all here."

Jermaine looked up and could see that Lenny Cartwright was, as usual, well ahead of the other two boys. Lenny was physically mature compared to the rest of them—he already had some hair in his armpits, which impressed them to no end. He was the strongest, and he proved it daily. Any encounter with Lenny was usually followed by a stinging slap to the backside, a bruising knuckle sandwich to the arm, or a purple nurple—a painful twisting of the nipple. Lenny thrived on spooking, teasing, bullying, and just about anything else that would ensure they all understood who the top dog was. Lenny was the protector, the brave one—the alpha male. While Jermaine was the natural leader, all decisions made by the group had to be ratified by Lenny, and the boys were fine with that.

Once Lenny reached Base Camp, as was his habit, he ejected himself off of his bike while it was still moving at a fast pace, allowing it to continue on without him. Jermaine smiled as he watched Lenny walking nonchalantly toward him. It was like a scene from an action movie—the calm-and-cool hero walking toward the camera, ignoring the mayhem behind him as the bike smashed into the large elm tree on the other side of the shed. Lenny sat down beside Pudgy and grinned. "'Sup, boys."

Bernie Maclaren arrived soon after, riding a well-worn silver-and-black bicycle. He had built it from scratch after his father had told him he hadn't yet earned the right to have a proper "store-bought" bike. Undeterred, over the course of a few months, he had gathered and assembled the parts necessary to create one himself. It wasn't pretty, but it rode like the wind; all the boys had been impressed with his ingenuity.

Bernie was the smallest one in the clan. Even though he was almost half the size of the others, Bernie was a year older, having repeated kindergarten. His nickname, Big Balls, had come from Lenny years ago. None of them reckoned his balls were any bigger than anyone else's, but his pint-sized frame made it seem like he had an enormous package, and it just stuck.

"He's all prick and bones," Lenny used to tease. "Prick and bones with two basketballs."

While most people in town called him JP, Bernie was the only one who called Jermaine by his real name. His mom and Jermaine's mom were "besties" when they were growing up, so he heard Jermaine's mother call him by his full name often enough. It just seemed natural to him, and Jermaine liked it when he did; it felt familiar.

Despite Bernie's tiny frame, he had the deepest voice of all of them, which seemed odd to folks when they first met him and peered down at the diminutive boy speaking. "Who knows," Jermaine had often commented, "maybe it's because he has big balls."

"Hey," Bernie said, his oversized green helmet wobbling on top of his head as he sat on the ground on the other side of Jermaine.

"Hey," Pudgy and Jermaine replied in unison.

Duncan Simpson was the last to arrive "Whaddup, boys?" he yelled happily to no one in particular, letting his bike drop haphazardly to the dusty ground. Jermaine always laughed at Duncan's painfully pitchy, verging-on-breaking voice. An inevitable, involuntary crack would often rudely interrupt his sentences, awkwardly collapsing them into a lower octave.

Duncan was by far the tallest member of the clan, made to look even taller by his long, slender neck with the thin white puka shell necklace his parents had brought him from Hawaii dangling below his protruding Adam's apple. His bulbous head appeared to balance precariously atop his skinny-as-a-bean-pole body. He was pale all year long, and his skin appeared almost transparent.

Duncan was nerdy, awkward, fearless, and, Jermaine thought, funny as all get-out. Duncan once stuck a firecracker up his ass and lit it in front of everyone, just to see if it would make him jump. It did, and they all had visited him at the Providence Health Clinic for the next two days during his recovery.

Once all the boys had assembled beside the shed, Jermaine stood up. "Pudgy's got something to tell us. Let's head into Base Camp."

The boys followed Jermaine as he pushed through the creaky wooden door. Jermaine closed it behind them, and they sat down on their designated milk crates. Though the dank, dusty shed was small, it was the perfect size for their clan. There were two windows on the side walls, which allowed for light in the summer. In the far corner, there was an old metal desk on which they would often light candles when it was too dark to see anything. Jermaine looked over at his friend. "Okay, spill it, Pudgy. What's going on?"

Pudgy's blue eyes were bulging with anticipation above his rosy cheeks. His bright ginger hair, as was his preference, was shaved close to his skull. He wore his favorite *Captain America* T-shirt, accented with the various food and grass stains collected over time. Pulled high on his ample tummy were his baggy silver basketball shorts. On his feet were his go-to green flip-flops, worn down on the inner edges.

Pudgy slowly stood up and began to dramatically recount what he'd overheard from his mom's phone conversation with Becky Green's mother. It was a rare occasion when he was the center of attention, and he relished the moment.

"Becky's mom was startled awake Sunday morning by Becky's frantic screams. 'Mom! Dad! Wake up!' she'd screamed." Everyone knew he was embellishing it a tad, but it seemed appropriate. He had always been a good storyteller.

"She was beside herself. Absolutely unconstotable."

"Inconsolable," Jermaine corrected.

"Huh?"

"Never mind. Go on."

"Right...anyway, when they settled her down, they found out that she'd been waiting for Margaret down at the hopscotch court at the bottom of Birch." Pudgy lowered his voice and began slowly moving in a circle, making eye contact with each of his friends. "It was early in the morning, and she'd been all alone."

Duncan, Lenny, Bernie, and Jermaine all unconsciously leaned forward toward Pudgy. Jermaine felt a slight chill of goose bumps race down his arms. Pudgy could certainly spin a yarn.

"Seems she was practicing on her own while waiting for Margaret."

All four boys nodded. It made sense; they all knew Becky and Margaret were inseparable.

"That's when she heard—now this is the weird part..."

Jermaine could tell that Pudgy seemed to pause not only for effect but because he was still not fully confident on how to properly explain the next bit.

"Heard what, bozo?" Lenny asked anxiously. All the boys knew that patience was never one of Lenny's strong suits.

"Well, that's the crazy thing," Pudgy continued, undeterred. "Seems it was footsteps—following her own footsteps." Pudgy winced, as if it even sounded weird to him now that he'd said it out loud.

"*Whatcha* mean footsteps, Pudgy?" Duncan asked, his voice cracking halfway through the question.

Pudgy appeared to think about it for a second, then looked over at Duncan. "Stand up, Dunc."

"Huh?" The clan knew that Duncan wasn't the quickest horse on the racetrack, but he was always game.

"Just stand up for a sec."

Duncan looked around at his friends, then stood up. His orange tank top was ridiculously loose on his tall, scrawny frame. Duncan's mass of curly brown hair only accentuated his height. Lenny had once reckoned he was well over seven feet tall, but Bernie and Jermaine had measured him last May, and he had topped out at five-ten-and-a-half. They both agreed it was still an impressive height for a thirteen-year-old. "Okay, now what?" Duncan asked.

"Move over here so there's some space." This was getting interesting, and the boys quickly shuffled their milk crates backward, giving Pudgy and Duncan more room.

Pudgy then pulled Duncan close to his chest but facing away from him, and Duncan seemed to tower above Pudgy. "Okay, now take two steps forward," Pudgy ordered.

"Why—" Duncan was about to ask when Lenny yelled, "Just do it, dickweed."

Duncan shrugged his shoulders. "Okay, okay…one, two," Duncan counted out as he took two full steps forward.

Pudgy waited briefly, then took two exaggerated steps right behind him, ensuring everyone heard him pounding his feet onto the shed floor.

"I don't understa—"

"Now take three more steps and then stop," Pudgy directed. Duncan did as he was told, this time in silence.

One step, two steps, three steps…

Pudgy hesitated, then did likewise.

One step, two steps, three steps…

"I don't get it," Duncan confessed. "Becky was followed by someone?"

"That's the thing." Pudgy lowered his voice again. "There wasn't anyone there. She'd looked around…but nothing. Still, every step Becky took, she could hear one following shortly after."

"What're you saying, Pudgy?" Jermaine asked. The boys all looked over at Jermaine, then back at Pudgy.

Pudgy cleared his throat as Duncan took his seat again. "Becky told her mom that when she had decided to run toward her bike to go home, the footsteps ran behind her as well."

The four boys again all leaned forward toward Pudgy.

"And…" Pudgy's voice was now an almost inaudible whisper. "When she got on her bike and began pedaling, she could hear the footsteps running behind her…*all the frickin' way home*."

The silence in the cabin was palpable. This was just about the freakiest thing Jermaine had ever heard, and he could see on the faces of his friends that they felt the same way.

Pudgy continued. "My mom says Becky hasn't been out of her bed ever since. Her folks were worried sick that she'd gotten a fever or something, and they even called the doctor. But get this…the doctor said she's fine."

"Holy moly," Bernie exclaimed.

"My mom says Becky apparently swears what happened is the God's truth."

Jermaine knew that Becky Green was one of those know-it-all, little do-gooder types—"precocious," as his mom had often described her. But he also knew that it was unlike her to make stuff up. Unlike Duncan Simpson, who once told his teacher that his father had earned a Purple Heart even though he'd never set foot out of Whatcom County.

No, one thing was evident to Jermaine: Becky Green was no liar.

The shed felt muted. No one seemed to know how to respond. After a few minutes of silence, it was Duncan who spoke first. "No harm in searching the area, is there, boys?" Duncan was always the first one up for an adventure. Without hesitation, they were all in. Curiosity and boredom were the combustible fuel that generated most adventures for their clan.

Within seconds, they'd mounted their bikes and were racing toward Birch Street with Farmer Granger's knee-high corn slapping at their legs along the way. Lenny took his usual position at the front—*pole position*, as he liked to call it. He was soon followed by Jermaine, Duncan, Bernie, and finally Pudgy—desperately attempting to cling to the peloton.

It was July in Providence, and adventure was in the air.

Chapter Two

As he always did, Lenny dismounted his bike before he'd come even close to a full stop—allowing it to continue on without him, wobbling and weaving and eventually careening with a loud *bang* into a tree some twenty feet from where he stood. It always gave him a chuckle, and he smiled widely. One by one, the clan pulled up behind him. Pudgy was panting heavily as he dismounted, finally joining the others at the hopscotch court.

"Whatcha think, JP?" Duncan asked, gazing at the foreboding forest surrounding them.

Jermaine also surveyed the thick woods on all three sides of the dead-end road and waited until he was satisfied that all appeared as it should. Though he noticed it was unusually quiet, he could sense no imminent danger for the clan. "Let's split up and look for footprints or any sign of someone in the woods. Whoever was following Becky could still be in there, so be careful. Let's go in about fifty feet or so. Keep close enough so that if you find something, you can yell and we'll all hear."

Everyone nodded. It sounded like a solid plan.

"Duncan, you and Lenny take the north side here." Jermaine pointed behind him. "Bernie and Pudgy can go south." He moved his arm toward the other side of the road. "I'll take the end of Birch."

Again, the clan nodded and shuffled into their designated teams, each secretly glad that they had a partner.

"Let's meet back here in twenty minutes. Remember, if you see anything, scream out loud so we'll all hear you."

"Whoop! Whoop!" Duncan hollered happily. He loved adventures.

❖

Once they had dispersed, Pudgy tried desperately to keep up with Bernie but soon lost sight of him. There was a lot of deadfall, and the thick ferns made progress difficult for everyone. Pudgy was soon panting heavily again and eventually stopped to catch his breath. "Hey, Bernie, can you hear me?"

"Yup. I'm up here." Bernie's deep voice echoed from the steep slope above him. Pudgy could tell he was falling behind Bernie.

He may have been the smallest in the clan, but no one questioned Bernie's bravery. When given a task, he would be hell-bent on accomplishing it—no matter what the danger. While most believed Bernie's dogged determination emanated from constantly having to prove himself due to the obvious fact that he was so much smaller than everyone in his grade, the clan knew that it was more than this. It was because of his dad.

Bernie's father was a harsh man. Bernie's older sister got off easy compared to what Bernie had to go through at home. Stacking wood, cutting the lawn, cleaning the eaves, or digging fence posts, each day there were at least two or three jobs for Bernie to complete before he could hang out with his friends. His sister *may* have had to help her mom around the house a little, but claiming she had piano lessons to prepare for, or a test she needed to study for, allowed her to easily manipulate her parents. Most of the chores inevitably fell on Bernie.

Bernie never complained. The boys were always impressed with his stoicism. They knew—as Bernie knew—it was always best to avoid agitating his father. Bernie's dad was prone to dark mood swings.

"Don't get too far ahead. I can't keep up," Pudgy yelled, scrambling over a fallen log. He was panting from the exertion of moving through the thick foliage. "Bernie?" Pudgy yelled as he stopped. "Bernie, I'm going to turn ba—"

Bernie suddenly appeared from behind a tree up ahead. He was smiling and carrying something white. It took a while for Pudgy to recognize what it was. He soon realized it was the skull of a small animal, perhaps a raccoon or a squirrel. Bernie was holding it up in front of his face and moving the jaws up and down. "Hello, Pudgy," Bernie teased. "Do you want a kiss?"

"Too funny, Bernie." Pudgy sat down on a stump to catch his breath. "You see anything?"

Bernie was about to answer when the most horrific scream came from behind them. It sounded like Lenny.

Bernie dropped the skull and began to bolt toward the scream.

"Hey, wait up, Bernie," Pudgy pleaded, standing and pulling his silver shorts up as he began to follow. But Bernie was already out of sight.

❖

Another scream. "Help! Help!"

Jermaine could hear the others running toward Lenny from deep within the woods on either side of him. "Hold on, Lenny," he screamed.

"Help!"

Jermaine then heard Duncan, who'd obviously arrived on the scene first: "You bastard!" Jermaine could just make out the sound of the other boys yelling as well as he pushed through the final mass of thick cedar boughs.

"You stupid idiot!" It was Duncan again.

When Jermaine finally arrived, Lenny was on the ground, rolling around in laughter. The other boys were standing around him, fuming.

"Not funny, Lenny. Not funny at all," Bernie scolded.

"What the hell you doing, Lenny?" Jermaine asked.

"Ha! Come on, JP. I had you all fooled. Scared the crap outta all of you. Haha!" Lenny's eyes were watery from laughing so hard.

"What's going on?" Pudgy was completely out of breath.

"Just Lenny being a douche again," Bernie explained calmly. "Come on. Let's get back to the bikes."

"I scared all of you guys. Joke's on all of you!" Lenny said defensively as he got to his feet and brushed himself off. "I had you all believing I was gettin' murdered. Ha!"

"Douche."

❖

It was after Dr. Lewis's second visit to Becky Green's bedside that she'd suggested to the girl's bewildered parents that it would be best for Becky to see a specialist; more specifically, a counsellor or a therapist—perhaps even a psychiatrist. It had been three days now, and whatever hallucination or delusion Becky had experienced last Sunday had scared her enough that she'd remained unwilling to leave her bed. She wouldn't even go to the bathroom; her mother had to provide her with a bedpan. Gladys Green was hysterical. She couldn't believe the difference in her beautiful Becky.

Even her brothers, Blaine and Bobby, had feigned sympathy, even going as far as bringing her a *Cool Magazine* with Taylor Swift on the cover that they'd bought at Langmaid's Grocery. They knew this wasn't like Becky; though young, she was usually so unfazed and independent.

Margaret had visited a few times. She was as confused as everyone. When she had arrived on Birch Street last Sunday to meet Becky, she'd assumed Becky had been late, so she played a bit of hopscotch on her own. When Becky hadn't shown up by nine, Margaret had gone to look for her at her house. It was then that she'd learned what had happened—like her parents, she was a little freaked out that she'd been playing on Birch Street on her own as well that very morning.

When Becky's folks had questioned Margaret about what she experienced on Birch Street, she explained to them that she neither saw nor heard anything when she was there. Margaret was frightened for her best friend. Becky had always been the confident one—and her idol.

That first night, Gladys had visited her daughter's room before going to bed. Becky was still wide awake and staring out the window.

"Hey, baby-girl. How ya doing?"

Becky was pale and disoriented. She turned and looked at her mom. "Mommy, I'm scared."

Gladys sat on the bed beside her and began stroking her forehead and cheeks. "I know you are, baby-girl. But you're just having some bad dreams. You're gonna get better. I promise." Gladys forced a smile and leaned down to kiss her daughter's head.

"Mommy, will the Follower come into the house too?"

"The Follower?" Gladys asked softly, swallowing hard. She had begun to shiver.

"I hear it outside."

Gladys instinctively looked out the window. It was dark, and the air was motionless. She tried to steady her nerves before responding. She felt short of breath, and she had never been so confused. "Outside, honey?"

"I can hear it walking around the house. It's waiting."

Gladys pulled her daughter close to her chest. She could feel her own heart beating against Becky's head. She was beyond frightened and felt helpless not knowing how to protect her daughter. She didn't want to ask but knew she had to. "Waiting for what, baby-girl?"

Becky pulled away from her mom so she could look up at her. Her face was pale and gaunt. She was shaking, and sweat had formed into tiny beads on her brow. Tears were welling in the corners of her eyes.

"Waiting for me to walk again."

❖

Jermaine's mother spent most of her days playing online poker, bingeing Netflix, and sipping vodka from a coffee mug. Summers were the worst, as Jermaine was around enough to witness how inebriated—and agitated—she became as the day wore on. His mom usually prepared dinner just after lunch while she was still relatively sober. It would be ready for his dad to heat up when he got home; she would—more often than not—already be in bed at that point, feigning sleep when he returned. The next day she usually claimed that she'd had a migraine, or tummy ache, or some other nonsense. Jermaine knew that his dad knew, though they never talked about it. Truth was, they rarely spoke about anything.

As soon as they were sixteen, Jermaine's two older brothers had left for fairer climes, both looking for work in California. His dad was a welder for True North Pipelines, spending five long days each week in Chandler, about a two-hour drive from home; he rarely got home before eight o'clock each night.

When all was said and done, Jermaine's daily adventures with his best friends in the world were the only thing that kept him sane. While he loved his folks, the clan was his *real* family, and he adored each and every one of them.

❖

It was her fourth consecutive day and night without getting out of bed. Becky still struggled to sleep, and she could not get comfortable, tossing the damp sheets off her body when she was too hot, then dragging them back over her when the shivers started. She looked at the ballet dancer clock on her bedside table. It was two thirty in the morning.

Becky listened to the gentle breeze outside her second-story window. She could just make out the leaves on the giant oak tree shimmering silver and gray in the moonlight.

She was busting for a pee and tired of using the pot her mom had provided for her. She thought about it. The bathroom was only halfway down the hall from her bedroom. *Just a short distance.*

She listened again for any sign of the Follower. All was silent.

Come on, Becky. You can do this.

Becky sat up in bed and turned on the light. She then slowly shifted her legs over the side until her feet were only a few inches above the floor.

Fifteen steps, tops. You can always run back if you hear anything, she thought, urging herself into action—willing herself to face her fear.

Becky shuffled her bum closer to the edge—ever so slightly. Her toes were now almost on the floor. She listened for any sound of footsteps outside. All she could hear was the prattle of leaves outside her window in the cool evening breeze.

❖

Bernie still had on his green bike helmet as he sat at Jermaine's kitchen table—he often forgot to take it off when he finished biking. They both had just polished off a bowl of Cheerios and were now joyfully slapping together peanut butter and jelly sandwiches.

Jermaine's mom "had a headache" and was watching the *Waco* series in the den. The boys were going to meet at Base Camp after lunch to discuss plans for the afternoon. Lenny wanted to go fishing in Swift Current Creek and maybe catch some frogs for bait. Pudgy thought that was a good plan and was game. Despite their aversion to her, Duncan, Bernie, and Jermaine wanted to visit Becky Green to see for themselves how messed up she was. Weird things like this didn't happen much in Providence, and it might be pretty cool to see.

The clan would have an official vote, and as was their rule of law, majority would win. There was a good chance visiting the Greens' house would be on the agenda.

"Pass me the jelly," Jermaine said.

Bernie had already made his sandwich and had taken a massive bite out of it. Peanut butter dripped down his chin onto the table. He smiled at his friend as he slid the sticky jar toward him.

"What do you think happened to Becky?" Jermaine asked, unscrewing the jar and jabbing his knife into it.

Bernie swallowed and took a big gulp of milk. He wiped his face on the sleeve of his hoodie. "Beats me. Probably gone nuts."

"Yeah, maybe. It's just not like her, though, you know?" Jermaine wasn't convinced. Something spooky had happened to Becky Green, and he wanted to learn more.

"Maybe some creeper was hanging in the woods and she just didn't see him," Bernie said.

"And ran behind her all the way home? And she didn't see him when she looked back? It just doesn't make sense."

Bernie licked a blob of peanut butter from his knife. "It's messed up, that's for sure," he mumbled.

Pudgy, Lenny, and Duncan were already at Base Camp when the other two boys arrived after lunch. All of them were outside enjoying the sun. Pudgy was leaning against a tree, reading his latest Cosmic Ghost Rider comic, Lenny was sitting on the steps of the shack, whittling a stick with his jackknife, and Duncan was attempting, with limited success, to do handstands against the outside wall.

"Hey, JP. Hey, Big Balls," Lenny greeted without looking up from his handiwork.

"Whatcha making, Lenny?" Bernie croaked as he dismounted his bike.

"Spear. For catching frogs," Lenny replied, as if it should have been obvious.

"Cool," Bernie commented, taking a seat beside him—his green helmet still on his head.

Duncan gave up on the handstands and joined Bernie, hitching himself in tight beside Lenny to watch him work. Lenny was good with his hands—just like his dad, who was a logger. In his spare time, his father loved to carve wooden sculptures with his chainsaw, and the Cartwright property was scattered with horses, cows, ducks, and pigs, all carefully—*and loudly*—crafted.

"So whatcha say, boys?" Jermaine thought it was time for a vote.

"Fishing," Lenny offered, again without looking up.

"Pudgy?"

"I'm with Lenny. Who wants to go visit a girl, anyway? Fishing for me." Pudgy looked back at his comic.

Jermaine laughed, then looked at Duncan. Tufts of grass were sticking out of his curly hair and wedged into his puka shell necklace from his many failed handstand attempts. "Dunc?"

"I wanna find out about the footsteps. I say we visit Becky."

"Me too," Bernie added.

"That makes three of us," Jermaine said with a smile. "Guess we're heading to the Greens' place, boys."

"Ugh," Pudgy protested, but he knew the rules.

"Okay," Lenny agreed begrudgingly. "But we're fishing after, deal?"

"Deal," Jermaine agreed.

"Up, up, and away!" Duncan chirped happily, jumping up and dancing toward his bike like a madman.

❖

Becky Green's mom answered the door. It was obvious she'd been crying. Her eyes were red and swollen. All five of them immediately felt bad for disturbing her.

"Hi, Mrs. Green. Sorry to bug you. We were just wondering how Becky was doing. We heard she'd had a bad experience," Jermaine said calmly. The rest of the boys were glad it was him speaking. He was good with words, and they knew Mrs. Green liked him.

"I see," Gladys Green said softly. She held a Kleenex to her nose and closed her eyes. "She's not doing well, Jermaine. She took a turn for the worse last—" Gladys began to cry again; she was obviously distraught. All the boys, except Jermaine, looked awkwardly down at their feet.

"Who is it?" Mr. Green's voiced boomed from behind her.

"It's Jermaine Prescott and the boys," she replied with a sniffle, turning her head.

"What do they want?"

"Just checking on Becky." Gladys looked up again and tried to smile at the boys. She leaned forward and lowered her voice. "Jermaine, you all should run along now. Dr. Lewis is on her way over here again."

Jermaine nodded. "Yes, Mrs. Green. Tell Becky we just wanted to check in on her. Let us know if you need anything."

"Thanks, Jermaine. Thank you, boys."

With that, all five boys made their way back to their bikes they'd left scattered across the Greens' front lawn.

"Time for some fishing," Lenny announced.

Jermaine stopped at his bike and looked back at Becky Green's large white house. The drapes of her bedroom were shut tight.

❖

By noon the next day, the news had spread to every household in Providence. Becky had been taken by ambulance to Bellingham. Pudgy had heard it was for something called "psychiatric evaluation."

Pudgy's mom had briefly spoken with Gladys Green. She was beside herself with worry. Apparently, Becky had experienced another episode—this time much, *much* worse.

The clan immediately planned to assemble at Base Camp for Pudgy's update. They couldn't get there fast enough, though they'd had to wait until Bernie finished mowing the lawn. It was half-past two when they finally sat down together in the shed. Pudgy waited until they were silent before he stood up to speak. He hiked up his silver shorts and took a deep breath. He was beginning to like his new role as town crier.

"You know when Mrs. Green told us yesterday that Becky had taken a turn for the worse? Well, guess what happened?" Pudgy paused for effect. Jermaine could tell he loved milking a good story.

"What, bat fart?" Lenny asked, obvious frustration in his voice.

"Well, it was the night before we visited. It was late at night—sometime after two in the morning—when everyone was still fast asleep. Her parents were startled awake by Becky's screams. She was hollering at the top of her lungs and running down the stairs!"

The boys sat still on their crates. Jermaine looked around at his friends. This was getting crazy.

"Her dad ran to try to find her, but she'd already sprinted out of the house. He looked everywhere, up and down the entire town. He finally found her, and get this…" Pudgy paused again.

Lenny looked as if he were going to burst. "What, dipshit?"

"He found her at the end of Birch Street."

"Holy moly," Bernie said. The group let out a collective breath.

"She was hollering to nobody, 'Leave me alone! Go away!' She was hysterical. Mr. Green had to grab her and hold her tight because she was trying to run into the woods. He had to carry her all the way back home."

"Holy moly," Bernie whispered again.

The boys were quiet, attempting to digest this latest bit of news.

"That's some crazy stuff," Duncan mumbled.

"Sure is." Pudgy lowered his voice. "Apparently the footsteps happened again. And know what she called it?"

It was obvious that Lenny was going to lose his mind, so Pudgy continued.

"She called it the Follower."

Chapter Three

The news out of Bellingham was not good. According to Pudgy's mom, Becky Green required round-the-clock sedation as they ran the blood work and monitored her vitals. Gladys Green had hastily found a cheap motel near the inpatient center in the behavior health unit—a twenty-bed section on the main campus of PeaceHealth St. Joseph Medical Center. No one was sure how long Becky might be staying there.

Becky's brothers and father remained in Providence, and nobody saw much of them. Pudgy figured they were just passing the time watching the idiot box and waiting for Mrs. Green to call. It seemed the entire town was as confused as the Greens. How could something so personality-altering happen so quickly?

As the days passed, the clan eventually fell into a routine again. It was an unusually hot July, and swimming in Swift Current Creek was on the agenda each afternoon. Duncan liked to do backflips off the small embankment—or *backflops*, as Lenny called them. With his tall frame awkwardly spinning through the air like a flailing pretzel, legs and arms akimbo, he would inevitably splat down on the surface of the water horizontally, rather than executing the intended vertical entry, much to the delight of the clan. It caused no end of laughter from the boys. "He puts the ham in hammy," Bernie once described Duncan, and it was true. He was a master mood-lightener and first-class entertainer.

The days were long and the evenings warm. It again felt like a great time to be a kid in Providence. It was just when calm had returned to the area that news of Pickle Town's disappearance reached them.

❖

"Little Pickle" Town was seven years of age. She was the only child of Dave and Morgan Town, the owners of Your Town Hardware, a small, cluttered store smack-dab in the middle of Providence. Your Town Hardware was the go-to place for any "bits 'n' bobs" needed on any given day.

"Hey, Dave, you got any three-quarter-inch CPVC? I need about a hundred feet."

"Yup."

"Hey, Morgan, I'm looking for that doohickey that connects to the end of my vacuum. You have one?"

"Yup."

It was uncanny that a shop so small always seemed to have that one particular *thingamabob*, *thingy*, or *whatchamacallit* that the good people of Providence needed. The Towns were gold in Providence, and when news got out that Little Pickle was missing, every able man, woman, and child immediately headed to their house on Maple Street. By the time Officer Thompson had driven in from the police station in Musgrove, the search was already on.

It was just after three o'clock in the afternoon when Pickle had headed out to walk Taco, their aging beagle, around the block. At about quarter-past three, Mrs. Town had heard Taco scratching at their front door. There was no sign of Pickle. Dave and Morgan spent the next twenty minutes running around the neighborhood and knocking on doors. No one had seen her.

As soon as they were convinced Pickle was well and truly missing, Dave Town hastily organized the surging group of volunteers into units and devised a rough search plan. Morgan would stay at home in case Pickle showed up and to meet the police when they eventually arrived. Everyone was asked to keep their cell phones close by and to ensure they had loaded the

Towns' home phone number into their contact list. Morgan would arrange a phone tree if there was any news.

Jermaine Prescott suggested to Mr. Town that he and the boys could concentrate on the woods around Birch Street. They'd already gotten a good understanding of the terrain from spending so much time in the area. Mr. Town nodded weakly; he was obviously distraught.

❖

As they were racing on their bikes toward Birch Street, Jermaine yelled out to the others that they should search in their original groups—the ones they used when looking for Becky's follower. He also reminded them that they should stay really close to each other and ensure they always had visual contact.

"Told ya," Pudgy yelled at Bernie between heaving breaths. He clearly didn't want to be left behind by Bernie again.

"And no funny stuff, Lenny. This is serious," Jermaine warned.

As they rounded the corner to Birch Street, Duncan pulled ahead of the others and popped a wheelie, balancing on his rear tire. "Whoop! Whoop!"

Once they had all reached the hopscotch court (and Lenny's bike had finished tumbling and flipping over the curb after he'd jumped off), all five boys quietly broke off into their groups and headed into the woods, making sure they were always checking for each other visually and vocally.

Jermaine worked his way alone up the small embankment at the end of the road. As he had found the previous time, there was little room to maneuver through the thick undergrowth. He stopped and looked to his right; he could just make out Bernie's green helmet through the trees. Pudgy would be just behind him, no doubt.

Jermaine looked to his left and saw Duncan awkwardly moving under a large cedar limb. He was about to keep going when he heard Lenny's voice.

"Found her!"

"What? Jeepers," Duncan yelled. "Hey, boys! Boys! Lenny found her!"

"You better not be fooling around again, Lenny," Pudgy screamed from fifty feet away.

This time Lenny wasn't joking. Jermaine and Duncan were the first to arrive beside Lenny. Little Pickle was sitting on a log right in front of him, her feet tucked up underneath her. She was crying and shaking. "Hey, Pickle," Lenny whispered as he moved closer.

Pickle didn't look up. She just stared at the ground, whimpering softly and sniffling.

Jermaine couldn't believe what he was looking at. How the little girl managed to get herself lost in the woods like this was beyond him.

Lenny moved right up to the tiny girl. "Hi, Pickle. It's us. Lenny, Duncan, and Jermaine. You okay?"

No reaction.

By the time the other two boys arrived, Lenny had already lifted Pickle up into his arms. She was freezing cold and shaking violently. "Call her mom, JP. Tell her to bring a car," Lenny demanded. He was already walking back down the embankment, weaving his way under and over the thick foliage, heading toward Birch Street.

Jermaine pulled his cell phone from his pocket as he followed Lenny back toward the bikes. As he dialed the Towns' home phone number, he knew Lenny was going to be a hero.

❖

"Catatonic." That was how Dave Town described Pickle's state to the small group of neighbors still gathered outside their house that evening. The sun had long ago set, and, as was the norm in many parts of the Pacific Northwest, the cool evening air descended on Providence in a sudden wave. Despite the hour and the temperature, people were keen to show their support for the Town family. There was also an ulterior motive. One that nobody would publicly admit. But it was there—like an itch that wouldn't go away until it was rubbed. Beneath their hushed whispers, there was another sound. That of their own inner voices, deep within the confines of their minds. What they really wanted to know was if Becky Green's "issues" were at all related to Pickle Town's "issues." And if they were, then *what the hell was going on with the children of Providence?*

Dr. Patricia Lewis side-stepped the small gathering as she exited the Towns' home and quickly made her way to her car. There was an immediate hush as she left; they knew enough not to ask her any questions, and she knew enough not to offer anything. It was a private matter. It was the Towns' story to tell.

Recently graduated, young, and single, Dr. Lewis was begrudgingly putting in her required time in this rural charge until her dream job in Seattle, or Portland, or LA—or wherever—became available. Providence was nice enough and the folks were kind to her. But it wasn't the kind of work she'd originally gone into medicine to do. She liked the action of the city, the sound of screaming ambulances, and the adrenaline-inducing mayhem of an ER unit. She preferred it on the front line.

To Dr. Lewis, the surrounding area, which included Providence, Pulltown, and Musgrove, was only a stopover at the beginning of her career. It was to be a sleepy, hassle-free commitment where she could gather some experience, get back some energy that medical school had sucked from her, and do some extra studying on the side.

As she walked down the Towns' pathway toward her car, she had a sinking feeling that whatever was occurring with Pickle and Becky might only be the beginning. She'd heard of mass hysteria in medical school. *Psychogenic illness*, as she recalled. She knew that there could be an epidemic-like, rapid spread of hysteria once a community got caught up in something. Sure, it's only two kids, but both had suddenly turned into sniveling messes and seemingly lost their minds with no discernible explanation. Was this the tip of an iceberg? Lewis hoped to hell not.

Closing the door of her Honda Fit, Patricia Lewis turned on the radio, hoping for some nice jazz or a few golden oldies to soothe her nerves. These two cases had tested her mettle—*and* her ability. She was about to start her car when she looked up and saw Dave Town running toward her.

He was crying.

❖

The coroner's report stated that Pickle Town died at 9:47 p.m. Her cause of death was nebulously determined to be from traumatic shock, though even the coroner was reticent about the explanation. However, from a purely scientific point of view, it was clear that Pickle's body had simply shut down. Her blood pressure had fallen so rapidly that the flow of oxygen to her vital organs—more specifically, her brain and heart—had been drastically reduced in a matter of minutes. He had never seen the like in someone so young and healthy—for no apparent reason.

Dr. Lewis had been with Pickle when she died, only minutes before the ambulance from Pulltown had arrived. She had been shaking violently and was cold as ice when she suddenly stopped. Her eyes opened wide, and she looked over at Lewis as her breathing ceased. The horror in Pickle's eyes had shaken the doctor to the core.

The funeral was to be held in a week and a half, on the first weekend of August. The Towns requested that, in lieu of flowers, a fund be set up in Pickle's name. This money would be donated to the ASPCA; Little Pickle loved animals—especially Taco.

The day after Pickle's death, the boys decided to assemble at Base Camp to chat things through. Lenny in particular had been unusually quiet ever since her death was announced; they could tell he'd been deeply affected by Pickle's passing. What initially had been a euphoric moment for them—finding a lost girl—had quickly turned into a devastating loss for the community. It felt like a giant pall was hanging low over Providence.

Jermaine waited until Pudgy had closed the shed door before he spoke. "You boys did well finding Pickle. Lenny, you were amazing. You were a hero." Jermaine could tell Lenny was hurting, but he also knew he'd never admit it.

"Whatcha think is goin' on, JP?" Duncan asked quietly. "I mean, first Becky and now Little Pickle?"

"And both of them on Birch," Bernie quickly added, his baritone voice echoing loudly in the shed. He could barely see past his helmet, which was riding low on his forehead.

"Yeah, that's crazy weird, don't you think, JP?" Pudgy asked.

Jermaine *had* been thinking about it. A lot. It certainly seemed a strange coincidence that not only had Becky been playing hopscotch on Birch Street when she first heard the Follower, it was also where she was found the night she ran away. And recently, Little Pickle had been found in the woods just off Birch Street.

Pudgy was right. It was crazy weird.

"Dunno," Jermaine replied. Unless he had a good idea of what he was talking about, he'd always chosen to be a person of few words.

The boys sat for a minute pondering the events of the last few weeks. They were all lost in their own thoughts when Duncan's loud voice exploded through the silence.

"Who wants to see me light a fart?" Duncan always had a way of breaking the ice. With the recent heaviness lately, they all agreed it might be good medicine for them to see Duncan light himself on fire again.

"What is it with you and lighting things near your butt, Duncan?" Lenny asked, half smiling.

"A Blue Angel, baby! Whoop! Whoop!" Duncan yelled, pulling a lighter from the stash of Base Camp supplies collected over the years in the top drawer of the metal desk beside him.

❖

Archie Truscott was eighteen years old and had Down's Syndrome. He was the youngest of three children. Like most older siblings in Providence, Archie's older brother and sister had since moved away, leaving Archie living at home alone with his loving parents, Tammy and Yarl Truscott. They knew he would be living with them their whole lives.

Archie was a kind-hearted, popular member of Providence. He often hung out at Langmaid's Grocery, helping bag groceries. Everyone loved Archie and his positive outlook on the world.

Pudgy was riding his bike to Langmaid's when he noticed Archie, who had been walking toward him, suddenly turn right and begin to head down Birch Street. Curious, Pudgy picked up the pace, rounded the corner, and caught up to Archie when he was only partway down the street.

"Hey, Archie. Whatcha doin'?" Pudgy pulled alongside Archie and slammed on his brakes, which caused Archie to stop as well.

"Hi, Pudgy. That's a nice bike," Archie observed. He was smiling, like he always did.

"Thanks. Where you headed?" Pudgy unconsciously looked toward the end of Birch Street.

"One day I want a bike like that one."

Pudgy grinned. "I'm sure you'll get one someday, Archie."

Archie's smile widened, and he again began walking. Pudgy dropped his bike and ran after him. "Hey…hey, buddy. What's going on? Where you going?"

Archie stopped again. "I don't know." He seemed confused and looked more serious. "They're leading me here."

Pudgy felt a chill go down his spine. He quickly surveyed the woods on either side of them. "Who's *they*? Who is, Archie?"

Archie rubbed his head and looked back at Pudgy vacantly. "I don't know."

Pudgy knew he had to get him out of there. "Hey, you wanna ride my bike? I can help you. We can go to Langmaid's. Would you like that?"

Archie grinned. His eyes were beaming with joy. "You mean it, Pudgy?"

"Yeah, come on," he said, grabbing Archie's hand and leading him back toward his bike. As he helped Archie get his balance on the seat, he chanced one more glance behind him at the thick, dark forest. He wondered what was happening to his town.

❖

It was the next day when Pudgy visited Langmaid's Grocery to stock up on some wine gums that he saw Archie sitting on the bench on the covered porch outside. He had his hands over his ears, and he was rocking back and forth. His eyes were closed, and he was mumbling to himself.

Archie's mother, Pam Truscott, was just coming out of the store as Pudgy arrived.

"Hey, Mrs. Truscott."

"Morning, Pudgy. Sorry I can't chat. Archie's having a bad day. Not sure what's got into him," she explained, hurriedly taking one of Archie's hands. He pulled it away and immediately put it back over his ear. "See what I mean?"

Pudgy sat down next to Archie and touched his leg. Archie opened his eyes and looked at him. He was still rocking back and forth and mumbling.

"Archie, do you want to ride my bike again?" Pudgy asked loudly. "You can ride it to your home."

Archie stopped rocking and looked over at the shiny red bike that was leaning up against the wooden porch post in front of him. He nodded and reluctantly pulled his hands from his ears. Mrs. Truscott smiled at Pudgy and mouthed, "Thank you."

Once he had Archie on his bike, he walked beside him, holding the bike firmly as Archie slowly pedaled. Mrs. Truscott walked on the other side of the bike.

"Just don't understand it. He's been acting like this for over a day now."

"Maybe it's just a fever or something," Pudgy lied. He knew deep down that it could well be something else. Something he didn't really want to think about because it scared the *bejeezers* out of him.

After Pudgy helped him through the front door of his house, Archie immediately ran to the couch in the living room and sat down with his feet tucked underneath him. He held his ears, closed his eyes, and began rocking again.

Mrs. Truscott looked worried. She again thanked Pudgy and moved to sit beside Archie. Pudgy let himself out, closing the door behind him. He needed to talk to the boys.

❖

The clan met at Base Camp after lunch. They listened as Pudgy described what he saw with Archie. After some debate, the consensus was that perhaps they were all getting a little high-strung from everything. It was probably a coincidence. Just because Archie was acting weird didn't mean he had met the Follower, whatever that was.

"Besides," Lenny added, "we all like Archie and all that, but he is…you know, a retard."

"Down's Syndrome, Lenny. Nobody says *retard* anymore," Pudgy corrected. "But remember I said I saw him heading down Birch Street yesterday. Still a coincidence?"

No one spoke for a while. It was Jermaine who broke the silence. "Chances are Archie had heard about Becky and Pickle, and he got confused and went to Birch Street. Who knows? What we need to do is clear our heads. It's summertime, let's have some fun today and forget about Becky, Pickle, and Archie for a while."

"Whoop! Whoop!" Duncan hollered.

Bernie smiled. "Whatcha thinking of, Jermaine?"

"Not sure. Any suggestions?"

"Could finish the bike jump out at Knotty Point," Pudgy offered. "And watch Duncan bail again."

The others laughed, remembering the classic Duncan moment when he missed the landing and ended up head down in a blackberry bush. It took the four of them to get him out relatively unscathed.

"That could be good," Jermaine replied.

"My dad's carving a moose. Even put a prick on it, like the real thing. You should see it. It's gotta be a foot long," Lenny said, holding his hands apart to emphasize the length.

"Cool," Bernie chirped. "We could go see the prick first and then head out to Knotty Point. I gotta be back by four o'clock, though, as my dad wants the hedges clipped before supper."

"Okay, hands up for that plan. The prick, then the point," Lenny said.

All five boys had their hands in the air. It was time for an adventure.

❖

Lenny's dad was at the far end of the backyard and busy working on the moose sculpture when the boys arrived. He was dressed in a tight T-shirt, his muscles bulging beneath. His dirty overalls hung loosely off his taut body. He was wearing large yellow ear protectors, so he didn't hear them arriving. The boys dropped their bikes and moved closer, observing him deftly maneuvering the chainsaw underneath the massive life-size moose sculpture.

Simon Cartwright looked up when he noticed the boys approaching but didn't stop what he was doing. He offered a slight nod and continued working. The boys all stood about five feet away and leaned down to look below the belly of the enormous moose. Lenny hadn't lied; the pecker was impressive.

After a while, Lenny signaled that it might be best to head back to the bikes. The noise was deafening, and they only had a bit of time to work on the bike jump before Bernie had to head home.

They grabbed a couple of shovels from Lenny's garage and jumped back on their bikes. They would be at Knotty Point in twenty minutes. They agreed that a quick stop at Langmaid's Grocery for some candy would be essential.

As they arrived, they noticed a stranger—an older woman—sitting on the bench outside Langmaid's. She appeared to be alone. "Looks like a drifter or a gypsy," Lenny whispered to Jermaine as they pulled up to the store and dismounted. Lenny's bike kept going and careened into the concrete base holding the large propane tank beside the store.

"One of these days you're gonna kill somebody with that bike, Lenny," Jermaine commented as he hopped up the steps beside him.

They all nodded politely at the exotic-looking black woman as they entered the store. The odd diversity of her attire was an assault to the senses.

She wore a long multicolored cotton dress with a well-used gray woolen sweater pulled tightly over top. A bright red-and-orange headscarf held up her graying dreadlocks in an unkempt mass on top of her head. Dark mascara was worn thick and purposeful around her eyes. Silver jewelry dangled from her ears and wrists, and a small silver nose ring was looped through one of her nostrils. Deep, weathered crevasses lined her dark face and bespoke her age—giving her a wise, otherworldly look. Her teeth were white as pearls as she smiled warmly and waved at the boys as they entered the shop.

Mrs. Langmaid was behind the till as they entered. Lenny had once suggested to the boys that she was about a hundred and fifty years old. She was ancient, that was for sure, but most of the boys didn't think she could be that old.

The boys secretly referred to her as Mrs. Yep-uh-haa, because it was usually the only thing she ever said.

"I'd like some licorice."

"Yep, uh-haa."

"And maybe a Snickers."

"Yep, uh-haa."

"All I got is ten bucks. Can I charge it to my mom?"

"Yep, uh-haa."

"Oh, never mind, I found some change. Here."

"Yep, uh-haa."

Her gray hair would tumble over her face, and her crooked fingers would shake as she pressed with all her might on each of the keys on the large antique till, triggering its familiar *cli-cling* sound as the drawer opened so she could make change.

Today Lenny asked her if she knew who the lady was on the front porch. Mrs. Langmaid shook her head without looking up. She rarely made eye contact.

"Must be just somebody passing through," he suggested.

Mrs. Langmaid shook her head again. She briefly looked up and pointed out the window across the street, toward the Breaches' house. Lenny noticed that their "Room for Rent, Nightly or Weekly" sign had been taken down from the front window.

"She's staying at the Breaches'?" Lenny asked.

"Yep, uh-haa," Mrs. Langmaid said, reaching a hand past Lenny and taking money from Pudgy, then handing him his comic book.

As the boys left the store, they all snuck another glance at the peculiar woman sitting on the bench. She smiled again as they mounted their bikes. Bernie and Duncan carried the shovels this time; Jermaine and Lenny promised to carry them home. They all knew Pudgy would struggle, so they never asked him to carry it.

It was time to head to Knotty Point.

❖

The next morning, Jermaine Prescott woke up late. He'd had trouble sleeping; an unnerving sense of dread kept him awake most of the night, and no amount of tossing and turning would rid him of it. His mother was in the kitchen when he finally came down. She looked as though she'd had a worse night than he'd had.

"Dad left already?"

"Two hours ago. You slept in."

"Yeah. Tired, I guess."

His mom nodded. "Toast?"

"Sure," Jermaine replied, sitting at their large kitchen table. It used to be a place of joy when his brothers were still living at home. Family meals were something to look forward to. It was a time when their mom had engaged with them, and their dad seemed to have more time on his hands. Now, like the table itself, Jermaine felt abandoned and empty.

"What's on today?" his mother asked without looking at him directly. He knew she was trying to hide her red, swollen eyes.

"Dunno. Lenny wants us to fish with him at Swift Current Creek," Jermaine lied. He had no idea what the boys wanted to do today.

"Fun," she replied, feigning interest. "I've got another migraine, so I'm going to go lie down for a while. Your toast should be ready soon. Love you." With that, she offered a quick smile, wrapped her housecoat tight around her, and left the kitchen; the strong, stale scent of her heavy perfume lingered after she left.

By ten o'clock, Jermaine had pulled up to Bernie's house on his bike. His friend was digging a trench beside the walkway that led to the backyard. "Hey, Jermaine," he greeted with a smile.

"Whatcha doing?"

"Dad wants a trench drain," Bernie replied flatly.

"For what?"

"Helps get water away from the house." Bernie's short dark hair was wet with sweat.

"When you done?"

"Dunno. Maybe a half hour? Wanna help?"

"Sure."

"There's a pickaxe around back. You can loosen the dirt for me."

"Cool," Jermaine said, rounding the corner of their house.

After five minutes of silent digging, it was Bernie who suggested what Jermaine had been thinking about most of the night. "What do you say we check out the woods around Birch Street again today? You know—just in case we find something."

Jermaine didn't reply right away. He wasn't yet convinced it was a great idea. On the one hand, there were too many unanswered questions, and fumbling around in the woods might not make things any clearer. It might only serve to stir up confusion and suspicion from folks in Providence.

On the other hand, what if they found something—whatever that something was? One thing seemed obvious: Birch Street and the surrounding woods seemed to have drawn—*lured?*—Becky Green and Pickle Town to it.

And maybe even Archie Truscott, had it not been for Pudgy diverting him. But why? Besides, the boys could also be susceptible to whatever was lurking there.

"I say we stay clear until we know more," Jermaine finally offered. "Folks might get freaked by us poking around just yet."

"Yeah. I guess," Bernie replied.

After they'd finished the trench, they hopped on their bikes and headed to Base Camp. When they arrived, Pudgy was already sprawled out on the grass outside the shed, reading a comic book and chewing on a long thread of red licorice. Lenny was practicing throwing a spear at a tree. Duncan hadn't arrived yet.

"Hey, Lenny," Jermaine called out.

"Hey, JP. Hey, Big Balls," Lenny replied, picking the spear up and examining the point. "Seen Duncan?"

"Nope. I thought he'd be here by now," Bernie replied, shifting his green helmet back on his head and sitting down beside Pudgy. "Got another piece of licorice, Pudgy?"

"Sorry, was my last one," Pudgy replied without looking up.

"Whatcha wanna do today, guys?" Jermaine asked.

"Hunt frogs," Lenny quickly replied. "Or squirrels, or something. This spear is a killing machine."

Pudgy looked up from his comic. "Pine Street. Check in on Mrs. Baldwin. Jackie Parr said he caught a glimpse of her in the bedroom yesterday."

"Really?" Lenny turned around to look at Pudgy.

"Yup. Didn't see anything, but you never know." Pudgy turned back to his comic. He loved ones with lasers and robots.

Bernie suggested heading out of town to ride the logging roads on Smoke Mountain.

Pudgy stuck his tongue out and blew it hard. "Pass on that one, Big Balls."

Jermaine smiled. "Okay, when Duncan gets here, we'll have a vote."

❖

Duncan Simpson knew he was a little late to meet up with the clan, so he was riding fairly quickly down Main Street. He was almost past Birch Street when out of the corner of his eye he saw something at the end of it, near the hopscotch court. Something small and brown.

Slamming on his brakes and leaving a juicy skid mark on the road beneath him, he stopped and turned to get a better look. It was a dog, and it was barking furiously at the woods at the end of the road. Duncan turned his bike toward it and rode down the short dead end. He soon recognized the dog. It was Taco—Pickle Town's dog.

"Hey, Taco," Duncan said softly, laying his bike down on the hopscotch court and moving slowly, trying not to frighten him. "Hey, buddy." The dog seemed oblivious to his presence and continued to bark frantically toward the forest.

"What's up, little guy?" Duncan stood beside Taco, and despite the heat, he felt a rush of goose bumps shiver up and down his body. He then leaned down and gently stroked the old beagle's head. It was hot and wet. He'd obviously been there awhile.

Duncan looked up at the woods to try to determine what it was that Taco was going nuts about, but there was nothing other than the tall cedars and thick foliage surrounding the pavement. Then Taco abruptly stopped barking. Duncan looked down at his eyes; they had gone foggy and gray.

At first Taco wobbled, and then he slowly crumpled to one side onto the hot pavement.

"Taco?" Duncan reached down to feel him. The dog had stopped breathing.

The sudden silence was unnerving, and Duncan looked up again; it seemed like the trees were even closer now. He decided that he would pick Taco up and walk him back to the Towns' house. There was no way he could ride with him—Taco was just too big; he would collect his bike later. *Poor Mr. and Mrs. Town were going to be devastated—again*, Duncan thought. Duncan felt horrible for them and dreaded having to be the one to tell them.

Duncan scooped Taco up in his long arms, careful to support his head on his bicep. The dog felt heavy, the way dead things do, and Duncan pulled him close to his chest. It was when he turned and began walking toward his bike that he heard the footsteps behind him.

Chapter Four

When Duncan hadn't shown up at Base Camp by two o'clock, Jermaine and Lenny both texted him. When they didn't get a reply, Jermaine suggested they go for a ride and have a look around Providence for him. They would start at the Simpsons' house at the end of Main Street; chances were his folks had left him a list of chores to do, though Lenny suggested that Duncan had probably blown himself up by sticking some dynamite up his ass. Nonetheless, they decided to have a look anyway.

As they were riding by, it was Bernie who spotted him sitting on the curb at the bottom of Birch Street. It looked like Duncan was cradling something in his arms. "Hey, hold on, boys. There he is."

All four of them slammed on their brakes. Duncan was sitting alone at the end, staring at the ground. His long, pale legs were crossed underneath him on the curb. He appeared to be holding a dog.

❖

Lenny reached him first, dismounting his bike at full speed, letting it torpedo into the dense undergrowth at the end of the road. He trotted up to Duncan and came to a jump stop. "Whatcha doin', Dunc?" he asked. Lenny bent down. "Hey, is that Taco?"

Duncan sat motionless, hugging the dead dog tight against his chest. The other boys arrived right behind him, dropping their bikes near the hopscotch court, and moved beside Lenny. "Duncan?" Jermaine leaned forward. "Is that Taco? What happened?"

Duncan said nothing.

"He's not speaking, JP." Lenny stated the obvious.

"Taco looks dead," Pudgy observed, wheezing a little from the brisk ride.

"Duncan? Hey, Dunc, it's us," Jermaine said, sitting down next to his friend and putting his arm around him. Duncan was sweating profusely. His eyes were glazed, and it was obvious that he'd been crying.

Lenny sat down on the other side of him. "Dunc?"

Duncan didn't look up.

"Hey, buddy. What's going on? What happened to Taco?" Jermaine asked.

Nothing.

"Talk to me, Dunc." Jermaine was whispering now. He rubbed Duncan's shoulders. "Tell us what's happening."

Duncan slowly lifted his eyes and looked directly at Jermaine. "It happened." His voice was barely audible.

"What happened?" Jermaine asked, looking up at the faces of his friends. They all seemed as confused and frightened as he was.

"Footsteps…"

"What footsteps, buddy?" Jermaine whispered. He immediately wished he hadn't asked. He knew the answer.

"The Follower."

❖

Try as they might, they could not convince Duncan to unfold his legs and stand up. He kept shaking his head and squeezing Taco's limp body close to him. Lenny suggested they just grab him and haul him to his feet, but Jermaine said no. They had to get him to come to his senses.

"How about we help you to your bike? We can all ride like the wind to Base Camp," Jermaine suggested quietly.

Duncan peered up at his friend. After a moment, he nodded in agreement.

"Okay, let's leave Taco down here on the ground. We can get him later," Jermaine instructed. Duncan released Taco into Jermaine's arms and watched him gently lay the dead dog on the grass beside the curb.

Lenny then took control, bossing the other boys into position around Duncan, ensuring they could all get a hold of the tall boy in order to hoist him up. When they were set, Lenny did the countdown. "Three, two, one—lift."

Duncan quickly rose to shoulder level. The four boys carefully walked him toward his bike. When they were standing beside it, Pudgy reached down with one hand and lifted it so it was upright. They carefully lowered him onto his seat.

"Okay?" Bernie asked.

Duncan nodded again.

"All right, boys, let's give him a push, then let's get on our bikes," Lenny suggested. "One, two, three—*push!*"

Duncan almost lost his balance with the sudden acceleration but managed to gain control. He began to pedal, at first slowly, then rapidly. Pudgy, Jermaine, Lenny, and Bernie followed suit, jumping on their bikes and taking off after him. They would be at Base Camp in ten minutes.

❖

By the time the five boys had reached the abandoned shed at the far end of Farmer Granger's cornfield, Duncan was a complete mess. He had been screaming the entire bike ride, lifting his feet up to kick at the air—his body flailing wildly on his bike.

"Go away! Leave me alone! Stop it!" he had screamed incessantly; his eyes were wild, and he was terrified. All four boys rode beside him the whole way, attempting to calm him down and urge him on. When they eventually arrived at the shed, Duncan jumped off his bike and stood motionless on the dusty dirt path in front of Base Camp.

The boys dismounted and immediately encircled their friend. Each one of them was scared to death and worried for Duncan. "What the hell is happening," Pudgy asked no one in particular. They'd never seen their happy-go-lucky friend ever act this way, and it was freaking them all out. *Big time.*

Duncan was hyperventilating and staring vacantly at the ground. Lenny moved closer and gently put his hand on Duncan's shoulder to calm him. "It's okay, buddy. We are all here with you. You're safe."

Jermaine decided to take control. "Let's carry him into Base Camp. He can sit on the desk in there."

Without hesitation, the four boys sprang into action, lifting Duncan high enough above the ground that his feet didn't touch but low enough to maneuver his tall frame through the front door of the shed. He offered no resistance.

Once inside, they gently lowered him onto the rickety desk against the far wall. One by one the boys pulled their milk crates close to the desk and sat down; all of them were breathing heavily and sweating—both from the intensity of the ride as well as from the thick humidity of the impending rainstorm.

"Whatcha think, JP?" Lenny asked. Everyone was looking for an explanation. If anyone would have one, it would be Jermaine Prescott.

A rumbling of thunder reverberated across the cornfield. The air was heavy and thick; the clouds were building to the west, and it was getting darker in Base Camp.

Jermaine was quiet for a moment. He looked up at Duncan, his long, scrawny legs dangling over the edge of the desk, six inches above the floor. His arms were wrapped tightly around his chest, and he was shaking. His friend's mound of curly brown hair was wet from sweat, and his pale skin looked translucent in the ambient light of the shed. "How you doing, Dunc?"

Duncan looked down at Jermaine. His eyes were filled with dread. "Followed me…here," Duncan whispered.

Jermaine nodded. "I understand." He looked at the other three in the room, then back at Duncan. "We are in this together, Dunc. You're not alone, understand?"

"That's right. All for one, and one for all," Bernie quickly offered, pushing his green helmet well back on his head.

"So shall it ever be," Pudgy added with a forced smile. He pulled a small pack of Skittles out of the front pocket of his shorts, ripped it open, and poured some in his mouth. He always ate when he was nervous.

"We're right here with you, buddy," Lenny added, standing up and looking out the window beside him. It was brown and dusty from years of neglect, and a large spider web covered the entire pane. "Rain's coming, JP. Whatcha wanna do?"

Jermaine stood and peered out the window himself. In the distance he could just make out the dark clouds racing across the menacing sky. The storm looked like it was going to be a big one. He knew that they should probably get Duncan home, but he also knew that Mr. and Mrs. Simpson were away for the week, visiting his dad's mother in Eugene, Oregon. Duncan's older brother, Kevin, was the only one around and the person in charge. Kevin worked at the gas station most days and was probably not at home. The last thing they wanted was to leave Duncan on his own right now. "We'll wait it out here," Jermaine stated, sitting back down and reaching out and rubbing Duncan's leg.

"I gotta head out for a bit. I got some chores. I'll come back here right after I'm done, I promise," Bernie said, glancing at his watch. Jermaine pulled his cell phone out and looked at the time; it was almost four thirty. Rain or no rain, he knew that Bernie's dad would kill him if he didn't get the recycling collected before supper. There was no rhyme or reason why it had to be done before supper. It just did.

Pudgy and Lenny looked at each other. Jermaine could tell that they were thinking the same thing: anyone heading out there alone after all they'd been through had some nerve. Say what you will about little Bernie "Big Balls" Maclaren, they all knew he was one brave son of a gun.

After Bernie had departed Base Camp, the remaining clan members sat in silence. There wasn't much more anyone could say. All of them understood that their lives had been changed forever.

❖

Bernie Maclaren took the shortcut across Farmer Granger's cornfield, maneuvering his bike through the rows of stalks as he made his way toward Providence. The wind was picking up, and he was determined to get home before the rain hit. When he finally reached Main Street, he stood up to coax the maximum speed out of his homemade bike, pounding his short legs against the pedals.

He was almost at Birch Street when he suddenly remembered Taco. They'd left the poor bugger lying on the grass at the base of Birch Street. The thought of leaving the dog out in the pouring rain made him uncomfortable, and he reluctantly slowed down as he reached the corner, coming to a complete stop at the top of Birch Street.

Bernie could hear the thunder rumbling behind him. The storm was almost upon him, and the wind had picked up dramatically. The thick branches in the forest at the end of Birch Street were moving willy-nilly, violently whipping in every direction.

The last thing Bernie wanted to do was to venture down to the end of Birch Street on his own, especially after witnessing what had happened to Duncan. But then he thought about the Towns and how much they'd been through lately with the death of their Little Pickle. They deserved to know about their dog.

Taco's only a hundred feet away. A quick pick up and turnaround. You barely have to stop. You can do this, Bernie thought.

The first large drop of rain sounded like a loud slap on his helmet. The dank, ominous smell of the approaching summer storm filled the humid air. Thunderstorms in this part of the Pacific Northwest were a rarity. Their occurrence brought an added sense of expectancy.

Don't do it, Bernie. Just go to the Towns' house and tell them where they can find Taco. Leave him there, Bernie, another voice in his head urged. *It's their problem. Not yours.*

Another crack of thunder and more raindrops.

Screw it, Bernie thought, getting back up on his bike and frantically pedaling toward the spot where they'd left the dead dog.

A blinding flash of sheet lightning sizzled above him, quickly followed by a nerve-shattering *CRACK!* as the thunder cannonaded around him—the inevitable grumbling, moaning sound of its echo dissipating into the distance. Bernie pedaled harder.

Only a few more feet.

The rain was now ricocheting off the pavement in giant explosions of silver. Bernie could barely see as the pellets pounded painfully against his face. As he approached the end of Birch Street, he swerved toward the curb, leaned back, and jumped his bike up onto the side of the road into the tall grass that lined it, slowing down as he approached the place where they'd left Taco.

Bernie knew he'd have to stop—ever so briefly—in order to scoop the heavy beagle up. He'd no intention of staying longer than he had to. He wasn't sure what the plan was in terms of carrying the dead dog; perhaps keep him balanced on his knees somehow. He'd work it out when he got there.

Bernie scoured the area ahead as best as he could in the conditions, not wanting to chance riding his bike on top of Taco. To his left, he could make out the dark outline of the hopscotch court beneath the rivulets of water racing down the street beside him and knew he must be near the spot. It was then that he saw a white object sticking out of the grass ahead of him. It appeared to be the exact spot that Jermaine had put the dog down earlier that afternoon. *Why's it white?* he thought, squeezing the wet brakes on his handlebars, causing his bike to shudder and slide until he came to a full stop. He then slowly stepped off his bike.

KA-BOOM!

Another powerful thunderclap erupted above him; Bernie instinctively ducked, his green helmet falling over his eyes. The wind picked up again, whirling around him in unpredictable gusts and causing the long tufts of grass to shiver and dance around him.

Bernie's heart jackhammered against his chest as he pushed his helmet back again, attempting—with little success—to wipe the deluge of water from his eyes. The rain lashed down around him as he leaned forward, trying to determine what the white object was in front of him.

He then realized what he was looking at. "What the—" His whisper was lost in the loud wind.

Bernie swallowed hard, briefly looking up at the swirling forest surrounding him. It took every fiber of nerve to remain focused enough to turn his bike around, jump back up onto it, and begin hightailing it away from Taco, from the hopscotch court, and from Birch Street altogether.

Bernie was not going home after all. He would head directly back to Base Camp. They were not going to believe what he'd just seen.

❖

The rain was pummeling the tired wooden roof of Farmer Granger's shed. The walls whined and creaked like an old galleon. Duncan still hadn't moved from his perch on top of the desk.

"How ya doing, Dunc?" Pudgy yelled above the din, wrapping his hoodie around the shoulders of his friend.

Duncan shook his head slowly. He wasn't doing well.

Jermaine had found some candles among their stash in the drawer of the desk and lit four of them; the light, though minimal, was comforting. The distant clap of thunder and subsequent drone of it rolling through the valley eased the tension somewhat. The worst of the storm had passed.

Ten minutes later, Bernie burst through the Base Camp door unexpectedly, frightening his friends half to death. He moved directly to the middle of the room and stopped. He was soaking wet, and his eyes were as wide as saucers.

"What the heck, Big Balls," Lenny yelled.

The sudden entry caused Pudgy to drop his pack of Skittles onto the wooden floor, spilling brightly colored candies in every direction across the room. "Jeepers, Bernie. You scared the crap out of me!"

Jermaine was perplexed. "You done your chores already? What's going on?"

Water was dripping from Bernie's soaked clothing and forming a puddle beneath him. "Taco," he mumbled vaguely.

"What about him?" Jermaine asked calmly. His friend was acting peculiar.

"I went down to get him. I thought, you know, that we shouldn't leave him out in the rain," Bernie said.

Lenny, Pudgy, and Jermaine all looked at each other and then back at their friend. Jermaine knew they were all thinking the same thing: Bernie had gone down to the end of Birch Street.

Alone.

"I went to where you put Taco down in the grass, Jermaine," Bernie explained, his deep voice quivering. "But—" Bernie paused. It was obviously too weird to explain.

"What, Big Balls?" Lenny chimed in impatiently.

"He's nothing but bone. A complete skeleton. No fur, no flesh…nothing. It's like he's been dead for years," Bernie explained awkwardly. It was evident he was still trying to digest what he'd seen himself.

"Whaddya mean? Like an animal got him?" Pudgy asked curiously. Jermaine nodded as well. He was equally confused how a dead dog left just over an hour ago could now be a skeleton.

Bernie shook his head. "No. Not like that at all. It's like it happened years and years ago. It's a faded white skeleton of a dog. In the exact position where Jermaine left Taco."

Duncan pulled his legs up onto the desk and crossed them beneath him. He hugged himself tight again and began rocking back and forth.

Jermaine stood up and placed an arm around Bernie's small shoulders. He was soaked to the skin. "You okay?"

Bernie nodded. "Yeah. Just freaked out, you know?"

Jermaine hugged him close. Bernie was one brave kid.

"Jeepers creepers," Pudgy added. "What the heck's going on in Providence?"

No one seemed to have an answer. That is, until Duncan broke the silence.

"The Follower."

Chapter Five

It was nearing seven thirty, and Pudgy stated what was on most of their minds. "We can't stay here all night, guys. I'm hungry, and my mom has been texting me wondering where I am. What are we gonna do?"

Jermaine had devised a plan. Duncan would stay with him tonight; he'd explain to Duncan's brother that he was having a sleepover. They would ride like the wind to his house—Jermaine's mom would likely be half-sauced in front of the television. She wouldn't notice things were amiss; the boys could help get Duncan in and then head to their own homes.

"Bernie, let's leave the Taco story here at Base Camp. From now on, you saw nothing and heard nothing about the dog. Make sense? The Towns will just have to deal with a missing dog."

Bernie nodded. "Roger."

Jermaine knew that Bernie's main worry now was trying to explain to his father why he hadn't returned earlier to tend to his chores. He had never been allowed to have a cell phone—the only member of the clan without one. His father just expected to see him at the required time. Period. It might not be pretty for Bernie when he got home.

"Duncan, do you think you can ride?" Jermaine asked.

Duncan didn't reply. He was looking paler as the afternoon wore on, and Jermaine knew it was going to be a long night.

Lenny stood up. "Dunc, let's get you on your bike. We gotta get going now."

"Whaddya say, buddy?" Jermaine moved in front of his friend, staring into his vacant eyes.

Duncan eventually nodded in agreement. He appeared to understand that staying in the shed all night was not a good option.

After a few clumsy attempts, the clan managed to carry the lanky boy outside and balance him on his bike. The ground was muddy and slick, and after a gentle push, he began pedaling on his own. The rest of the boys jumped on their bikes and quickly caught up to their friend.

Duncan was already yelling at something beside him.

❖

Jermaine was right about his mother. They could see the flickering of the television's light coming from the den, and when they peeked in, she appeared to be fast asleep in the chair. When all was clear, as quietly as they could, they carried Duncan up to Jermaine's room. Once there, they plopped him on the bed.

Jermaine walked them back downstairs and saw them out. "Thanks, guys. I'll keep you posted if I need you."

They all nodded. They were well and truly freaked out. "Thanks, JP. Good luck," Pudgy said, turning with the others and picking up his bike. Lenny volunteered to ride to Duncan's house to let his brother know about the impromptu sleepover.

By the time Jermaine got back upstairs, Duncan was asleep on his bed, so he pulled an extra blanket and pillow from the hallway closet and lay down on the floor. He would work out the details of explaining it all to Duncan's brother and his own parents in the morning. Now, he was exhausted and more than a little frightened.

He must have fallen asleep fairly quickly, because the next thing he was conscious of was the morning light beaming through his window onto his face. It felt warm and comforting, and he lay there with his eyes closed for a minute, enjoying the peace. Then his eyes shot open.

Duncan!

He suddenly remembered that Duncan had spent the night and sat up to look over at his friend.

"Dunc?"

The bed was empty. Jermaine looked around his room, but his friend was nowhere to be seen.

And the bedroom door was open.

❖

Jermaine searched his entire house. His dad had already left for work. His mom was in the den, sitting in her pink housecoat and holding a large silver coffee mug. He vaguely heard her mumble good morning to him as he descended the stairs.

Within minutes he had jumped on his bike, noticing Duncan's was still lying in the front yard where he'd dropped it last night. He headed straight to the Simpsons' house, not sure how he would explain things to Duncan's brother, Kevin. He'd cross that bridge when he got there.

As he was passing Langmaid's Grocery, he saw the same crazy-looking lady sitting on the front porch even though the store was yet to open

He suddenly thought she might have seen Duncan, so he swerved his bike toward her and came to a stop by the front steps.

"Excuse me, I'm Jermaine. I'm wondering if you might have seen my friend come by here. A tall, skinny guy named Duncan."

The woman leaned forward and smiled. "Strange things happening all around these parts." Her voice was deep. Her accent was thick and exotic.

"Pardon me?" Jermaine's mind was racing, and he was sick with worry.

"Kids going missing, hearing strange sounds. Footsteps leading them places. Makes them go insane, methinks."

Jermaine was about to leave, but something about her made him curious. She seemed to know a lot considering she'd only just arrived. "What do you know about these things?"

"More than you'd think. Let's just say it's why I'm here." The woman sat back and smiled again. "I haven't seen your Duncan friend. You better hurry, though. Chances are he's next."

Jermaine's eyes were wide with fear as he tried to comprehend what the crazy woman was going on about. He knew one thing. He had to find Duncan.

Jermaine quickly turned his bike around and began to pedal away. He could hear the crazy woman yelling behind him. "You best hurry now, *mon ami*."

❖

It was already half-past eight in the morning by the time Jermaine had pulled into the Simpsons' driveway. He dropped his bike on the lawn and ran to the front door, pounding on it with all his might.

A few moments later, Kevin opened it. He appeared to be about to head to work. "JP? What the hell is all the banging about?"

"It's Duncan. He slept over last night, but when I woke up, he was gone. Did he come here? Have you seen him?" Jermaine was breathless.

Kevin smiled. "No, I haven't seen him. Probably went to that stupid fort you nerds have out on Granger's farm or something. I gotta go to work. Let me know if you find him." Kevin brushed past Jermaine, closing the door behind him. He then stopped, as if he had something more to say; he looked back at Jermaine and smiled again. "Oh, when you see him, tell that gnarly grommet that it's his turn to cut the lawn this week."

Jermaine watched Kevin walk down Main Street and tried to figure out his next move. He had a bad feeling about this, and deep down he knew it might have something to do with Birch Street.

He decided to stop at Bernie's house first. When he arrived, Bernie was already outside sorting the recycling beside the house. Jermaine knew that he'd have been punished for not being home on time to do it last night. Bernie looked up as Jermaine coasted into his driveway.

"Bernie, Dunc's gone," Jermaine said before he'd even come to a full stop. "I need help looking for him. This is getting insane."

Bernie's mouth dropped open. "Okay, give me a minute to finish this up, and then I'll tell Mom I'm heading out."

Jermaine pulled out his phone and texted Lenny and Pudgy. He told them to meet up with him and Bernie at Base Camp as soon as they could.

By ten o'clock the four of them had assembled in the shed. Jermaine told them all that he knew. He also told them about his weird encounter with the crazy lady at Langmaid's Grocery. She seemed to know things, which the others also thought was bizarre.

"It's like she understands what's going on here or something," Jermaine explained. "She actually said it's *why* she's here."

After a moment, Pudgy suggested they all do one thorough ride through the entire town just to make sure Duncan was actually missing and then meet again back at Base Camp. They had to be positive that Duncan wasn't just walking around somewhere. They all knew he wouldn't be, but they agreed they had to be sure.

"Okay. Let's split up and do it in sections," Jermaine suggested, taking charge. "Lenny, you're the fastest, so you take the area north of Langmaid's. Bernie, you take the east side of Main Street, from Langmaid's south, and I'll take the west side. Pudgy, you got the south end."

"You got it," Lenny said and began to head back outside toward his bike. "Meet you all back here when you're done."

"One more thing," Jermaine called out. "None of us is to go down Birch Street alone, understood?"

They all nodded. No one had any intention of going anywhere near Birch Street.

❖

By the time the last boy had returned to Base Camp, it had become plainly obvious to all of them that Duncan was truly missing. Things couldn't be more dire. Duncan's parents were out of town, and they knew that they had to tell an adult immediately. All of a sudden this had gone from strange and surreal to deadly serious.

They all agreed that Pudgy's mom was probably the best one to begin with. She was also the most "connected" parent and would rally the town pretty quickly for another search and rescue mission. The four boys got on their bikes and reluctantly headed toward Pudgy's house.

Mrs. Murtland was a friendly woman and a doting mother who loved nothing more than when her son brought his friends home. She loved to bake cookies and spoil them rotten—one of the reasons why Pudgy's house was the most popular one for the boys.

From her kitchen window, Mrs. Murtland could tell something was amiss the moment she watched them plopping their bikes down on the lawn. Duncan wasn't with them, and they all looked *way* too serious and quiet. She hurriedly wiped the flour off her hands onto her apron and trotted to the front door to greet them.

"What's wrong, boys? Why the sad faces? Where's Duncan?" She was looking directly at her son. "What is it, honey?"

"Duncan's gone missing, Mom. We think he may have gotten the same kind of virus or whatever as Becky and Little Pickle. He was acting all strange," Pudgy blurted out.

"Oh, my goodness." Mrs. Murtland covered her mouth with her hands and moved to hug her son. "Are you sure?"

Jermaine jumped in. "We're sure he's missing. That's all we really know, Mrs. Murtland. He slept at my house last night, but he was gone by morning. We can't find him anywhere," Jermaine said. Then he added, "But he was acting strange before that, that's for sure."

"I see." Pudgy's mom took a step back to gather her thoughts. "Good heavens, boys, you must be worried. Come on in and sit down." She opened the door wide, and they followed her into the living room.

Lenny took the big comfy chair like he always did. Pudgy, Jermaine, and Bernie sat beside each other on the couch—noticing the extra space with Duncan missing. "Now start from the beginning and tell me everything. Don't leave anything out," Mrs. Murtland demanded, taking her seat on the piano bench.

❖

The frenzy began with Pudgy's mom's call to the police and the arrival of Officers Thompson and Plant not thirty minutes later. Thompson had advised her on the phone not to get Providence "all riled up" like what had happened when Pickle Town went missing. He wanted time with the boys to ask some questions before the floodgates opened.

When the police car eventually pulled into the Murtlands' driveway, the boys were sitting at Pudgy's kitchen table sampling his mother's fresh-out-of-the-oven raspberry tarts. Pudgy's father had hurried home from his job at the feed store after his wife had called. He was also halfway through a tart when the doorbell rang.

By the time Officers Thompson and Plant had entered the Murtlands' front door, three of their neighbors were already walking toward their front yard. It was hard to keep a secret in Providence.

Thompson and Plant refused the kind offer of a raspberry tart as they sat down at the table with the boys, though Officer Plant kept his eye squarely on the plate most of the morning. He was a sucker for sweets.

Like Pudgy's mom, the policemen wanted a step-by-step account of what happened with Duncan Simpson. By the time Jermaine had finished his story, the officers knew they had another weird one on their hands. It didn't bode well for them having a quiet weekend back in Musgrove.

They understood that the proverbial poop would be hitting the fan on this one—big time. The officers could see it now: the throng of in-your-face media arriving by the busload; search and rescue trucks with all their gadgets combing the vicinity; police tracking teams and other special units sweeping through the streets and surrounding area; out-of-towner gawkers smelling blood and seeking a thrill; and the most revved up of all—the locals.

All hell was about to be unleashed on Providence, and it was clear that there would be little peace for a while. At least until they found Duncan Simpson—dead or alive.

Duncan's parents were notified by the police that their son was missing and immediately headed home from Oregon. They were understandably inconsolable, and their devastated neighbors were streaming into their house to offer their support. Duncan's older brother, Kevin, carried with him an enormous guilt for not acting on Jermaine's fears earlier. He hadn't thought it was that serious. He could hardly face his parents.

By the middle of the next week, the prophecy of Officers Plant and Thompson had come to fruition. The entire town of Providence had been transformed into a makeshift command center. Search parties were organized; dog tracking teams were sent into the woods; and helicopters continuously buzzed overhead, searching for any sign of the missing boy.

A week and a half later, the search was officially called off. Other than one tracking dog briefly following a scent in the woods just past Birch Street, there were no clues as to where Duncan Simpson had gone. He had simply vanished, and the police had no explanation. Nobody did. For all they knew, he had been kidnapped and taken to another state. It was a mystery.

The county sheriff met with the Simpsons privately to let them know that they were heading home. He told them that Officer Thompson would remain in the area and would check in on a daily basis. They were sorry and disappointed they couldn't offer more assistance.

The Simpsons were religious folks and spent a lot of time with Reverend Parker at the Methodist church, finding consolation in his words. Their closest friends joined them in prayer whenever they were needed. They all found solace in the ritual of gathering. This was going to take a lifetime to get over—if ever.

The clan was devastated. When the search had been officially called off, Jermaine suggested a meeting was in order at Base Camp. He wanted time with his best friends to reflect on things. None of them could believe that Duncan Simpson—that tall, lanky, messy-haired, adventure-loving lug of a boy might never be with them again. It was too much to take in.

❖

Pudgy arrived last. The intense August sun was beating down relentlessly on Granger's shed, so they decided to meet outside beneath the shade of the large sycamore tree beside Base Camp. They sat in a tight circle facing each other.

Lenny was the first to speak. "I can't believe it. Just ain't frickin' right, you know?"

The boys nodded. It went without saying.

Lenny continued. "I mean, he was so crazy funny and, like…it just doesn't make sense."

Bernie looked up at Lenny and nodded. "Base Camp won't ever be the same without Dunc." His deep voice piercing the still afternoon air.

"We gotta see if *we* can find him, right?" Pudgy said. They had all been frustrated with not being able to participate in the initial search for Duncan. "Too young," the police officer in charge of coordinating the search efforts had observed. Pudgy looked at Jermaine. He was their leader, and if anyone would know what to do, it would be him. "I mean, we can't just give up, can we, JP?"

Jermaine had been twirling a stick on the ground, drawing circles in the dirt and listening to his friends. His own mind was unclear at this time. There were too many options, and he knew none of them would have a favorable outcome if acted upon.

Jermaine looked up at Pudgy and smiled. "I say we hang tight for a while. No sense charging off looking for Dunc if we don't know where he is," he said, pausing briefly before continuing. "Or what we're up against."

Lenny shook his head and blew air out of his mouth in disgust. "Well, that sucks. Seems to me we gotta do everything we can to find Duncan, don't ya think?"

There was no response. Nobody was sure what to do.

Jermaine spoke up. "Not yet, Lenny. We don't know where he is. What good will come if one of us…well, you know. I don't think we should chance it now. Not yet, anyway."

Lenny stood up and brushed the dirt from the knees of his jeans. He was scowling. "Bull crap. Don't you think you'd want Duncan and us to look for you if you'd gone missing? I mean, come on, JP."

Jermaine sat quietly for a moment. He wasn't going to rise to Lenny's bait. With all the best intentions in the world, he'd seen how revved up Lenny could get once he was fixated on something.

"Not yet, Lenny," he calmly repeated. Like always in these kinds of anxious situations, Jermaine's calm demeanor allowed the tension to begin to diffuse and dissipate. The boys could feel it. Even Lenny gave a *whatever* shrug and moved to lean against the thick trunk of the sycamore tree.

They sat quietly for a few more minutes. None of them had anything more to offer. The heaviness of the situation was becoming overbearing. It was Bernie who finally broke the silence.

"Guys, I gotta get back to paint the fence or my dad'll kill me. Besides, I gotta crap somethin' chronic!" It was one of his favorite lines and never failed to make the boys smile.

Even today.

As the sun was setting on Providence that evening, the four boys made sure that they returned home before it got dark. They all missed Duncan terribly and were scared to death for him.

❖

The next morning, after finishing his chores—mainly collecting the garbage and dealing with his mother's empty vodka bottles, dumping them into the large blue bin beside the house—Jermaine hopped on his bike and made his way to Langmaid's Grocery.

During the night he had begun to think about the crazy lady who spent her days sitting outside Langmaid's Grocery and was determined that he should speak with her—though unclear what exactly about. He couldn't believe he didn't mention her to the police. But in all the confusion, she had simply escaped his mind.

The weird-looking woman with her mismatched attire, weathered skin, and warm smile seemed to know something about…*something*. And now, in the clear-headed light of day, Jermaine thought he should try to find some answers. He wouldn't tell the boys unless he'd found out something of interest.

As he arrived, he was surprised to see Archie Truscott sitting with the crazy lady. They were chatting away happily. Jermaine was taken aback by the change in Archie. He seemed upbeat, completely void of the fear and anxiety he'd shown previously.

Jermaine dismounted and leaned his bike against one of the poles holding up the overhang of the front porch. He cautiously ascended the steps, taking off his helmet as he walked. "Hey, Archie. How's it going, buddy?" he asked, perplexed at the change in his demeanor.

"Hiya, JP." Archie was smiling, obviously pleased to see him.

Jermaine knelt down in front of Archie, putting his hands on his knees. "You look great, Archie."

"Thanks. You look great too!" Archie was beaming.

Jermaine then looked over at the exotic stranger sitting beside Archie. She winked. He was at a loss for words.

"Say, JP, can I ride your bike? It'd be fun," Archie asked hopefully.

"Sure thing. You can ride it on your own if you stay right in front of us here," Jermaine replied. It would give him a chance to speak with the strange lady.

Archie clapped his hands and wiggled with happiness. "Thanks, JP." He got up and ambled down the stairs toward the bike. They watched as he slowly began riding in wide circles in front of Langmaid's Grocery.

"You're wondering why Archie appears to be better." It was a statement.

Jermaine looked up at her. Something about her made him feel calm. He nodded.

"Silly me, please let me introduce myself. My name is Guylaine Cloutier," she said with her strange accent. She held her hand out. He noticed the black nail polish and the stack of silver bracelets ascending her arm from her wrist. "I'm a harbinger, soothsayer, fortune teller, clairvoyant, and psychic. I read tarot, palms, horoscopes, and tea leaves. I can be contracted for séance and spirit board services. Some call me a witch doctor, but I prefer healer, and I'm at your service!"

Jermaine's mouth dropped open, and he reluctantly shook her hand and took a seat beside her. He had no idea what she had just said to him.

She continued. "I come from clear across the continent. Louisiana. Near New Orleans. Acadian descent, Cajun by birth, with a whole lotta African American added over the years." She smiled and gave a chuckle. "I'm a bit of a mongrel, I'm afraid."

Jermaine stared at the spectacular woman beside him. "I…I come from Providence. Right here."

"Ah." She smiled fully again. "*C'est vraiment si beau ici.*"

"Huh?"

"You are very lucky, Jermaine. It is lovely here."

Archie spun around in front of them again and tried to wave, which caused the bike to wobble and he almost lost control. "*Wheeeeee!*" he screamed, heading around for another circuit.

The lady continued. "His mother was worried about him. He wasn't doing well. I just showed him a little mind trick. Gave him a little *gris-gris*."

"Huh?"

"A talisman, you know. He's not completely well—may never be—but it helps that he is…shall we say, limited," the woman said, pointing to her own head. "He can't overthink things."

Jermaine said nothing, but he wanted her to continue.

"I've seen this many times before. As I told you when I first saw you, it's why I'm here." The woman looked over at Archie. "This won't end here, you know. Not until he's stopped."

Jermaine didn't understand. "Who? Archie?"

The woman looked back at Jermaine, then shook her head and smiled. "No, *mon ami*," she said, "this is much bigger than you can imagine. And you are a young boy who shouldn't be concerning yourself with such things."

Jermaine was more confused than he had ever been in his life. People appeared to be going bonkers all around Providence; Becky Green had lost her mind, Pickle had died, Bernie said Taco had turned into bones on Birch Street—and one of his best friends had been missing for nearly two weeks. And now this freaky old hippie woman was talking about stopping someone. His mind was going to explode.

Archie swung back in front and jumped off the bike, leaning it back against the post. "Thanks, JP. That was cool!" He was beaming as he waddled up the steps toward them. He pulled a small stone from his pocket and rubbed it. "See what Guylaine gave me? It gives me superpowers," Archie chirped proudly.

The woman looked at Jermaine and lowered her voice. "You'd best stay clear of all this mess, Jermaine," she warned. "And make sure you keep away from the outskirts of town—especially near the edges of the forest."

That afternoon Jermaine met the clan at Base Camp. Lenny suggested jumping off the bridge into Swift Current Creek to get their minds off things. They all agreed that it would be a good idea, even though Duncan wouldn't be there to entertain them with his miraculous "backflops."

That night, the horrific news that Becky Green had died that afternoon in the hospital in Bellingham spread like wildfire around Providence.

Chapter Six

Pudgy had gleaned all the details from his mom. Becky's mother had called her the following day in floods of tears. Her baby girl was dead.

When all four boys eventually arrived at Base Camp that afternoon, Jermaine asked Pudgy to tell them everything.

Pudgy stood up, hiking his silver shorts into position high around his belly. Three pieces of red licorice were dangling out of his front right pocket. A comic book was curled up and sticking out of the left one.

He cleared his throat and began. "They called it a heart attack. But it was more than that," Pudgy stated. He stopped briefly, seemingly for effect.

"What do you mean?" Lenny asked anxiously. Jermaine could see he detested Pudgy's dramatic pauses.

"They'd had to strap her down on a guy's knee in the hospital room," he said.

"What the hell?" Lenny asked. He looked like he was going to lose it.

"Or maybe it was a guy-knee."

"What the heck is a guy-knee, Pudgy?" Bernie asked. He looked over at Jermaine for explanation.

"I think it's called a gurney, Pudgy," Jermaine offered.

Pudgy shrugged and continued. "She was having convulsions and screaming. They had to tie her down real tight. She was yelling at something to get away from her. Her mom said she'd completely lost her mind."

"Holy moly," Bernie said.

"The doctors sedated her, but it was too late. Her heart finally gave out, they said. Too much stress on her all this time. The funeral will be in a week," Pudgy said, sitting back down on the milk crate.

Bernie shook his head in disbelief. "First Pickle and now Becky. Holy moly."

Jermaine thought of Becky being tormented by the thought of something coming after her all day long—every day. It had been like that ever since she'd gone to play hopscotch on Birch Street at the beginning of the summer. It seemed so long ago.

He then thought about what the crazy lady had said to him the day before: *This won't end here, you know. Not until he's stopped.*

He knew he needed to learn more from the old woman before mentioning anything to the clan. For now, he would just try to keep them on level ground.

❖

Margaret Cleaves sat with Becky's family in the front row of the crowded church. Becky's older twin brothers wore matching blue suits and sat on either side of their father.

Reverend Parker read the eulogy, and everyone was beside themselves with profound sadness and growing confusion. Losing two young ones from a town as small as Providence had shaken the community to its core.

Pudgy and his parents sat directly behind the Greens. Lenny and his folks sat beside them. Jermaine sat with his mom. His father was away for work.

Understandably, Duncan's parents, Doris and Shane Simpson, weren't attending. They knew that they might soon be organizing a memorial service for their own son. They were not giving up hope just yet, though.

After Becky's casket was removed and on its way to Musgrove for cremation, Jermaine walked back to his house with his mother in silence. When they arrived, out of the blue she asked to speak with him and told him to have a seat at the kitchen table while she made tea. This took Jermaine by surprise, as she rarely said more than two words to him.

As they waited for the kettle to boil, she sat down opposite her son and reached across the table to take his hand. "Jermaine, you gotta promise me something," she said. She looked anxious and completely serious. Her eyes were red and shadowed with dark circles. "You gotta promise me you'll never, *ever* go into those woods beyond Birch Street."

Jermaine was confused. Not only did his mother's passionate plea scare him, it was the conviction of her tone. Knowing that he and the boys might soon head out to look for Duncan, he couldn't make the promise. "Don't be silly, Mom. Don't worry about me."

"Promise me, son." The seriousness of her voice was chilling.

"Mom, what's going on?"

His mom pulled her hand away. The kettle began to whistle, and she stood up and went to the counter. She plopped a teabag into two mugs and poured the hot water in. "Jermaine, honey. There are things you just don't know and can't know. I just need you to promise me," she said, returning with the steaming mugs.

"What things, Mom?" Jermaine asked, leaning over to open the door of the fridge beside him and grabbing the milk. He then looked across the table at his mother. She appeared so much older these days. He realized he'd never really known her to be happy. She always seemed to be without joy in her life.

His mom was reluctant to say more. "I have my suspicions. One day when you're older, I might explain. I just need to hear you say you will never go into those woods."

Jermaine could see the fear in her eyes. "Okay, okay, Mom. I promise," he said, picking up the mug with his right hand. His left hand remained behind his back with his fingers crossed.

"Good," his mother said, breathing out a sigh of relief. "Thank you. Now drink your tea. I've got a bit of a migraine coming on, so I need to lie down in the den." With that, she got up and walked into the next room. From where he sat in the kitchen, Jermaine could hear the gentle *clink* of a bottle. He knew she was adding some comfort into her mug of tea.

❖

It had been over two weeks since Duncan was last seen sleeping on Jermaine's bed. The mood in Base Camp was getting worse. At their core, they were boys of action, and they wanted to do something—*anything*—to find their friend.

"I think we need a vote," Lenny said. "Let's see who is in favor of going to look for Duncan. And see who is too chicken."

"I agree," Pudgy said. "I'm tired of sitting around. For all we know, Dunc is lost somewhere and needs our help."

"So where you gonna look for him, huh?" Bernie asked, his helmet pushed back on his head. "You just gonna wander around in the woods for him until nighttime comes? That doesn't sound like a brilliant plan to me."

It had the desired effect. Silence again descended on the shed. Eventually, it was Jermaine who spoke next.

"I'll make you guys a deal. Give me a few days to come up with a plan. We can vote on it at that point, but I just need a few days."

Pudgy, Lenny, and Bernie all looked at each other. Then one by one they nodded. It was obvious to Jermaine that they considered it a fair proposal.

Bernie and Pudgy had chores to do, so they left immediately. Lenny soon followed, deciding he wanted to haul some logs into the yard so his dad could teach him how to carve with a chainsaw.

Jermaine sat at Base Camp on his own for a while just thinking. He then had an idea. It was time to head back to Langmaid's Grocery.

On his way, he happened to see her out of the corner of his eye. She was halfway down Birch Street, sitting in the tall grass on the left side and staring at the end of the road.

Jermaine turned his bike and cautiously approached her from behind. "Miss Cloutier?"

The woman turned and smiled. "Hi, Jermaine. Call me Guylaine."

"Whatcha doing here?" Jermaine stopped his bike beside her. He didn't like being anywhere near this street.

"Just watching. Observing."

"Watching for what?"

Guylaine didn't answer. She didn't need to.

"The boys wanna go looking for Duncan. I won't be able to stop 'em for long," he decided to tell her. He was curious about what her reaction would be.

"That would be a damn foolish thing to do now, wouldn't it?" Her voice was suddenly stern. She turned her head again to look at the woods.

Jermaine moved beside her, still straddling his bike seat. "What is the thing? What needs to be stopped?"

The woman looked up at Jermaine. She had stopped smiling, and the seriousness in her eyes surprised Jermaine. "You don't mess with what you don't understand."

Jermaine thought about it for a minute. He remembered her initial conversation with him. "You said it's the reason you're here."

Guylaine nodded. "True, but that is my business. Now get back on your bike, Jermaine. Stay well away from this area."

Jermaine didn't move. He couldn't. He needed to learn more. "Has this happened other places?"

Guylaine didn't answer. She sat in silence staring at the woods.

"Is that why you're here? Have you seen it before?"

Still no answer.

"Guylaine, one of my best friends is missing. Two girls have died. Me and my friends are gonna get answers somehow." His heart was machine-gunning in his chest. He'd never spoken to an adult like that before.

Guylaine slowly faced Jermaine. He could tell in her eyes that she admired his pluck. "Jermaine, all I'll say is I travel across the continent tracking these things. It happens more often than you think. I keep on top of local press. Little nuggets are what first appear. I know what's coming before it gets too big. Like with the inexplicable circumstances surrounding Becky Green's illness followed by Pickle Town's death. Once I read about it, I had a good idea that it was happening here."

Jermaine got off his bike and sat down beside her. "What *is* happening here, Guylaine?"

Guylaine again looked at the woods. Jermaine waited quietly until she spoke. "I call them inbetweeners," she said matter-of-factly. "Neither dead nor alive."

Jermaine wasn't sure he had heard her correctly. "Did you say inbetweeners?"

Guylaine nodded. "Rogue spirits. Vengeful and without remorse."

Jermaine felt a chill go up his spine. "I don't—"

"You can't understand," Guylaine interrupted, anticipating his confusion. "Nobody does." She then chuckled. "I scare people most of the time. They don't get it either. I come to observe and advise, but they think

I'm a prophet of doom or a lunatic. Sooner or later, I usually get run out of town."

Jermaine studied the eccentric woman. Something about her made him feel at ease. "I need to learn more if I'm gonna save my buddy," he said softly.

"You're not going to do that, Jermaine," she replied. "It's most likely too late for Duncan at this point. I'm sorry, *mon ami*."

Jermaine's heart sank. He couldn't believe how blunt she was; he refused to believe Duncan was gone. "At least we have to try," he whispered.

Guylaine nodded. She understood. "Don't be getting yourself involved, son. No good will come of it, I promise you that."

Jermaine sat quietly beside her. The trees were gently swaying in the woods at the end of the road. It all seemed so peaceful. Serene even.

"I believe his name is Mordecai. That's all I know at this point."

Jermaine was puzzled. "Mordecai? Who is Mordecai?"

"The thing of which we should not speak."

❖

Pudgy had once written a poem for a school assignment, and he'd read it aloud to Lenny. In the poem he declared that Providence was "a nice place to grow up in, but a toilet to grow old in." Even Lenny knew that rhyming poems shouldn't have the same two words doing the rhyming, but he knew what Pudgy was getting at. It used to be that everybody who was old enough and fit enough to leave Providence had already bolted; but now, it wasn't even a good place for young people anymore.

Simon Cartwright handed the chainsaw to his son and told him to start it up and try shaving a bit off the top of the log. Lenny was about to pull the cord when, out of the blue, his dad asked him if he'd ever talked to that weird lady that hung out at Langmaid's Grocery with Archie.

"Nope. I've seen her there lots, though. Why?"

"Stay away from her. She introduced herself to me today. Said all sorts of weird things, like she was a card reader, and a horoscope this-and-that. All sorts of mumbo jumbo. She just seemed crazy, that's all. Now crank it up and let's get started."

His dad was a man of few words, but when he did speak, he meant what he said. And Lenny knew well enough never to question his authority. He had no plans on speaking with the crazy lady.

Not long after, Pudgy arrived at Lenny's house. He watched and waited until Lenny had finished his carving session. Lenny turned off the chainsaw, pulled off his safety glasses and ear protectors, and wiped the sawdust-laced sweat from his brow. Pudgy noticed how even at a young age, Lenny's muscles looked defined. Just like his father's.

"Hey, Lenny."

"What's up, Pudgy?" Lenny asked, laying the saw on the ground. His father was now at the far end of the property working on his own sculpture.

"Whatcha making?" Pudgy asked, looking at the curious gashes and gouges all over the log.

"Not sure yet," Lenny replied defensively. "Just working on my technique, that's all."

"Cool," Pudgy noted. "Say, I've been thinking."

"Yeah? What about?"

"About Duncan. It's driving me nuts not doing something about him. I'm tempted to go looking myself."

Lenny knew Pudgy was stretching the truth, as there was no way on God's green earth that he was going in those woods alone. "Yeah, bugging me too. JP says give him a few days. Let's see what he comes up with."

"I guess. Just hard not doing anything, you know?"

"Yup," Lenny replied. "I need a soda. Come on inside. You want one?"

"Sure do, thanks," Pudgy replied, following Lenny into the house. His mom was in the kitchen and greeted him warmly. "Hi, Pudgy. How are you today, sweetheart?"

"I'm good, Mrs. C, thanks. How are you today?" Pudgy was always polite and smooth when talking with adults.

"Just fine, thanks. You boys want some banana bread?"

"You bet!" Pudgy declared. Lenny smiled and helped his mom get the cutting board and a knife.

"What adventure do you boys have planned for today?"

"Dunno yet," Lenny replied. "We're meeting at Base Camp at noon. We'll take a vote then."

❖

As he was on his way to base camp, Bernie noticed Archie sitting on the front steps of his house. He was holding his ears with both hands and rocking back and forth. He looked both in pain and scared. Bernie yelled out to him. "Hey, Archie." But he received no response. It was just like Pudgy had described. It seemed that poor Archie was suffering immensely, and it filled Bernie with both sadness and dread.

Bernie was the last one to enter Farmer Granger's shed, as he had to trim the hedge before he could come out. He had trimmed it last week, but his father was a particular man and wanted things "just right," especially when it came to how the property would be perceived by his neighbors.

When he finally arrived, he explained to the others what he had seen on the front steps of the Truscott house. That's when Jermaine said something that made them all look at him strangely.

"Darn. He was just getting better too. That lady gave him a talisman, and it seemed to have worked." It came out of Jermaine's mouth before he could filter himself. He realized as soon as he said it that he'd have some explaining to do.

"What lady?" Lenny asked curiously. Jermaine could tell that he knew—they all did. Lenny just wanted him to say it.

"That lady that's been hanging around Langmaid's," Jermaine replied sheepishly.

"You been talking to her, JP?" Pudgy asked.

"A bit. She gave Archie some kind of stone or rock or something to help him deal with—you know—the sounds and stuff."

"Sounds? You mean the Follower," Lenny stated boldly.

Jermaine understood that it went without saying that they had never kept anything from each other. *Ever.* Lenny just wanted everything out on the table.

Jermaine didn't answer at first. They all appreciated the gravity of the situation and that Archie was in great danger.

"My dad says the lady is a kook. We should stay clear of her," Lenny added.

Jermaine knew he was quickly running out of time with his friends. He needed a plan, and he needed it soon. It was time to dig down a little more with his mother. She seemed to know something—something sinister and secretive. He could feel it. He would also try to see if Guylaine would toss him any more nuggets of information as well. He would take anything now.

Pudgy broke the tension. "Look what I got," he said proudly, leaning over and slowly pulling a wooden board out of his backpack.

"What's that thing?" Bernie asked, curious about the strange letters and numbers all over the large square piece of wood.

"An old Ouija board. My dad got it at a yard sale. Bought it for a laugh."

"A what?" Lenny asked, leaning closer to inspect the strange object. "What's it for?"

"I Googled it. It's for communicating with dead people or spirits and stuff like that." Pudgy passed the board around so they could all admire its exotic detail. "It comes with this doohickey as well. They say it's called a planchette. It's what you use to speak to them." Pudgy pulled out the small piece of wood with a tiny circle cut in the middle. He held it up for all of them to admire.

"Pudgy, why you want to get everyone riled up with that nonsense, huh?" Jermaine asked.

Pudgy stared his buddy down. "Well, if it were up to me, we'd have already gone looking for Duncan. I thought that while we were waiting for you to come up with some stupid plan, we could see if we could find him this way." Pudgy's voice was cracking, and tears had formed in the corners of his eyes. He wiped both eyes with the backs of his wrists. "Besides, what if it works?"

Lenny and Bernie looked at each other and then over at Jermaine. Lenny spoke first. "I'm in. I say we try."

"Me too," Bernie said.

Jermaine looked around the shed at his best friends in the world. *Why not*, he thought. *What was there to lose? It may buy a bit more time.* "Okay. Why don't we meet back here after supper? I gotta cut the lawn this afternoon. Say seven o'clock? Deal?"

"Deal," the boys shouted in unison. At least they were going to try something.

Bernie led the way out of the shed. "I gotta head home now too. I gotta crap somethin' chronic!"

As usual, it brought the house down.

❖

After he had finished mowing the lawn and had put away the mower, Jermaine made his way into the kitchen to get a glass of water. He was determined to confront his mother. He remembered her strange, almost frantic anxiety and trepidation about him going into the woods beyond Birch Street. She knew something, and he was determined to find out what it was. He—they—were running out of time. It was already after four o'clock, so there was a good chance that she would already be a little tipsy, which would perhaps make it easier for him to get information from her.

His mom was sitting in her housecoat in her big chair, watching *Breaking Bad* on Netflix. Sure enough, she was holding her coffee mug. Jermaine walked in and sat down on the sectional couch beside her—something he rarely did while she was watching the television, having her refreshment. She looked up at him, confused as to why he would be there.

He knew an ambush would offer the best opportunity for success. He took a deep breath before he spoke. "What do you know about the woods past Birch Street, Mom? I know you know something." Jermaine's voice was strong and determined.

His mother looked at him with shock, then slowly took a sip from her mug, grimacing slightly as she swallowed. She shifted to face the television screen again.

"I'm not leaving here until you talk to me, Mom," Jermaine announced, leaning over and grabbing the remote control from the coffee table and turning the television off.

She turned back toward him and glared intensely, but she didn't say a word. Eventually her face softened, and she spoke. "You're not thinking of going in those woods, Jermaine. You promised me—"

"Tell me what you know," Jermaine interrupted. He was unflinching and steadfast in his resolve.

His mother returned her gaze back to the blank television screen, taking a larger gulp from her mug. He remained silent. After a moment she let out a long breath. Jermaine could see her hands shaking. "Okay. But you can never breathe a word of this to anyone, okay?"

Jermaine nodded.

"Promise me."

"I promise," Jermaine replied. He could hear his own heart pounding in his chest.

She sat silently for a few more moments before mustering up the courage to begin. "I'm not sure if it's at all related. It was, like, years and years ago, when I was not much older than yourself. I was seventeen."

Jermaine leaned forward toward his mother. She looked tired and frightened.

"He was older than me. By a lot. I mean a *real* lot," she began. Clearing her throat before continuing. "My parents didn't know I was seeing him. I was in love with him, but they could never know." She moved her head further away from her son and looked out the window. The clouds were moving swiftly above the hedge tops.

"He was a hunter. Most of the year he lived in Pulltown. That's where I first met him—at a coffee shop when I was still in high school. But come the season, he would spend months at a time at some old cabin in the woods. On a creek. He said it was called Skagit Creek, though I'd never heard of it then, or since." Jermaine's mom leaned back and inhaled deeply before taking another sip, wincing as it burned its way down her throat.

"Go on, Mom," Jermaine urged, rubbing his mother's arm with his hand. He couldn't remember the last time he had hugged or even been this close to his mom. It made him feel sad.

"He told me a story about the cabin. I couldn't believe he could live there alone after hearing the story. But he was brave. Brave and handsome," she said, hinting at a smile.

She took another long breath, and Jermaine noticed the mug shaking in her hand. "Anyway, he'd told me about something he heard from another hunter who'd stayed at the cabin years and years before him. It was a story that makes my skin crawl to this day." His mom paused to take another breath. "Seems a young boy wandered up to the cabin out of nowhere. Like, I mean *out of nowhere*, you know?"

Jermaine nodded. He could feel a chill rise up the length of his body, and the hairs on his arms and the nape of his neck tingled.

"Bobby—that was my boyfriend's name—Bobby told me the hunter thought the boy must've been lost or abandoned or something. A young boy. Couldn't have been older than seven or eight. But the cabin was miles upon miles from any civilization. He just couldn't figure out how he'd gotten there. The boy didn't speak a word either." His mom took another sip from the mug and swallowed hard.

"What happened?"

"That hunter kept a diary. Some other hunters a couple of years later discovered the cabin and found the diary. The last thing he wrote in it was about the boy's arrival and how odd it was. They also found the hunter's bones on the porch—right there at the cabin where he'd died."

"I don't understand," Jermaine said. Trying to figure out how this all related to her older boyfriend, Bobby—or to anything else, for that matter.

His mom turned and looked at him. Her face was pink and puffy, and her eyes were red and frightened. "Know what else they found in the diary?"

Jermaine shook his head.

"He'd been writing about some old grave behind the cabin he'd discovered. He reckoned it was dug by the person who originally built the cabin or something. Anyway, the weird thing was, every day there seemed to be fresh dirt on the grave. He could even smell it in the air. There was no explanation for it. No animals seemed to be digging at it. It perplexed the hunter, and he wrote about it lots in the diary."

Jermaine waited until she took another slow gulp from her mug, wiping her mouth with the sleeve of her housecoat.

"I'm telling you all this because of what Bobby said the last time I ever heard from him, before he went missing. He'd called me from the satellite phone that he'd take with him when he went out into the wilderness for months on end."

"Satellite phone?" Jermaine asked.

"Before cell phones. He worked as a mining prospector in the winters. The company he worked for let him use it for emergencies. Once a month during the summers he would give me a quick call and repay the company that winter. It was really expensive, but he…we felt it was worth it." His mom pursed her lips and slowly released her breath—as if to steady her nerves. Jermaine could see how hard this was for her.

"What did he say?" Jermaine's voice was weak, and his heart was racing.

"Said a young boy had knocked at his cabin door that morning. Scared the living daylights right out of him. Bobby laughed and told me it reminded him of the old hunter's story. Said he was standing there all soaking wet in, like, shorts and a tie or something crazy like that. Bobby said the boy seemed to just want to sleep. Said he was sleeping on the spare cot when he called me. He said the boy told him his name. I'll never forget it. Said it was Mordecai."

Jermaine's heart nearly leapt out of his chest. He felt suddenly dizzy and hot. He became disoriented, like he'd been spun around and around and left to gather his senses.

His mother continued as if she felt relieved to divulge her dark secret after all these years. "Bobby also decided to share with me that he'd discovered a grave the week before—out behind the cabin—and it had fresh dirt on top. Now if that's not enough to make you lose your mind, I don't know what is." Jermaine's mother put her mug down and wrapped her arms around her chest. Her whole body was shaking. "I could tell Bobby was a little freaked out about it all. I told him to get out. I said, *Bobby, get away from there right now!* He just tried to calm me down and told me I was overreacting."

"Jesus, Mom," Jermaine said, leaning back on the couch. He noticed he was also shaking.

"He then promised me he would leave in the morning. That's the last I ever heard from him. I kept listening to the news for anything about him being found. All I heard was that he was a missing person. He was never found."

"Did you tell anyone? The police?" Jermaine asked.

His mother looked at him and matter-of-factly said, "How could I? Your grandparents would have killed me for dating an older man. I couldn't breathe any of it to a soul. Besides, by the time I'd come to my senses, the police were already looking for him. Regardless, I've been consumed with guilt ever since."

"Does Dad know?"

His mother shook her head. "I've never told him. And I shouldn't have told you. I don't know why I did." She grabbed her mug again and took a final swig, emptying it and swallowing loudly. "Keep this to yourself, Jermaine. Promise me."

Jermaine nodded. His pulse was still racing as he tried to gather his thoughts. When he felt he could leave his mom, he got up and walked to the kitchen, trying to make sense of everything that he'd just heard. Even more confusing, why did Guylaine Cloutier also seem to know who Mordecai was? And, on top of it all, what did this have to do with Birch Street, anyway?

He remembered Guylaine's words of warning to him: *Don't be getting yourself involved, son. No good will come of it, I promise you that.*

He would skip dinner. He couldn't face food right now, so he walked outside and got on his bike. He needed to head to Base Camp. He needed some time to think before the others arrived.

❖

Pudgy was the last one to come through the doors, and Lenny already had a handful of candles lit and had placed them on top of the rickety desk that was pushed up against the wall of the shed. He wanted to set the mood. While it was still relatively light outside, Lenny thought the ambient light of Base Camp made for a perfect setting for speaking with ghosts. He was keen to get started. He'd never done anything like this before. None of them had. It felt edgy and exciting.

Pudgy walked in and placed the board down on a spare milk crate that had been moved to the middle of the room—the fact that it was Duncan's milk crate did not go unnoticed. The boys all pulled their own milk crates in close, making a circle around the strange board. Pudgy was the one who'd researched it all, so they waited for his instructions.

"Okay, this little piece of wood here is the communication device. When we begin, we all gotta put our hands on it—real gentle—but only when I tell you to."

The boys all leaned forward for a closer look. It appeared to be just that: a little piece of wood.

"Now, here on the Ouija board, see there're letters, numbers, and some words. *Yes* or *no* are the obvious ones, and *goodbye* for when it's over or when you want to end it."

"End it?" Lenny asked.

"If you want it all to stop," Pudgy explained. "It's what I read on the internet, anyway."

"So we say those words on the board, or what?" Lenny asked. He was physically strong, but he wasn't the quickest when it came to understanding instructions.

"No, Lenny. Our fingers are going to gently touch the little piece of wood here and follow it where it wants to go."

"Sounds lame, but whatever."

"We'll go around the board with the piece of wood a couple of times to get it warmed up and to get a feel for it."

"So then what happens?" Bernie said.

"I will ask it *yes* or *no* questions. That way whoever we're speaking with can give us answers easily. Sometimes the spirit may try to spell something out, so usually we'd have somebody with a pen and paper ready to write it all down," Pudgy explained. He'd obviously researched this well.

"I'll do it," Jermaine volunteered. Pudgy nodded and pulled a notebook out of his bag along with a pen and handed them to him.

"You're sure about this?" Jermaine asked. He was still completely rattled from everything he'd recently heard from his mother.

"We can always shut it down. If we want to bail, we move the wood to the *goodbye* part of the board. Then it's over. Simple as that," Pudgy replied confidently.

"So what are we gonna ask it?" Lenny asked. He was obviously eager to give it a go.

"I've come up with a few questions. Let's see how it goes. Everyone ready? Okay, no talking from now on. Just me, okay?"

Bernie and Lenny nodded nervously. Jermaine sat still.

"Okay, Lenny and Bernie, put your finger here beside mine. Don't press down hard. Just real light," Pudgy instructed. The two boys followed his instructions.

"Let's move around clockwise a couple of times."

"Wait, which way is that?" Lenny asked.

"Just follow my lead. Ready? Here we go," Pudgy said, watching as the planchette began to move in a big circle.

When they had gone around a couple of times, they stopped again in the middle. Pudgy then closed his eyes and told the others to do likewise. "We are here to ask a few questions. The first question is, is anybody there?"

Jermaine watched with curiosity as his friends waited for some kind of sign. He had his pen ready in the faint chance that something might happen.

"I ask again, is any—" Just then the planchette moved quickly toward the *YES*.

"Holy moly," Bernie exhaled, his eyes now wide open.

"Shhh, Bernie. No talking," Pudgy instructed. "Keep your eyes closed."

Jermaine felt the hair on his neck stand up and quiver. The entire room felt cold and full of static electricity.

"We are here as friends," Pudgy continued; his voice was cracking and shaky. He now kept one eye open himself. "We have a few questions for you if you don't mind. We are seeking news about our friend. His name is Duncan Simpson. Do you know the person I am talking—" Again the wooden pointer pulled their hands across the board.

YES.

Jermaine breathed out slowly. This was getting beyond freaky. He shuffled his crate in closer toward the others. *Don't be getting yourself involved, son. No good will come of it, I promise you that…*

"Are you Duncan Sim—" Suddenly their hands moved to the other side of the board.

NO.

Jermaine looked up at the other boys. Pudgy's eyes were open, and all of their faces were pale.

Pudgy continued. "Are you friendly?" he whispered.

The planchette moved to the middle and then back again.

NO.

"Holy moly, Pudgy. I think we should stop this," Bernie whispered.

"Shhh, Bernie. Give it some time. We want answers," Lenny demanded. Jermaine could tell he was trying hard to act brave, but it was obvious that he was also downright freaked out.

Pudgy cleared his throat. His voice was barely audible now. "Duncan Simpson. Is he alive?"

The planchette hovered and shook for a moment. Then it began to move.

NO.

All four boys looked at each other. Pudgy continued. "Who are—"

Suddenly the planchette shifted to the alphabet part of the board and began darting quickly between letters. Pudgy called them out for Jermaine to write down.

"D-E-A…" Pudgy paused before the last one. "D."

"Dead," Bernie said. "Holy m—"

The planchette moved again, this time quicker. Pudgy called out the letters. "D-U-N-C-A-N-D-E-A-D."

"Duncan dead," Jermaine repeated. "It's saying that Dunc's dead."

The planchette moved back to the middle of the board. None of them seemed sure what to do next.

It was Jermaine who spoke again. "Ask it for its name, Pudgy."

Pudgy nodded. "What is you—"

This time the planchette jumped out of their hands and began moving rapidly on its own between letters. Pudgy called them out as fast as he could. The planchette moved furiously around the board and then suddenly flew across the room, smashing into the wall of the shed. The candles flickered and almost went out.

The boys were too terrified to say anything initially. Then Lenny flipped the board off the crate, and it tumbled across the room, ending up tilted against the wall beside the planchette. "Enough of this crap," he said, standing up and moving away from the middle of the room toward the candles.

Pudgy looked over at Jermaine. "Did you get it? Did you get all the letters?"

Jermaine sat staring ahead of him without moving. "You okay, Jermaine?" Bernie asked, leaning over. "Hey, buddy, you okay?" Bernie looked down at the notebook. He gently took it from Jermaine so he could read what was written.

"What's it say, Bernie?" Lenny asked.

Bernie looked confused. "I think it says Moreci or something," Bernie replied, trying to decipher Jermaine's scribbles. "Whatever that means."

"It's Mordecai," Jermaine whispered, looking straight ahead. "And he's the boy we're looking for."

❖

As the boys prepared to leave Base Camp, Jermaine told each of them that he was almost set with a plan. He knew they were bewildered and confused by all that had transpired; be said that he would tell them more later, but he needed one more day. More importantly, he told them that they should definitely, and secretly, begin preparing for a journey. He also urged them to say nothing to anyone about what had occurred that evening.

The next morning Jermaine headed straight to Langmaid's Grocery. The bench outside was empty, so he popped in briefly to speak with the owner.

The bell above the door announced his entry. "Morning, Mrs. Langmaid," Jermaine offered.

She glanced up briefly and smiled awkwardly.

"I was wondering if you've seen that lady, Ms. Guylaine Cloutier, today. The woman who's been hanging around for a few weeks. Have you seen her?"

"Yep, uh-haa."

Jermaine moved toward the counter. "Do you know where I can find her, Mrs. Langmaid? It's important," he said.

Mrs. Langmaid pointed down Main Street.

"She's down there? How far?"

Mrs. Langmaid wiggled one of her crooked fingers as if to say, *A fair way down.*

Jermaine understood what she was indicating. "She at Birch Street, Mrs. Langmaid?"

"Yep, uh-haa."

Jermaine thanked her and raced out of the store. Jumping on his bike, he began pedaling hard down Main Street. He needed to speak with Guylaine immediately.

When he arrived at Birch Street, he could see her sitting in the grass in the same place she had been before—partway down on the left, staring at the woods at the end of the road. He pulled his bike up beside her and dismounted. He then sat down next to her without saying a word.

"Hello, Jermaine. What brings you here on this fine morning, honey?"

"Mordecai," he responded flatly.

"I see," she said, smiling at the determined boy beside her. She admired his gumption. "What about Mordecai?"

"He's a boy. A boy who never died properly or something like that. He's out there and has been for a while," Jermaine said, pointing at the woods ahead of them.

"My, my, I see you've been doing some research."

"He might have killed one of my best friends. I need to know how he can be stopped before he gets others."

"I see," Guylaine replied but said no more.

"It has to do with a grave, doesn't it?" It was more of a statement than a question.

Guylaine glanced back at Jermaine. "Well, look at you. I'm impressed," she said.

"Please, ma'am. I need to know."

Guylaine took a while before she responded. She'd never encouraged anyone to take on an inbetweener—*ever*. But she knew by the look in his eyes that he was one to seek the truth whether she helped him or not. "The grave is the clue. Inbetweeners are agitated because they haven't been put to rest properly. It happens on occasion. They eventually go rogue and will kill and feed off of all life-forms until their grave is consecrated. No one's sure why."

Jermaine listened intently. It sounded like a vampire movie or something out of a fantasy book. "Consecrated?"

"Well, that's a Judeo-Christian term. Most religions have some form of purification ritual," Guylaine said.

"Can you speak English? I'm only a kid," Jermaine reminded her politely.

Guylaine smiled and stood up, stretching her back and letting the sun warm her face. She closed her eyes and breathed in deeply. Her colorful scarves waved in the breeze behind her. "Mordecai needs to be purified or he will keep killing. Ever wonder why the hunters stopped exploring this part of the woods years ago? No wildlife—none. All gone. All consumed."

Jermaine thought about it. It was true, he couldn't remember the last time he saw any sign of larger game whenever the clan had played in the woods.

"He's moved farther afield, and now he's found Providence. He's luring its residents into the woods. I sense him in there—he's close. He knows I'm here. He knows I know."

Jermaine was now just plain scared. The last few days had pushed him to his limits in terms of trying to make sense of it all. "How can he be purified?" he asked timidly, almost not wanting to hear the answer.

"I hear him—his echoes and vibrations. It's loud if you are trained to hear it. It screams from the woods." Guylaine wrapped her arms around her chest. "It's his grave. It's always the grave. Wherever that might be."

Jermaine's pulse was racing. He decided to keep his cards close to his chest. She didn't need to know what he'd learned from his mother. "What about the grave, Guylaine?"

"Inbetweeners like him were never buried properly—sure, the ceremony may have looked right, but for some reason, they never found peace. There's no logical explanation. A mutation, maybe." Guylaine chuckled. "There is more truth than folks know when they say 'RIP' when someone dies. It's everything."

Jermaine tried to get his head around what she was saying. How could a boy not be buried properly? And what did this have to do with the missing people?

"There's only two ways to stop inbetweeners. Either his bones have to be found and properly buried, or something much more disturbing has to occur."

Jermaine looked up at the enchanting woman. "What do you mean?"

"Sacrifice." Guylaine turned to look down at the boy beside her. She wanted to make sure he understood the magnitude of it all. Her voice was strong and defiant. "A blood sacrifice to appease the gods, or whatever you want to call it. It's been like this since the dawn of humanity. Not just an animal sacrifice—no, it has to have meaning for inbetweeners. Someone will have to die to make it all stop. Has always been thus. Don't ask me why, but our forefathers knew this. They understood. And this is the reason this is way too big for you, Jermaine. Go back to your friends, *mon ami*. I'm warning you. Leave this alone."

Jermaine sat quietly for a moment, then stood up and faced the unusual woman beside him. "How do you know so much about this, Guylaine?"

"Just do, that's all. Been following inbetweeners like this most of my life. Seem to have a knack for it—so did my momma, and her momma before her. Just trying to do my part to warn people. Though most pay me no mind."

Jermaine gazed at the thick forest at the end of Birch Street. He tried to sort through everything Guylaine had told him. He knew he had to take action, and after a few moments, resolved in his decision, he turned back toward her. "Thanks, Guylaine. You've been helpful," Jermaine said, suddenly leaning over and picking up his bike.

"Mind what I say, Jermaine. This is too big for you. Time will work this one out."

Jermaine smiled and got on his bike and began pedaling away. Guylaine sat back down and stared again at the woods. She could sense that Mordecai was close.

❖

That evening, when Jermaine called Bernie on his house phone, he used the code word that they'd used since they were eight: "Sherpa." Everyone who knew the boys understood what the code word meant—especially their parents and siblings—but the boys still thought it was cool to use, and they only used it when the situation undeniably called for it. Jermaine then texted Lenny and Pudgy the same word.

Just before midnight, they all snuck out of their houses and, in the cover of darkness, biked to Base Camp. Jermaine already had several candles lit by the time the boys had trickled in, taking their places on their individual milk crates. Jermaine had a laptop open and facing him.

"What's this about, JP?"

"Sit down, Lenny," Jermaine instructed. All the boys looked at Jermaine. It was unlike him to be so bossy.

"What I'm going to tell you will scare the crap out of you. It will also ask something of you that I'd totally understand if you turn it down. In fact, you'd be dumb not to."

"What the hell you talking about?" Lenny asked.

"Before I say anything, I have to have your word that this will never, ever be mentioned to anyone—*ever.* Is that a promise?"

All the boys nodded. Pudgy then said, "All for one, and one for all, remember?"

"So shall it ever be," Bernie added. It was their secret mantra. Part of their pact—they'd been reciting it since even before Base Camp had first been established when they were eight years old. They had watched the old *The*

Three Musketeers movie and heard the quote. They all had thought it pretty much summed up their clan.

Jermaine nodded, then proceeded to tell them the entire story that his mother had told him about the hunter in the cabin with the diary. Then he followed it with everything his mom had recounted about what happened with her boyfriend. He was sure to slow down when he explained how both deaths coincided with the arrival of a young boy.

The shed became suddenly silent. Jermaine thought it got colder. Pudgy, Lenny, and Bernie unconsciously shuffled their crates closer to the middle of the shed. Nobody said a word for a few moments. The flickering candlelight added tension to the already heavy atmosphere.

Jermaine then continued to tell them about Guylaine Cloutier and why she said she was in Providence in the first place.

And then he dropped the bomb.

"Remember the Ouija board?"

All three boys nodded. Jermaine knew that the events of the previous night had significantly rattled the clan. It had taken things to another level altogether.

"Remember the name it spelled out?"

They nodded again.

"My mom and Guylaine both mentioned the same name to me—Mordecai. He's the boy."

"Holy moly, Mackatony," Bernie exclaimed.

"Hump a lizard," Lenny added.

"For real?" Pudgy asked. "So you think this same freaky kid kidnapped Duncan?" It was obvious that Pudgy, like the rest of them, was attempting to piece together such a bewildering scenario.

Jermaine evaded the question. Instead he continued to tell them all he could recall about Guylaine's belief in rogue spirits and something called inbetweeners—what they've been calling the Follower. He then told them that she believed Duncan was dead.

There was again silence in the shed as everyone attempted to digest what they'd just heard. They knew Jermaine never said anything unless he felt it to be true; still, no one wanted to believe it. Eventually Lenny spoke. "But how does she know?"

"She seemed to know a lot about how this all worked. Anyway, she also told me the only way that inbetweeners can be stopped is through either finding their bones and burying them properly in the original grave or…some kind of sacrifice." Jermaine paused before continuing. "Specifically, a blood sacrifice."

"You mean like a chicken or something?" Lenny asked innocently. "I could do that. I could use my hunting knife," he added hopefully.

Jermaine shook his head. "If it has to be a sacrifice, then it has to be a human that dies."

"Holy moly," Bernie muttered again. "So one of us would have to die? You're kidding, right, Jermaine?"

Jermaine shook his head again. They all knew he was deadly serious.

"But we can find his bones, right?" Pudgy said. "I mean, all we have to do is find his bones and bury them, right, JP?"

Jermaine didn't answer. The likelihood of finding a boy's bones in those woods would be nearly impossible. It was at that moment they all realized what Jermaine was asking of them.

"How does the sacrifice work, Jermaine?" Bernie asked softly, his voice cracking.

Jermaine looked around at the boys and took a deep breath. "On top of his grave. She said it has to be on his original grave. But remember, she had no idea that I'd actually heard of the grave. And I bet it's the same grave the hunter and my mom's old boyfriend had found." Jermaine sighed. "And that's why I said you'd be dumb to get involved."

"What you're saying is we're talking suicide, then." It was Bernie who put it bluntly.

Jermaine didn't reply. He had said enough.

It was too much to comprehend all at once, and the boys again sat lost in their own thoughts, watching the candlelight cast long shadows that danced across the walls and ceiling. After a few moments, Pudgy spoke again. "Say, what's with the computer, JP?"

Jermaine reluctantly turned his laptop around so it faced the three boys. There was no internet connection, but he'd obviously taken some screenshots and wanted a bigger screen than his phone. He knew this would be a defining moment.

"Remember I told you that my mom had mentioned the hunter's cabin with the grave was near someplace called Skagit Creek?" They all nodded. "I searched for it and found it—it's in a small area called Mossy Gulch. Seems there's only a brief mention of it anywhere—usually when there were floods in the area. However, it shows up on a map. It's just a tiny area, and Skagit Creek passes through it in a valley about forty miles from here."

The boys all leaned forward to get a better look. It indeed appeared as a little blue line in some valley. "So I looked on Google Earth and then found Mossy Gulch and the creek, and I zoomed in up and down the area, looking everywhere for a cabin. It took me forever. It's crazy wild and pretty much nothing but trees, rocks, and the creek," Jermaine said. "Then I found a bit of an opening and discovered this." He clicked to the next screenshot, and the boys leaned forward even closer.

There was an insignificant brown dot on an embankment of a creek.

"What's that?" Lenny asked.

Jermaine clicked one more time, and the fuzzy picture had zoomed in even closer on the same location. They could see a dot about a hundred feet in from the creek, tucked just behind some trees. "Hey, it looks like a little house," Pudgy said, making out what appeared to be a square structure in the grainy screenshot.

Jermaine nodded. "A cabin. It's the only one in the entire area that I could find."

"You reckon that's the one?" Pudgy asked.

Jermaine shrugged. "Who knows, but it's worth a shot. It's all we got."

"Are you suggesting we go find the cabin?"

"Maybe."

"Are you nuts?" Lenny asked.

Jermaine looked up at his buddies. "I'm not sure what to do. Duncan's probably dead. That's the truth. We can't save him. But I keep thinking about Becky and Pickle. And I got a pretty good idea that Archie may soon follow. I'm not sure when, or if, it will ever stop."

Again, silence descended on the shed. The sheer enormity of what Jermaine was suggesting was emotionally overpowering. It was Lenny who spoke again. "So you're gonna go and kill yourself on his grave, is that it, JP? Is that the plan?" Lenny asked facetiously.

Jermaine didn't answer.

"You're not serious," Pudgy blurted out. "Tell me you aren't serious."

Jermaine looked at the wooden floor beneath his feet. He didn't know how to answer. He was conflicted, and now that it was out in the open, he began to doubt his own resolve.

"I'll do it." It was Bernie. He stood up, moved his helmet to the back of his head, and looked directly at Jermaine. "I'll go. Someone has to, or people will keep hearing footsteps and keep walking into the woods and never coming back." His voice was oddly steady and confident.

Jermaine stared at him in surprise. "Bernie, you don't—"

"You're crazy, Bernie," Pudgy interrupted. "You can't go wandering off into the woods looking for a cabin and a grave. You'll last about a minute."

Lenny agreed. "Yeah, a minute if you're lucky, Big Balls."

Bernie seemed unperturbed by the response. He shrugged his shoulders and remained standing defiantly.

Jermaine placed his laptop on the floor, then stood up and looked at Bernie. "Not if he's not alone."

Pudgy laughed out loud. "You're kidding, right?"

Jermaine was quiet.

"You think that if you're with somebody, you're safe? Like it can't get you if you're not alone? Is that your theory, JP?" Pudgy appeared exasperated.

Jermaine looked around at each of the boys in the clan, then stared directly at Pudgy before he spoke. "Think about it, Pudgy. The hunter, and then my mom's boyfriend, they were both alone when they saw Mordecai. And wasn't Becky by herself at the hopscotch court early that Sunday morning?"

Pudgy reluctantly nodded. "Sure, but—"

"And Pickle was out for a walk alone with Taco—and he probably didn't count—though he got done-in when he was alone later."

"I guess, but—"

"And remember Duncan went down Birch Street on his own to check on Taco? That's when it all began with him too. And, of course, there's Archie. I'm not sure when he was first, you know, in contact with it—but he was on his way down Birch Street *alone* when, Pudgy, you saw him."

Pudgy looked around at the others and said nothing. It was true. Nobody ever seemed to initially hear the Follower when they were with somebody else.

"But we were with Duncan when he was hearing all sorts of stuff while riding his bike with us," Lenny remembered.

"But that was after," Bernie interjected. "Once he'd been in contact. Same with Archie sitting on Langmaid's porch. Pudgy, you saw what it was doing to him. But we weren't around when it started. Jermaine's right. I bet if there are two of us, we'll be okay."

Pudgy took a deep breath and tried to recap what had just transpired. "So let me get this straight. Bernie, you just volunteered to go into the woods to find the cabin, right?"

Bernie nodded.

"Somewhere miles and miles from here. In the middle of nowhere, right?"

He nodded again.

Pudgy then looked at Jermaine. "And you think that if he's with somebody, he'll be fine, 'cause it can't get you if you're not alone?"

"Yes," Jermaine responded.

Pudgy continued. "And if you can't find some freaky bones and rebury them, then somebody has to kill himself on a creepy grave, right?"

Nobody responded.

"All this so this Mordecai kid is able to leave us all alone and die a normal kind of death? Does that sound about right, JP?"

Jermaine looked at the floor again. He knew it sounded preposterous.

"Are you nuts, JP?" Lenny yelled. He also stood up and looked around at his buddies. "I mean, come on, dude. You're saying more of us might need to die?"

Jermaine nodded, unwilling to meet his friend's eyes.

"Besides, do you think for a minute your mom and dad won't call the cops once you go missing too?" Lenny continued.

"That's true," Pudgy agreed. "You'd only be gone a few hours before your parents would freak out and call the cops. Everyone is freaked out anyway."

"And Bernie, your dad will flip a lid! He'd hunt you down and kill you before you got far," Lenny said with a wry chuckle.

Jermaine paused to let the tension subside a bit. He was still trying to get over Bernie's quick decision to volunteer for such a dangerous endeavor. He walked over to the desk with the candles and leaned over to look at them closely. He watched the flames flicker in the cool air. After a few seconds he spoke. "Bernie and I can say we're going to spend the weekend with Daryl Tanner in Pulltown. Our folks know we're school buddies, right?"

"What the—" Pudgy began.

"They'd understand that we'd need to get away from it all after everything that's been going on here. Heck, they'd probably even encourage it."

"It would buy us a couple of days," Bernie added. He obviously liked the idea.

"That's true," Jermaine agreed. He decided to keep it rolling while he had momentum. "We'd have a good head start before people began questioning things."

Pudgy leaned forward. His voice was quiet now. "But, JP, you're talking about you, or Bernie, maybe *dying*. Suicide. Are you serious about this? I mean, come on." His voice was shaking.

Jermaine could swear that a foreboding chill invaded the shed, penetrating the walls and pressing in on them. He smiled at Pudgy; he could tell he was as frightened as the rest of them. "I'm not asking any one of you to come with me." He looked over at Bernie. "I mean, us. All I'm saying is that can we live here if we didn't at least try? What would be the point, right? Just to watch others disappear? And then what? Huh?"

After a moment Pudgy screamed, "Jesus!" and it made everyone jump. His voice echoed off the walls and retreated into the darkness beyond

Base Camp. Then everything again fell silent. Just as Jermaine was turning away from the candles, he heard Pudgy's voice behind him. This time he was barely a whisper.

"I'm in."

Jermaine turned to look at him. "No, Pudgy, I don't—"

"All for one, and one for all, right?"

Jermaine said nothing as he looked at Pudgy. He could see tears forming in his eyes. He was shaking.

Lenny spoke next. "Well, who the hell is going to take care of you boneheads if I don't come along, huh?"

Jermaine looked over at Lenny. "You too, Lenny?"

"So shall it ever be."

The four boys slowly moved toward the middle of the shed. Jermaine looked each one of them in the eye. "This is crazy big. Are you all sure you want to do this?"

It was so quiet they could hear the faint sizzle of the candlewicks burning. It was Bernie who spoke for all of them. "When do we leave, Jermaine?"

❖

That night, as Jermaine lay in his bed, he tried to recount the various events of the day and how rapidly decisions had been made. In particular, he had been taken aback by how quickly Bernie had volunteered to find the cabin. Though he would have expected nothing less from his best friend, something in his haste made Jermaine question his ultimate motive. While he knew Bernie was a deeply empathetic and loyal person, Jermaine had a strong suspicion that proving himself to his father might be at the core.

Jermaine tried to imagine what dangers awaited the clan. He knew one thing: life in Providence would never be the same; it would change for good. In many ways, it already had.

The next day, it was obvious that the Pulltown excuse had worked like a charm. All of their parents had bought it and thought it was a grand plan. Lenny's dad even offered to drive them to Pulltown, as he had some work to attend to there. They would be at Daryl Tanner's for a couple of nights, and they had plans for some camping. There was sure to be some fishing and swimming at Lake Teshko as well. Just what the doctor ordered.

In reality, Daryl was a marginal friend, though he desperately wanted to be part of the famous "clan" from Providence. They'd hung out a bit, but really only during school time, and never during the holidays. So when Jermaine had called him up out of the blue to let him in on a little secret, he was thrilled. He'd asked Daryl to play along if anyone asked. And Daryl seemed eager to comply. Jermaine told him that after being dropped off at his house, he and the boys were actually going into Musgrove to visit some girls.

Obviously not wanting to be the one to spoil an epic adventure, Daryl agreed to perpetuate the lie. He would wait on his front lawn to greet Mr. Cartwright and the boys upon arrival. Both of his folks worked Fridays, so it was an easy-peasy no-brainer.

Jermaine had done his research. From Pulltown, Skagit Creek in Mossy Gulch was a hike of just over thirty-six miles. It would most likely take a couple of days—depending on terrain. He had packed a couple of compasses in case one broke—and like he had suggested to Pudgy and Lenny, he'd leave his cell phone at home, as he didn't want any possibility of being tracked.

All four of the boys had fairly substantial backpacks. Jermaine had outlined what he thought they'd all require for their adventure. He then designated tasks for preparation; the first one was that they were responsible for their own sleeping bag.

Pudgy would be in charge of the food. His job would be to purchase and pack four days' worth of supplies without raising suspicion. Jermaine and the others would reimburse him. "And no candy," Jermaine had demanded. Pudgy agreed, but all of them knew there would be some treats included.

Lenny was in charge of all essential survival gear. Not knowing how long they would be out there, it was important that they were well prepared. It was agreed that Lenny would secure a first aid kit, two ten-foot lengths of nylon rope, fire-making essentials, water bottles; one tent—the one they always used—was small but lightweight and would do the trick for the four of them; and a couple of hunting knives, just in case they were needed.

Bernie collected the camping supplies. One large tarp, a chlorination kit for water, a cooking pot, four bowls, and a few essential utensils.

Jermaine was the map guy. Orienteering had been a passion of his ever since he was a Cub Scout and had remained so ever since. He enjoyed using a compass and a map to challenge his navigational skills. Since he would have to leave his cell phone at home, GPS would not be an option.

He had already plotted a route, and using a topographical map that he'd printed off and had laminated at Langmaid's Grocery, he would be responsible for getting the clan to Skagit Creek—more specifically, to the hunter's cabin in Mossy Gulch. Getting home again wasn't part of the pre-planning. They would cross that bridge when they reached it.

Mr. Cartwright leaned over in the front seat of his Ford F-150 and slapped his son on the shoulder. "You boys have a good time. We'll be seeing you in a couple of days. Be good and be safe." With that, he waited until they'd all poured out of his truck and then drove away from the Tanners' house—honking his horn and waving his arm out the window at them.

Daryl Tanner jumped off his front doorstep, grinning from ear to ear. "Hello, guys," he said awkwardly. He admired the sheer guts in attempting this adventure in the first place. "So tell me about the girls in Musgrove. Do I know them?"

"Hey, Daryl. Thanks a lot for helping us out here. I know you didn't have to," Jermaine said. "We gotta run, but I swear we're going to make it up to you next year. I promise. And remember, if anyone asks, we're camping with you, okay?"

"So you guys are heading out now?" Daryl seemed disappointed. He'd hoped for a chance to hear all about the naughty exploits they'd been planning with the Musgrove girls.

Jermaine looked back at Daryl. "Gotta run, Daryl. We're already late, and we're getting a ride from a friend up in town. See you later, and thanks so much, buddy."

The boys all turned and began to quickly walk across Daryl's lawn to the road and toward town. Once they were just over the ridge of the hill and clearly out of sight of the Tanner house, Jermaine stopped and checked the bearings on his compass. "Okay, we head into the woods here. I'll keep checking every once in a while." He looked around at his friends, first at Pudgy Murtland, then at Bernie Maclaren, and finally Lenny Cartwright. They were the closest people to him in the entire world, and he knew this was the moment of reckoning. He took a deep breath and held his arms up, inviting them in for a hug. They each did the same, forming a circle in the middle of the road and holding each other tight.

"Everyone still good to do this?" Jermaine asked. "No shame in backing out now."

Nobody spoke. Until Bernie.

"I gotta crap somethin' chronic!"

Part Two

Into the Woods

Chapter Seven

Lenny Cartwright was eight years old when he was given his first knife by his father. It was a hunter's knife, with an impressive jagged ridge on the top and a lethal, razor-sharp blade beneath.

The boys in the clan had been suitably impressed, and Lenny had brandished it with pride whenever he could. In the eyes of the clan, Lenny was the coolest, toughest kid they'd ever met. To a person, if they ever went to war, they'd choose Lenny to be with them in the trenches over anyone. Lenny was that type of person: loyal, resolute, and brave.

While Lenny was the brawn, Jermaine was clearly the brains of the group. Soon after the shed had been claimed on the far side of Farmer Granger's cornfield, it quickly became apparent that Jermaine was the *ipso facto* leader—the go-to person for advice and direction. A reality that remained unchanged throughout the years.

Jermaine always seemed to possess a steady, calm demeanor. He observed all angles before offering an opinion. When he did finally speak, he would always choose quiet, thoughtful words to advance an argument and to find reason in any situation. When it came to any decision, the boys all looked to Jermaine for ratification.

Pudgy was funny, empathetic, helpful, and grounded. Being a part of such a cool clan was the greatest thing that had ever happened to him. *All for one, and one for all* was something that he took to heart in every way possible. No one in Base Camp would ever doubt Pudgy's loyalty and devotion to the clan.

Bernie was more complex. His selfless, courageous, caring personality was complicated by his strained relationship with his father. He never felt that his father loved him, and this tested his confidence. It also drove him closer to the boys in the clan. He knew that his friends accepted and loved him unconditionally.

With Duncan seemingly gone forever, they all knew that the strength of their bond would be tested beyond comprehension. The first few minutes of their journey had already proven to be a challenge, as it was immediately apparent that it would be tougher going than they had anticipated.

Much tougher.

❖

Even after a mere five hundred feet, they were virtually exhausted from scrambling over the many fallen trees, dodging thick branches, and escaping the tangles of the various vines, ferns, and unyielding, waist-high undergrowth beneath them. No topographical map in the world could have prepared them for the density of the foliage.

They had never explored the woods outside of Pulltown. In the past, they had always gone hiking and biking in the terrain west of Providence—past Birch Street. When they were younger, they spent a lot of time in those woods and got to know the landscape. But the topography here was different—much more challenging to navigate. The foliage as well seemed denser and demanded greater exertion to pass through.

Lenny led the way, trying as best he could to forge a path for everyone. Jermaine followed, compass in hand, periodically shouting out directions as Lenny pushed through the thick vegetation ahead of him. Pudgy and Bernie took turns bringing up the rear. After an hour, it was Bernie who suggested a water break. No one complained.

They found a long, moss-laden log and sat closely beside each other in a line, passing a water bottle between them. No one said a word. It was now becoming increasingly obvious to the boys that it would take longer than a couple of days to get to Skagit Creek.

Despite the tough going, they'd managed to remain close enough to each other, always within sight. According to Jermaine, it was the one rule—*the only rule* that mattered. So far, it seemed to be paying off.

After a twenty-minute rest, Lenny decided it was time to get going. Pudgy found a sweatshirt in his backpack and pulled it on, helping to protect the Band-Aids that Lenny had already applied to some deep scrapes and cuts on his arm. As he threw his pack onto his back, he told Bernie that he would take up the rear for a while.

❖

Guylaine Cloutier began making her way back up Birch Street and toward her temporary accommodations at the Breaches'. A significant part of her life had been spent on the road living this way—in insignificant dusty, one-horse towns like Providence; or meandering through quiet suburbs near urban sprawls; or trekking across farm fields near the various middle-of-nowhere, sleepy hamlets that dotted the continent. Rarely in cities, though. Cities were too loud and chaotic for anyone to notice anything was amiss. Cities were impersonal, and the missing were deemed to simply be missing—probably kidnapped, gunned down, overdosed, or runaways.

Guylaine only ventured to new locations when she felt she could help. To places she could potentially get people to listen, where she could make a difference. People might listen in a town like Providence. But now it only seemed to be a young boy that actually heard her. She knew Jermaine understood. She could sense it in him, and it made her sad.

At home, her evenings were typically spent scanning the infinite number of local news stations and newspapers from across the continent and separating the chaff from the wheat. She had become quite adept at deciphering the chatter, differentiating the run-of-the-mill disappearances of loved ones with the oddities—the ones that didn't sit right with the locals. The ones that just made them scratch their heads. The ones that were followed by another one, and perhaps another—*yet again.*

Back in the day, Guylaine's momma and her *mawmaw* didn't have the resources she had now. There was not the easy benefit of internet, newswires, and such. They relied on word of mouth. Over time—albeit a great deal of time—news would eventually filter down to their cabin in the delta because somebody knew somebody, and that somebody knew somebody else who would recommend her *mawmaw* and momma. People knew of these wise women living in southern Louisiana who could help. These women understood what needed to be done.

But times changed, and the visionaries like her had become sideshow spectacles and outliers. Their talents were seen as nothing more than street-performing claptrap and gibberish. Freaks.

While Guylaine continued to be drawn to places like Providence out of sheer duty, she was more often than not maligned, teased, and blamed for the inexplicable occurrences that were taking place willy-nilly in a community. It was wearying, but she knew she had no choice. It was her calling.

If not me, then who? she often thought.

As she ambled past Langmaid's Grocery, she realized it had been three days since she'd last seen Archie Truscott. She was aware that his talisman would have only lasted awhile; it was a temporary mind trick—a placebo, nothing more. There was little else she could do. She knew that eventually he would have to go. He wouldn't be able to resist the footsteps leading him down Birch Street. The inbetweener would get him. Locking him up and tying him down would do nothing more than make him go utterly mad. Eventually his body would succumb to the terror.

❖

Dr. Teddy Mitchell had been a dentist in Musgrove his entire professional career. After Teddy had retired, he and Emily, his wife of thirty-eight years, had moved back to Providence, the place where they had both grown up. They had purchased and restored a quaint white rancher on Arbutus Avenue, where now they both spent the majority of their summer days puttering around their impressive garden.

Teddy Mitchell was a creature of habit, and most days he could be seen going for a run-walk, or *light jog*, as he liked to call it, down Main Street. He always took the same route. From his house he would head north until he got to the edge of town and turn down Blarney Crescent. Once Blarney hit Main Street, he would then turn and head through the center of town along Main Street, past Langmaid's Grocery, Your Town Hardware, and the church, eventually turning east and circling back home along Aspen Street.

But not today.

Mrs. Glenys Brothwell was walking her two pugs on Main Street and was about to say good morning to Dr. Mitchell when she noticed his "light jog" had suddenly turned into a rather frantic run; by the time he was almost upon her, it had become a full-out sprint.

Aghast, Mrs. Brothwell stopped in her tracks, pulling her pugs' leashes toward her as he raced past her. She then watched him make a sudden right turn on Birch Street. His erratic behavior was bewildering, and the terror in his eyes had completely frightened her. He was yelling and screaming and flailing his arms out beside him. It scared the living daylights out of her.

Watching in shock as the dentist disappeared down Birch Street, Mrs. Brothwell hurriedly waddled to the corner just in time to catch a glimpse of the dentist entering the woods at the bottom of the road. Her pugs had begun barking incessantly, and she quickly picked them both up to calm them down.

❖

Guylaine Cloutier left the front porch of Langmaid's Grocery and slowly made her way to Archie Truscott's house. She hadn't seen him for a few days and wanted to see if she could help in any way. She knew that Tammy and Yarl Truscott were aware that she'd been somewhat successful in helping their son before, but she was unsure how they would react when she knocked on their door.

It was Yarl who answered. "Hey," he said. He didn't invite her in.

"Mr. Truscott, I just wanted to see how Archie was doing. I've not seen him lately."

"Not great," Yarl answered suspiciously. "Look, lady, I'm not sure who—or what—you are, but this is a private matter. Thanks for checking in, but it's best if you don't anymore." He began to close the door.

"I only want to help, Mr. Truscott. I've seen this before, you know."

Yarl stopped closing the door and stared at the older woman in front of him. She was dressed in exotic clothing and bejeweled from head to toe. "What did you say?"

"The Follower. He hears the Follower. It's trying to get him to leave your house. To go to the woods. I know what's happening to him."

Yarl didn't know how to respond. She could see he was confused. When he spoke again, his voice was soft and sad. "He hasn't eaten or slept in days. He keeps crying." Yarl's own voice cracked with emotion. "Dr. Lewis isn't sure what's happening."

"It's nothing she can help with. There's nothing you can do. It will run its course one way or another," Guylaine explained, trying not to sound too harsh but wanting to be honest. "Here, please give him this." Guylaine reached out her hand. "Tell him it's from me. Tell him to rub it with both hands and then put it under his pillow at night. It may take some of the edge off." Yarl took the small, polished stone from her hand. "It's another talisman. Nothing more than a small rock, really, but it may buy him some relief and comfort if he believes in it."

Yarl Truscott peered at the shiny stone in his hand. He then looked up and mouthed, "Thank you," and slowly closed the door.

Guylaine made her way through town toward Birch Street. It was time to keep watch again. In the distance she could see Mrs. Glenys Brothwell clutching her two pugs and hurrying toward her. She looked utterly frightened.

❖

Officer Douglas Thompson eased his police car up the Mitchells' driveway and came to a gentle stop. He reluctantly stepped out and closed the door. He could see a crowd had already formed in front. He felt his gut tighten. *Here we go again*, he thought.

Glenys Brothwell was holding her two pugs—one under each chubby arm—and a group of anxious neighbors had surrounded her on the front lawn. Glenys was recounting what had transpired down on Birch Street while out walking Daffy and Dandy. "The poor things are still beside themselves with worry," she declared, cuddling the dogs closer to her ample bosom.

As Thompson moved toward the front door, he was still attempting to process what he'd heard from dispatch about Dr. Mitchell. *What the hell is going on in Providence?* he thought, reaching over to press the doorbell.

Inside, Dr. Patricia Lewis had just sedated Mrs. Mitchell and was checking her pulse for the third time. Glenys Brothwell had immediately called Dr. Lewis when Mrs. Mitchell had fainted at her own front doorstep after being informed about her husband's disappearance into the woods on Birch Street.

When Mrs. Mitchell was again conscious and able to speak, she eventually explained to Dr. Lewis that her husband had indeed been acting a little odd the last few days. She noted that he was a private man and didn't like to share what was on his mind. But she knew something was off with him.

She told her that the last thing that she could ever imagine was that he'd been "infected with this Follower nonsense." The more she thought about what might have happened to her husband, however, the more anxious and inconsolable she became. Dr. Lewis decided sedation was the best option.

Within a few minutes of Glenys Brothwell's terror-inducing description of what she'd just witnessed, a few of the brave local folks had begun to scour the woods beyond Birch Street. After a couple of hours, they had found neither hide nor hair of Dr. Mitchell. Just like the Simpson boy, the good dentist seemed to have vanished into thin air.

As he slowly returned to town, Thompson knew in his heart that the dog-and-pony show would be hitting Providence again within the next few hours. The entire area would become ground zero for yet another soul-crushing search and rescue operation.

❖

By late afternoon, they realized they needed to find a suitable site to set up camp for the night, as they were exhausted. Though by Jermaine's calculation they had only gone twelve miles, it had already taken its toll on all of them.

Pudgy had a few pretty nasty gashes on his forearms from his encounter with some bramble he'd gotten caught in. All the Band-Aids that Lenny had applied had peeled off, so they dropped their packs and Lenny pulled out the first aid kit to treat his wounds. It wasn't anything serious, but there was a fair bit of blood.

Bernie and Jermaine sat on the ground and studied the map. "I'm pretty sure we're right here," Jermaine said, pointing to the location. Bernie let his eyes travel along the length of the map toward Skagit Creek and could see they still had a significant distance to cover.

"If we don't get there by the end of the weekend, everyone will be out looking for us, you know," Bernie stated.

Jermaine nodded. It was true. It was already late Friday afternoon, and if the terrain continued the way it was, there was little chance of reaching the cabin until Sunday evening. And once Monday morning rolled around, questions would begin to be asked.

The place they had selected to be their campsite was relatively flat. There was enough room between the massive Douglas firs and Great Western cedars that surrounded them to pitch the tent and also give them a bit of space to move around.

They spent the first fifteen minutes stamping down ferns, kicking smooth small clumps of earth, and moving some of the fallen branches and decomposed logs to make the entire space more comfortable. At Lenny's suggestion, they then collected armfuls of moss and laid them on the area where they had decided to put their tent.

As Bernie and Lenny put up the tent, Pudgy had volunteered to be the chef and began to sort through his pack for dinner options, of which there were two: spaghetti and plastic pouches of tomato sauce, or Kraft Macaroni and Cheese. Jermaine dug a small hole that would become their fire pit. They would search for dry firewood in groups of two once the tent was up.

By seven o'clock, the sleeping bags had been laid out in the tent, the fire was lit, the water in the pot was boiling, and the boys had gathered around the warm glow, enjoying the comforting heat. Due to the thickness of the surrounding forest, it had become noticeably darker, and the damp chill that clung to the air had quickly descended into their campsite.

"So quiet here," Bernie observed. The lack of any sounds other than their own movements made it feel surreal. The silence was unnerving.

Pudgy pulled the cheese pouches out of the four boxes of macaroni and cheese and poured the pasta into the pot, giving it a stir with his wooden spoon. He threw the empty boxes onto the fire, and the ensuing flames caused the shadows to dance on the large boughs high above them.

"We should have enough water for another day's worth of hiking and to cook one more meal. If we see any other source tomorrow, we should do a refill just in case," Lenny suggested.

"Good point. Let's keep our eyes open tomorrow. I can't see any creeks on the map, but who knows," Jermaine said. He took a bowl and spoon from the stack in front of him and passed the others around. They were all getting hungry.

"You bring ketchup, Pudgy?" Bernie asked.

"Duh," Pudgy replied sarcastically. "Who can eat Kraft Mac and Cheese without ketchup?"

"What about milk?" Lenny asked.

"Got a packet of dried milk. When we strain the water, we'll leave some in the bottom. We can add the cheese at the same time," Pudgy replied proudly.

"Awesome," Bernie commented. He licked his lips in anticipation.

After they had eaten and rubbed the dishes clean with moss and a bit of water, they went to their packs to pull out sweatshirts or sweaters to put on, then returned to sit around the small fire. It was now well and truly dark, and all of them were constantly looking over each other's shoulders into the thick woods just beyond them—Jermaine couldn't help but feel that they were being observed. "We should get an early start in the morning," he said.

"How far do you think we'll get?" Pudgy asked.

"Depends on the terrain. I think we have a bit of a climb tomorrow," Jermaine replied, pulling his map from his pocket. "Once we get over the high point, after that, we can head down to the valley and hopefully follow that the rest of the way." Jermaine clicked his flashlight on and pointed it at his map. "Hopefully it will clear a bit once we're in the valley."

Lenny took his hunting knife from the sheath on his belt and began whittling a long branch he'd found earlier in the day. "Whaddya think we're gonna find at that cabin, JP?"

Jermaine only shrugged. He had no idea what they were going to find. Deep inside he was desperately attempting to come to terms with the supreme sacrifice one of them might have to make. It had consumed him ever since he had made up his mind about what needed to be done.

"I miss Duncan so much," Bernie suddenly said.

The group was silent. Nothing more could be added. They all watched as Lenny continued to carve his stick into a sharp spear, periodically holding it up to admire his own handiwork.

It was Jermaine who finally spoke. "We should head to bed. Let's all go and have a pee together, then call it a night."

❖

Most of Providence was quiet, and the residents had consciously locked their doors, double-checking they were secure, and gone to bed. They were shaken and confused; they knew that the next day would be a hectic one.

Officer Thompson drove his cruiser through town and then decided to head down to the base of Birch Street for a quick look. His headlights shone silver and yellow off the thick, dark branches ahead of him. When he reached the end, he stopped the car and turned off the engine.

On the seat beside him was a large and powerful searchlight. He picked it up, and as he opened his car door and stepped out, he flicked it on and pointed it to the forest beside him. There was a slight breeze, and the dark branches wiggled and danced. He moved the light from left to right, slowly and with purpose. *Whatever is happening in Providence, it seems to begin and end right here,* he thought, moving the light back in the opposite direction.

He knew the missing person report he'd filled out with Mrs. Mitchell and Glenys Brothwell had been nothing more than protocol. He'd radioed it all in and told the sheriff what he thought. Officer Ian Plant was already on his way out to help him handle the locals in the morning while they waited for the circus to begin.

His job tonight was to help calm the residents and to keep a vigilant eye on the town. *To serve and protect,* he thought, reaching for the car door and turning off his light. He was about to get into the car when he thought he heard something move in the woods ahead of him. He quickly turned his light back on and shone it toward the trees.

"Dr. Mitchell? Is that you?" Thompson moved his light from side to side.

Nothing.

"Hello?" Thompson stepped forward and leaned down, trying to see beneath the thick boughs that lined the street. The wind was picking up, and the limbs shivered and twisted in the breeze.

Come on, Dougie boy, get a grip. There's nothing there, he thought, convincing himself he was just imagining things.

Keeping an eye on the trees, he walked backward toward the car, then reached for the door handle and quickly opened it. As he got in, he snapped off the light again, placing it back on the seat beside him. He turned the key in the ignition, and his headlights came on. A clump of bushes ahead of him shimmied and then stopped. Thompson felt a cold rush of goose bumps roll down the back of his neck. The air felt electric and anticipatory. *It's just the wind. Get a grip, Dougie*, he thought as he put the car in reverse and did a final scan of the line of tall trees in front of him.

Suddenly the *ding, ding, ding* of his seat belt warning came on, making him jump. He quickly reached over and grabbed the strap, clicking it into place. His heart was slamming against his chest, and he took a deep breath to steady his nerves.

As he slowly continued backing up, he had the uncanny feeling that he wasn't alone.

Chapter Eight

Pudgy was the first to emerge from the tent, followed by Lenny. There had obviously been no need to animal-proof the packs in these lifeless woods, so they had left them just outside near the fire. Pudgy dug deep into his and pulled out four granola bars. As planned, breakfast would be a brief eat-and-run affair.

Jermaine came out next with his map and compass already in hand. "Hey," he said to the boys. Pudgy and Lenny nodded back.

Finally, Bernie crawled out, squinting in the morning light. He rubbed his eyes and yawned, then went to sit down by Lenny, who was examining his newly crafted spear. "Hey, Big Balls, want me to make you one of these bad boys? I can make it tonight for you."

"Cool," Bernie replied, smiling at his friend.

Behind them, without warning, Pudgy let out a terrifyingly primal, blood-curdling scream that pierced the morning silence. The three boys whipped around to see what was wrong. Pudgy had fallen over backward and was frantically pointing toward the woods beyond the tent. His eyes were wide, and he was ghost-white. The granola bars lay scattered next to him.

"What is it?" Lenny asked, leaping up and moving beside him, spear at the ready. The other boys followed suit, moving close to each other and scanning the woods.

"Did you see him?" Pudgy asked. He was breathing rapidly and shaking.

"See who, Pudgy?" Jermaine asked, searching the trees for any sign of life.

"A kid. A young boy—just standing there." Pudgy's eyes were beginning to water.

"Where?" Bernie asked, wishing he already had one of Lenny's spears.

"By the big tree there." Pudgy was still pointing toward the large cedar tree on the other side of the tent.

Lenny and Bernie slowly moved around the tent toward the tree. Lenny held his spear at arm's length in front of him and led the way.

"Be careful, guys," Jermaine warned. "Let's stick together." Jermaine grabbed Pudgy's arm and pulled him up from the ground. The four boys inched closer to the tree.

"About here?" Lenny asked.

"Yeah, right there," Pudgy replied weakly.

Lenny carefully walked around the entire tree and returned to his friends. "Nothin' here now," he said.

The four boys moved back toward the fire pit—eyes peeled on the forest that surrounded them. They stood together, panting and feeling the adrenaline coursing through their veins.

"Let's pack up and take the tent down. We need to get the heck outta here," Jermaine suggested, once again scanning the surrounding forest for any movement.

As they hurriedly took down the tent, Bernie looked over at his friend and quietly asked Pudgy what the boy looked like. The others stopped what they were doing to listen.

Pudgy was visibly shaking. "He was young—like seven or eight or so," Pudgy replied softly. His cheeks were flushed, and snot was running down from his nostrils. He wiped his nose with the sleeve of his hoodie. He looked frightened to death. "He was wearing shorts, I think. Like…blue shorts. And he had on a fancy shirt." He thought for a moment, obviously trying to remember more details. "And a red bow tie," Pudgy recalled. "He had these long blue socks and…oh, and shiny shoes. Black ones." A confused look then appeared on his face. "And he looked like he was all wet."

"Holy moly," Bernie said.

"What was he doing, Pudgy?" Jermaine asked.

"Just standing there." Pudgy paused, then continued. His voice was noticeably weaker. "Smiling. He was smiling at me."

The boys all looked at each other before getting back to work in silence, all the while keeping a close eye on the surrounding forest. This was quickly getting real.

❖

Whatever that silly rock was that the crazy lady had asked Yarl to give to Archie, it seemed to be working, Tammy Truscott thought as she sat looking at her son. He had slept most of the night and was still asleep when she'd come to check on him early in the morning.

Yarl had explained to her that it was some kind of talisman, whatever that was. Even if it was just a silly superstitious trick, Archie had believed it, and it was giving him some relief from the constant terror he'd been feeling.

It had been excruciating to watch her son suffer, and the brief reprieve was a godsend.

Tammy made her way downstairs. Yarl was pouring coffee for the both of them as she stepped into the kitchen. "Still asleep?" Yarl asked, handing her a mug.

"Yes, thank goodness," she replied. "I'll keep checking on him." She knew that Yarl would be leaving soon, likely for most of the day. He was eager to help with the search for Dr. Mitchell. They both knew that if they found some answers about the missing dentist, it may somehow help their Archie.

They had been phoning their other two children every day to update them on Archie's condition. Archie's older sister and brother were both married and had lives of their own now. But they were still a tight-knit family, and his siblings were deeply worried; they made their parents promise them they'd keep them in the loop.

After they'd finished their coffee, Tammy walked her husband to the door. He stopped and looked at her. "You'll call me when Archie wakes? Let me know how he is?" Yarl asked, leaning over and kissing her.

Tammy nodded and wrapped her arms around him. She wondered when, if ever, this nightmare would end.

❖

The new commanding officer of this, the second Providence operation, was a grizzled veteran named Cob Stanton—a no-nonsense, cut-to-the-chase, humorless ex-marine. "Get the job done and then get the hell out" was his approach to each and every case he worked on. Anything else was an utter waste of time. He was hand-selected by the sheriff to get the job done—quickly and efficiently. The last thing anyone wanted was an even bigger circus attraction in Providence.

Stanton stood at the bottom of Birch Street and tucked his thumbs behind his thick cowboy belt pulled tightly around his taut waist; he watched as the large trailer was unhitched from the police van and blocks were placed under each tire to prevent it from rolling into the woods. Since this was the last place Dr. Teddy Mitchell had been spotted, Stanton had decided that this would be the command center while they were in town. It would be his new home until he closed down the operation.

The previous evening, volunteers had been summoned by phone tree, and again most of the town's able-bodied men and women had signed up to help out with the search. They would begin to arrive soon, and when they did, they would be sorted directly into teams. Each group would have a search and rescue volunteer assigned to them who would spend an hour going over protocols and responsibilities.

Stanton had asked to meet the "local yokel, Johnny-on-the-spot," as he liked to refer to local law enforcement in these kinds of "middle-of-nowhere, one-horse towns." In this case, that person was officer Douglas Thompson.

According to Stanton's sources, Thompson was a handsome young cop with an easy smile and a solid reputation. He was well liked and seemed to have the trust of the locals. His sidekick, Officer Ian Plant, was a doughy wannabe with a penchant for sweets. He would also be joining them.

Stanton wanted to hear everything Thompson and Plant had on Providence and its surroundings, as well as the residents of Providence and their take on what the hell was happening around here. He wanted to better understand the lay of the land and, more importantly, what he'd gotten himself into.

Stanton signaled one of the support crew to fire up the generator as he unlocked the trailer. He grabbed the small railings on either side of the door and hopped up the two metal steps and inside the trailer. Flicking on the dull yellow lights, he moved further inside and looked around the dank trailer. He could see there was already a map of the area on the wall ahead of him. It was the same one that had been used when Duncan Simpson had disappeared. While Cob Stanton hadn't worked on that case, he would use a similar search strategy.

He looked to his right and, through a small open door, he saw the tiny cot with the thin mattress. It was obvious that he wouldn't be getting much sleep while this case was active. Across from him, he saw the tiny closet serving as the toilet and shower. He scowled and moved toward the desk to his left. Two technicians were hovering over it hooking up his computer monitor and ensuring he had internet service.

The K9 unit would arrive in Providence shortly, and they would take the lead before the locals destroyed what was left of any scent. *Idiots running around in the woods, chasing shadows*, he thought, stuffing a dab of chewing tobacco under his lip.

For this search, he had also requested a drone unit. This handy resource would use the latest thermal imaging cameras in three separate drones, hoping to spot something warm-blooded, alive, and roughly the same size as a missing dentist.

Beside the desk was a coffee maker and a microwave on a counter; below them, a small fridge. "Hey, Pete," he yelled, his gruff, whiskey-tortured voice penetrating the trailer walls. A few seconds later, a scrawny young officer opened up the trailer door and peered in. "Yeah, boss?"

"What's a guy gotta do to get a hot mug of java 'round here?"

The nervous man glanced over at the counter and realized some basic supplies were needed. "On it, boss," he replied as he disappeared from the trailer.

Stanton waited until the technicians were finished and satisfied that the Wi-Fi was working. They quickly left the trailer without speaking to the commanding officer. Stanton ambled over to the desk and sat down behind it. Leaning back, he looked around the miserable trailer. He was more determined than ever to make short work of this case so he could head back to the city.

❖

They began climbing almost immediately after leaving their campsite. At first the terrain began as a gradual incline and then soon became quite steep, and Pudgy in particular was struggling. The thick undergrowth remained awkward to navigate and demanded that the four boys zigzag in, around, and through the many obstacles in their way.

Jermaine constantly checked and double-checked his orientation, pausing often to ensure they remained relatively in line with their intended destination. By noon he figured they had only covered about seven miles.

"Time out," Pudgy yelled, sucking for air as he plopped himself down on a log.

"Hold on, boys," Bernie called out. "Rest time."

Lenny and Jermaine turned and came back to join them. They all let the backpacks fall off their shoulders onto the ground. It was hot and there was little air. The forest was quiet and expectant—*like it is anticipating us*, Jermaine thought as he attempted to find their location on the map.

"So whatcha think, JP?" Lenny asked after taking a swig of water from his canteen.

"I think we must be nearly at the top. Once we get there, it looks like it's straight down to the valley, and then we can follow that all the way to Skagit Creek." Jermaine wiped his forehead with his sleeve. "Everyone okay?"

All three boys nodded. Pudgy didn't look well, and the boys all knew it was primarily because of what—*or who*—he saw earlier that morning.

Jermaine continued. "We can probably set up camp in the valley tonight and make it to the cabin by midafternoon tomorrow if we push it."

The boys all sat in silence. The thought of reaching the cabin and actually having to confront the ultimate purpose of their journey was beyond frightening.

❖

Archie awoke with a yell. Tammy was in the den and dropped her book and ran up the stairs to his room. Her son had his feet tucked up under him on the bed. He was crying and rocking back and forth.

"Honey, I'm here," she said as she moved toward the bed.

"Mommy, Mommy, tell it to go away. Bad. Bad. Go away!" Archie screamed through his tears.

Tammy sat on the bed beside him and hugged him close to her. He was hot and wet with sweat. She suddenly thought of the talisman beneath his pillow and reached over to grab it.

"Look what I found, honey. That lady gave it to you, remember? She knows how to help you."

Archie slowly stopped crying and looked down at the small stone in her hand. He reached out and took it from her, still sniffling and shaking.

"Makes them go away?" he asked, looking at his mother.

"It helps, honey."

Archie cuddled the stone in both hands and slowly lay back down. "Don't like the footsteps, Mommy."

Tammy felt a shiver race down the length of her body. "I know, honey."

❖

From the top of Birch Street, she had watched them assembling. She knew there would be too many suspicious eyes on her if she tried to help out. She was an outsider; a few saw her as a curiosity, but most saw her as a shifty vagabond who was somehow connected to these events.

Guylaine Cloutier knew the efforts of the volunteers would be fruitless. It always was, but she came to watch anyway. *Without hope, what do you have?* she thought, walking toward her spot in the grass, halfway down Birch Street. *Absolutely nothing.*

It was why she kept doing what she did. Year after year. Town after town. State after state. It was all about offering hope and having hope.

Mordecai was very active, she thought. He was more active than most of the others had been. His appetite seemed insatiable, and he was brazenly aggressive. Guylaine knew that it would probably get a lot worse before it got better. Until someone dealt with his grave—wherever it was. In the meantime, she could only do what she did best: warn people, give advice when asked for it, and keep watching for signs.

The sun began to peek over the tops of the massive trees at the bottom of Birch Street, and it felt warm on her face. She could see a lot of activity happening around the trailer that was parked right beside the hopscotch court.

Becky Green's hopscotch court.

Locals and out-of-towners alike were milling about, drinking coffee, and fiddling on their phones, trying to keep busy before the proverbial starter's pistol would sound and they could run off into the woods and feel that they were actually doing something meaningful.

Tension was in the air. People were noticeably antsy and ready to get on with it. She knew that, ultimately, people were privately consumed with one thing: trying to make sense of what the heck was going on in Providence.

Guylaine could hear the crowd grow quiet, and many began looking up her way. She turned and looked beside her and saw six people slowly walking, arm-in-arm, down Birch Street toward the trailer. By the time they had reached the others, the murmur had become a hushed silence, and Guylaine figured she could have heard a pin drop.

She recognized them and was moved by their presence. Pickle's parents, Dave and Morgan Town, walked beside Becky's mom and dad, Gladys and Brian Green; and beside them, Duncan's folks, Doris and Shane Simpson. They were here to join their community in looking for Dr. Teddy Mitchell.

Guylaine admired their stoicism and their desire to help look for the missing dentist. She knew they were also here to find answers.

Or closure.

Or both.

❖

The K9 unit consisted of four dogs and their corresponding handlers. They were split up into two groups and had already been in the woods for over two hours, and other than the initial entry point that Glenys Brothwell had confirmed as where she'd seen Dr. Mitchell enter the woods, they found nothing. *Bloody locals trampling it all*, Commanding Officer Cob Stanton thought, spitting out a brown stream of soggy chew onto the ground.

The volunteers had been separated into five teams and were still getting briefed by their leaders. Though most of them had already been through the whole process recently in the search for Duncan Simpson, it was still a necessary exercise.

Officers Douglas Thompson and Ian Plant got out of their vehicle and walked toward the lean, gruff man standing just outside the command trailer ahead of them. They'd heard of Cob Stanton. Most cops had. From what they were told, after he had returned from active duty with the I Marine

Expeditionary Force in the early years of the Gulf War, he decided to pursue a career in law enforcement. Once there, it didn't take long for him to move up the ladder, and he was promoted to senior member of the Seattle Violent Crimes Division. A position he held for nearly two decades before he was moved over to his current gig handling situations like this one. He had quite a reputation throughout the entire state—in short, he was a jerk, albeit a jerk who tended to get results. They were both a little tentative as they approached.

Thompson was the first to stick out his hand to offer a welcoming handshake. He smiled warmly and introduced himself.

"I know who the hell you are," Stanton growled, looking with disdain down at Thompson's outstretched arm. He then turned and stomped up the trailer steps and pushed through the door. "Get up here so we can get down to business," he barked over his shoulder, his stern, weathered voice reverberating off the trailer walls.

Thompson looked at Plant and smiled again. This was going to be interesting.

❖

They had finally broken the back of the climb, feeling the relief in their legs as the terrain began to flatten out. The forest was still a challenge due to the thick undergrowth making it difficult to navigate—but their spirits lifted with the understanding that soon they would be descending toward the valley.

"Hey, Bernie, how's Pudgy?" Jermaine called over his shoulder. He was busy verifying his bearings on the map as he walked while at the same time making sure he didn't trip and fall flat on his face.

Bernie briefly glanced behind him and replied, "Hanging in."

"Lenny…hey, Lenny, let's find a place to rest. We could all use it," Jermaine yelled ahead at Lenny, who was pushing through the forest fifteen feet in front of him. Lenny had been invaluable in finding the easiest path around rocks, over deadfall, and through the thick undergrowth—all the while moving left or right, depending on Jermaine's instructions, as if Lenny were the driver and Jermaine his navigator in an off-road car rally. *We work well as a team*, Jermaine thought, stepping over yet another log.

"I see something up here," Lenny hollered. "A big boulder we can sit on. Might even get a view."

"Hey, Lenny, know what?" Bernie yelled at the top of his lungs.

"What, Big Balls?" Lenny's voiced echoed back through the forest.

"I gotta crap somethin' chronic!"

They all chuckled, and Pudgy picked up a branch and threw it at Bernie, hitting him in back. "You're such an idiot."

"Sticks and stones, Pudgy!" Bernie retorted.

By the time they had all dropped off their heavy backpacks and climbed up onto the boulder, a few drops of rain had begun to fall. They didn't mind a bit, as it felt wonderfully cool on their hot faces.

Pudgy, looking determined, began digging deep toward the bottom of his pack in search of something. Eventually, with a smile as wide as his face, he emerged, pulling out a flattened pack of Twinkies—holding it proudly above his head like he'd won a major trophy. "Score!"

Lenny laughed. "Awesome. Chuck me one of those bad boys."

"Me too," Bernie said.

Jermaine nodded at Pudgy. He'd take one as well.

After they had eaten and rested, Jermaine spread his map out on top of the flat rock face in front of them and the boys gathered around, watching the raindrops bead on top of the laminated topographical map.

"We're here," he said, pointing to a spot on the map just past where the contour lines were close together. "That's the hill we just climbed. And this is where we want to get to by tonight," he said, moving his finger past another stack of contour lines. "Once we get down that hill, we'll be in the valley. We should try to make camp there."

Jermaine looked over at Pudgy. He was pale and suddenly serious. It was obvious that he was again thinking about what he'd witnessed that morning.

Pudgy could still see the young boy in front of him. He was dressed in what appeared to be formal summer clothing, standing there dripping wet and staring directly at him. The boy's small body had appeared frail, and dressed the way he was, he looked like one of the nerdy boys protected by the Laser Robots in his comic books. There was something about the way he had been staring at Pudgy and smiling. He reminded Pudgy of a ravenous lion eager for a kill. Lethal.

But at the same time, the boy's smile also seemed more calculating than desperate—as if he were on a mission.

Why was he smiling? Is he toying with us?

But most of all, try as he might, Pudgy could not forget the look of the boy's emotionless, maniacal eyes. They appeared dark and lifeless—empty.

Pudgy couldn't shake a terrible feeling. He'd had it gnawing at him all day long. He was positive that all four of them were being led into this boy's trap—like a cunning spider, watching and waiting as his clueless victims climbed right into his web.

"You okay, Pudgy?" Lenny asked, shaking Pudgy out of his thoughts.

Pudgy nodded and took a drink of water. The wind was picking up, and the rain was beginning to fall harder. It was time to get going.

❖

Murphy's law, Commanding Officer Cob Stanton thought as he stood outside in the pouring rain, watching the Search and Rescue Drone Unit assembling their equipment in the foul conditions. He buttoned his dark blue raincoat tight around his neck and leaned back against the trailer. He had helped them determine locations for deployment in the forest in front of him based on the topographical maps. He almost felt sorry for the poor sods who had to stand in these dismal conditions with their gadgets as they searched every inch of the forest floor.

Almost.

The drones' thermal imaging cameras were capable of locating any warm-blooded life form in the forest below. They would search from an altitude of two hundred feet above the treetops and would maneuver, in crisscross fashion, over a two-mile radius around predetermined areas, scanning the forest floor for any sign of life. In particular, anything that might be the shape and size of a human.

Stanton spewed a brown stream of tobacco juice onto the number 2 of the hopscotch court below him, watching the torrent of rainwater whisk it away toward the sewer at the end of Birch Street. *Beautiful day to look for a body*, he mused, turning and heading back to the trailer. He was already truly tired of being in Providence, Washington.

Ten minutes later he finally felt the warmth return to his hands and feet, though the trailer seemed to have a permanent dampness to it that he detested. He pulled a fresh brown clump from the pouch of Red Man tobacco and plugged it inside his cheek.

He was turning away from the tiny window above the command center desk when he heard the knock on the door. "Come in," he snapped and watched as the two nervous officers awkwardly stepped in and pulled off their hoods.

Stanton slowly examined them—a quick character analysis. Thompson was tall. *A looker. Probably had the girls throughout his jurisdiction talking about him. Young. Probably still a virgin—if so, a wasted opportunity. Intelligent.*

He then turned his focus to his sidekick, Ian Plant. A man who had avoided eye contact ever since he'd arrived. *Squishy, like the Pillsbury Doughboy*, was Stanton's first impression. *Most definitely a virgin. Probably for life. And to top it off—dumb as a bag of hammers.*

Stanton rubbed the thick stubble on his chin and sat down behind his desk, grabbing his mug of coffee. "So, boys, tell me something."

"What's that, sir," Thompson replied. Officer Plant was too nervous to say anything. Both officers briefly rested their eyes on what appeared to be a major knife wound that ran from Stanton's right wrist all the way up his forearm.

"What the fuck is happening in Providence?"

"Sir?" Thompson asked, taken aback by Stanton's in-your-face persona.

"Don't play stupid, son."

"Right," Thompson said, clearing his throat before continuing. "Well, we're not exactly sure. But it *seems* to have been going on for a while."

"It?"

Plant looked over at Thompson. Stanton could tell he was glad his partner was handling things.

Stanton didn't invite them further into the trailer. He could see they looked awkward standing by the door, dripping wet. He was fine with that.

"It seems that people have been hearing things—you know, footsteps and such. And…they seem to be drawn to the woods here." Thompson pointed at the wall beside him. He knew that his performance thus far had been feeble at best. Truth was, he hadn't a clue what was happening to the people of this town.

Stanton suddenly released a mucus-filled, hacking cough that would have made Keith Richards proud. He then pulled an empty Coke can to his lips and released a gob of green and brown phlegm into the opening as he stared at the two officers. "So, tell me, then—if you're capable…" He leaned forward and glared at what he perceived to be a couple of rejects in front of him. "Why do you think the good people of Providence are suddenly getting up and sprinting into these goddamn woods? And once they do, why is it that they appear to go either batshit crazy, missing altogether, or dead?"

Plant again looked at Thompson, and he took the cue. "We're not sure, sir. Dr. Lewis—the local doctor who has been assessing the situation—I mean, she has, you know, been treating many of the victims—well, she's wondering if it's some kind of collective psychosis. Apparently, that can happen sometimes. Or, she said another explanation could be that it's a virus that affects them mentally. They are still doing tests, so we're just not sure."

Stanton stood up, pushing his chair away from him with the backs of his legs, and slowly walked around the desk, eventually sitting back down on the edge of it. He was now only a few feet from the officers. He folded his arms across his chest and leaned back. "I see. And do tell me, what kind of cockamamy theory is that? A virus? Jesus Murphy, man. Is this whole town stupid?"

Thompson and Plant didn't reply. They obviously knew better.

"You boys have been in charge of this area for a couple of years now, right?"

They both nodded sheepishly.

"You'd think you'd have come up with some better explanations than that one. In the meantime, I have a search—and hopefully a rescue—to attend to. Get back to me when you have something useful to offer." Stanton nodded toward the door.

❖

When they were back in their vehicle, Plant looked over at Thompson and shook his head. He was still in shock. "Crap, is he always in such a foul mood? What was that all about?"

Thompson smiled. "Just trying to save his own neck by doing his job. Don't take it personally."

"What an asshole," Plant said.

"Yup. Comes as advertised," Thompson said, starting the ignition and turning on the windshield wipers. They sat for a minute watching the scene unfolding in front of them.

They could see that the K9 unit had returned and the dogs had already been loaded into their crates in the back of the van. They knew that they would try again after they were rested and fed and a new area had been mapped out.

The search parties were about to head into the woods, and it was beginning to rain even harder. As they walked past the police car, a couple of the younger women in the first group gave Thompson brief, flirty smiles and waved. Like most people in the region, they thought he was just about the cutest thing they'd seen in Providence…*ever.*

Chapter Nine

Guylaine Cloutier stood by the fruit section of Langmaid's Grocery and looked out the window at the steady stream of cars, trucks, and various media outlet vans pouring into Providence. She had seen this scene play out many times before in towns across America. Once the media caught a sniff of something like this, they knew how to sensationalize it. It's the one thing they were good at. Soon it would be trending throughout the entire state; everyone would be keen on finding out the latest—mesmerized by the frenzied search for the missing locals and speculating on the mysterious cause of their disappearances. She knew it would be wise to keep out of sight for a while—a stranger like her in town was not above suspicion.

Guylaine moved toward the counter and placed her basket gently on top. "Just these today, Mrs. Langmaid."

"Yep, uh-haa.," Mrs. Langmaid replied, eyeing the two apples and then pressing the large keys down on her till. A loud *cling* filled the air as she rang up the total and pointed toward the top of the till.

"Here is a five. No change needed. Have a great day, Mrs. Langmaid," Guylaine said, handing her a bill and then heading toward the door. Her rented room was only fifty yards from Langmaid's Grocery, but the rain was becoming heavier and she knew she would be drenched if she ventured out as she was. "Say, do you have an umbrella that I could—" Before she could finish the sentence, Mrs. Langmaid, without looking up, had an umbrella in her hand and leaned it toward her. "Thank you so much, *mon ami*. You are so kind," Guylaine said, taking the umbrella from her.

"Yep, uh-haa."

❖

What a shit show, Cob Stanton thought, leaning against his wobbly desk in the cramped police trailer at the end of Birch Street. He had a bad feeling about the goings-on in Providence—like an undigested piece of raw meat, something in his gut turned and demanded attention. The weather added to his feeling of foreboding.

The incessant rain on the metal roof wailed above him, filling his new abode with a deafening barrage. The muffled knock on his door was a welcome relief from the relentless onslaught. "Come in," Stanton yelled above the din as he pulled the last Tums tablet from its plastic container and popped it into his mouth. His heartburn always acted up when he knew things were about to get real.

The man in command of the SAR Drone Unit, Billy Somer, stepped in. He was soaking wet and water poured off his long raincoat onto the faded cream linoleum floor. He flipped back his hood as he closed the door behind him. Stanton immediately noticed the look of confusion on his face.

"Everyone back?" Stanton asked, referring to the operators of the three drones.

Somer nodded. He still looked confused.

"And?" Stanton didn't have a lot of patience for subordinates who were inefficient with the use of his own time.

Billy Somer shrugged. "I don't understand."

Stanton was going to lose it. "Understand what? It was a simple question."

"Yes, everyone is back," Somer offered, but the look of disbelief on his face made it clear to Stanton that something wasn't right.

"What happened?" Stanton barked.

"Well, that's the thing," Somer replied. "Nothing."

"Nothing? So you didn't find the runaway dentist, is that what you're trying to say?" Stanton wasn't sure if Somer was drunk or just plain stupid. He reached down and picked up an empty Coke can from beside his desk. He then proceeded to release a stream of dirty brown tobacco mixed with spittle into the opening, wiping his mouth with the back of his wrist when he was done.

"Yes. No…I mean…no, we didn't find the dentist. In fact, we didn't find *anything*."

"Help me understand what you're trying to say to me, Somer." Stanton hated riddles.

"Never in my career have I experienced this. Nothing on the forest floor or in the trees above it. Nothing in the ten square miles we covered. No birds. No rodents. No animals. No dentist." Somer then slowly leaned back against the trailer door and folded his arms. He was obviously distressed. "Sir, it appears that there is *nothing* warm-blooded and alive in the entire area that we searched."

Stanton stared at the man in front of him as he attempted to decipher what he'd just heard. He realized then and there that his premonitions had been correct. *Yes siree, this was turning into a regular shit show in Providence.*

❖

The rain was falling harder now, and the warm wind had picked up considerably. The descent became even more treacherous as the ground beneath them turned muddy and slick. The trees whipped back and forth in the wind like they were being tugged to and fro, which made navigating their way down the steep slope perilous.

Jermaine stopped periodically in an attempt to check his bearings, but the combination of the weather and the difficult terrain made it nearly impossible. He decided to wait until they were further down into the valley before trying it again.

Like all the boys, ever since they'd entered the woods, he'd seen an unusual amount of animal and bird bones scattered throughout the forest floor. Each carcass had appeared to be picked completely clean. Anything that had once lived in these woods had succumbed to something. It then dawned on him that it was the same in the forest beyond Birch Street, though he'd never given it much thought before.

"Need a break," Pudgy yelled from behind, his voice quickly dissipating in the howling wind.

"What?" Jermaine called over his shoulder. He then stopped and looked up behind him. Pudgy and Bernie were twenty feet from him, and he could tell Pudgy was struggling. Jermaine then looked below him and called out to Lenny, who was further down the hill. "Hold on, Lenny. Break time again."

At first it appeared that Lenny hadn't heard him, but he soon stopped and turned to face Jermaine. He raised his hand and gave the thumbs-up sign. He then moved to his left where he found a relatively flat area and pulled off his pack and plopped it down in a puddle. A river of mud and debris now raced down the slope beside him.

A minute later all four boys were huddled together in the pouring rain. Pudgy was in obvious discomfort. "I think I twisted my ankle," he said, rubbing the top of his muddy boot on his right foot.

"You'll be all right, Pudgy," Bernie offered.

"I know. Just need a rest, that's all," Pudgy replied sheepishly as he sat down in the mud. Jermaine knew that Pudgy hated being the one who seemed to be holding things up all the time. He had always admired his pluck and grit.

Bernie pulled off his pack and sat down beside him. "Holy moly, it's rainin' hard." He looked over at Jermaine. "How much longer until we get to the valley, do you think?"

"Maybe a half hour or so. Not that much longer." Jermaine pulled out the plasticized topographical map from the front pocket of his pack and placed it on his knee. The rain was bouncing off the lamination and he wiped it with his raincoat sleeve before placing his compass on top.

They all saw it at the same time. The compass needle was spinning around wildly.

"What the—" Lenny blurted out.

"Must be the rain," Pudgy suggested. The compass needle then began to rotate even more quickly. Jermaine picked it up and gave it a shake, then placed it back on top of the map. The magnetized needle continued to spin out of control.

Jermaine then dug into his pack and pulled out his spare compass. “Must be broken,” he offered weakly, placing the second one on top of the map as well. The needle began to fly around wildly.

The four boys looked at each other, eyes wide and expectant. It was then that Lenny saw him.

❖

Dr. Patricia Lewis was beginning to feel like she might as well take up permanent residence in Providence. *Who needs the fast-paced city life when you have all this craziness right here?* she thought, stepping through doorway into the front hall of the Truscotts’ house, pulling off her wet raincoat and handing it to Tammy Truscott.

Archie had taken another turn for the worse and could do nothing but rock back and forth on his bed all morning, holding his ears with his hands. Lewis had brought some sedatives along that she hoped might alleviate his anxiety. Whatever was going on in Providence was way beyond her expertise. The similarities of the cases were unnerving, and she had no idea if it was an issue with an exposure to some kind of toxic chemical that caused the brain to react this way, or if it was a viral infection, or just plain hysteria. Whatever it was, it was scaring the hell out of the good folks of Providence—her included.

She had decided that Archie would have to be taken to Seattle to get blood work done and so he could be monitored more closely by experts; Dr. Lewis had already ordered transportation. She knew this decision would freak out the Truscotts, as they would have a vivid recollection of Becky Green being sent away and never returning. This would be hard news for the family.

After administering some sedatives to Archie, Lewis came back down the stairs. Tammy Truscott was standing in the kitchen. "Sleeping now," Dr. Lewis replied.

Tammy breathed out a sigh of relief. "Coffee?" Tammy asked hopefully. Dr. Lewis could tell that she was beside herself with worry; her husband, Yarl, was helping out with the search for the missing dentist, so she was trying to cope on her own as best as she could.

"Thanks, that would be great," the doctor said, taking a chair by the table. This was going to be a difficult conversation.

❖

No birds, squirrels, mice? Cob Stanton kept running it around and around in his head. *No skunks, raccoons, bears, elk, or deer? Nothing?* It just didn't make any sense at all. If it were one drone, he would have blamed it on faulty equipment. But all three drones? Something smelled rotten in the state of Washington.

One of his deputies had dropped off a cold box of Kentucky Fried Chicken that he'd picked up in Pulltown on his way to Providence. Stanton pulled out a mangy-looking thigh and bit into it. *Maybe that crap about a virus is true. Maybe something has chased away all forms of life in the area*, he mused, looking down at the soggy fries squished at the bottom of the box. *Or something has consumed them.*

Stanton thought of Officer Thompson. He seemed like a reasonable guy. Young and wet behind the ears, perhaps—but obviously keen to do right. It was time to get him to round up some of the local hunters for questioning. They'd know how long the game had been missing in these parts and where it was now.

❖

"Don't move," Lenny whispered. They were all huddled together, sitting in a circle, and Bernie, Pudgy, and Jermaine all looked up at their friend. He was staring intently toward the trees directly behind them as the rain pummeled his face. They could see the fear in his eyes.

"Is it him?" Pudgy whispered weakly.

Lenny nodded.

"What's he doing?" Bernie asked, his deep voice cracking.

Lenny shook his head and mouthed, "Nothing."

They heard it at the same time. A giggle. The kind made by a child who was hiding and being naughty. The type of giggle made by a mischievous kid planning things while believing that he was unobserved. A giggle made by kids with secrets. Then it stopped and was followed by the jarring sound of breaking branches and a frantic commotion in the woods behind them; they all swung around in time to see a large bough of a cedar tree violently flinging upward and then back down.

Then, just as suddenly, it stopped. All was still again.

Jermaine turned to look at Lenny and saw that he was shaking. He'd never seen his friend so unnerved.

"You okay, Lenny?"

Lenny nodded.

"The boy?" Jermaine asked.

Lenny nodded again. "Yeah. He was standing there."

The three boys looked at him, shifting closer together. The rain felt heavier, and it was loud upon their hoods.

"He was smiling," Lenny whispered, barely audible above the din.

Pudgy and Bernie looked at each other. It was Pudgy who spoke next. "Was he dressed up in fancy clothes?"

Lenny nodded again. It was hard to tell if it was rain or tears that rolled down his cheeks.

❖

Officer Thompson entered the trailer first, followed by Buck Bridges, the local tanner and legendary Providence hunter. Both men peeled back their hoods and stared at the ornery man behind the desk who'd made no attempt to get up to greet them.

Cob Stanton sank back in his chair and tucked his thumbs beneath his wide belt and sized up the hunter. "Bridges, I presume. Thompson here tells me you've been hunting around these parts for over thirty years." It was a statement, not a question. Stanton then stuffed a wad of chew between his lower lip and gum and used his cheek to move it into place.

"That's right," Bridges replied. Stanton could tell from the man's demeanor that he was in no mood to have been dragged from his armchair at home to be interrogated by an uppity cop from Seattle. "That why you hauled me out here in the rain? Just to ask me that?"

Stanton smiled. He appreciated a no-nonsense man. "Somethin' like that." Stanton pulled himself up out of the chair and stretched his aching back before slowly moving toward the large map on the wall beside him. "When's the last time you bagged something here?" He was making a large circle motion on the map around a twenty-mile radius at the end of Birch Street.

Bridges didn't move closer; he could see just fine from the door. "Ain't been nothing caught there for years. Hunting went dry there eons ago. We spend our time working the north side of town these days."

Stanton eyed the man closely and squeezed a spout of sludge from his lips into the Coke can he was holding. "I see. So why do you think the hunting went bad there?"

Bridges shrugged. "Beats the hell out of us. It started slowly, and then it all went quiet. Something must have scared the prey away. Maybe a large carnivore moved into the area, but we never saw no trace of it."

"No birds? Deer? Nothing in the entire area. That make any sense to you?" Stanton pressed.

"Look here, mister. I'm a hunter, I ain't no biologist. If the deer and bear go somewhere else, I follow 'em. I'm not one to ask questions—nature has its own reasons sometimes." Bridges glared at Stanton. He was done chatting. Luckily Cob Stanton felt the same way.

"Well, thanks for coming in, Mr. Bridges. Much appreciated on such a nasty day. Happy hunting," Stanton chirped sarcastically, moving back toward his chair. "You'll get him home safe and sound and out of this rain, won't you, Officer Thompson?"

Thompson nodded and turned to Buck Bridges. He felt a fool having dragged him out on such a dreary day. He knew he would catch an earful on the way back to the car.

❖

After Lenny's encounter with the boy and everyone hearing his unnerving giggle, the entire clan was again profoundly shaken. Even though the air was now getting chilly and they were wet to the bone, they were reluctant to get moving again. It was Jermaine who suggested it was time.

Lost deep in their own thoughts, they continued their descent of the steep mountainside, gradually falling back into their preferred formation—Lenny leading the way, Jermaine following, and Pudgy and Bernie taking turns bringing up the rear. Pudgy's ankle seemed a bit better, so they were able to keep relatively close to Jermaine.

Jermaine knew that when they reached the valley floor, he would have his work cut out for him attempting to navigate without a functioning compass. He would worry about that when the time came; for now he was focused on putting one foot in front of the other without wiping out and tumbling down the steep incline.

It took a lot longer than they had anticipated. After an hour of concentrated descent, Jermaine looked at Lenny, who had moved further ahead of them than Jermaine was comfortable with, and called out for him to wait up. With the howling wind and slashing rain, he could tell that Lenny hadn't heard him. "Lenny!" he tried again, but to no avail.

Jermaine then stopped briefly to look behind him to ensure Pudgy and Bernie were making progress. He could just make them out as they carefully maneuvered around various obstacles, attempting to descend the slope. They too were distancing themselves from the group. *But at least they have each other*, Jermaine thought, bracing himself against a small sapling.

Jermaine knew that he needed to catch up to Lenny so that neither of them would be alone, so he turned and looked back down the hill. It was at that moment that he heard a faint cry for help coming from below and saw Lenny. What he saw made his knees buckle beneath him, and he fell backward into the slope.

Lenny was looking up at him—terror in his eyes. He was trying to yell, but nothing came out of his mouth. On his back was the boy. His eyes were wild, and blood covered his face. He was frantically biting into Lenny's neck and clawing away at his back. The sheer speed and tenacity of the attack was mind-numbing.

"Lenny!"

Mordecai briefly looked up at Jermaine. His mouth was full of flesh. He smiled widely. Lenny's lifeless head now dangled limply on his chest. Then, as quickly as it began, the boy stood up, grabbed Lenny by the leg, and dragged him into the thick undergrowth, disappearing from sight in one swift movement.

"*Lenny!*" Jermaine screamed at the top of his lungs and began to run—as best as he could—down the slope toward where he had seen them. After only a few feet, he slipped in the mud and tumbled headfirst down the embankment, rolling and sliding and ultimately somersaulting his way down the steep hill, eventually coming to a painful stop against a large stump with a loud *thud*.

Jermaine was dazed, and it took a moment for him to come to his senses. When he felt he could manage it, he slowly sat up while at the same time looking into the woods beside him for any sign of Lenny.

The rain pelted his face as he moved his hands over his entire body to ensure that all of his limbs were still intact. Though sore, he was still in one piece. He quickly looked back up the mountain to see if he could catch a glimpse of Pudgy and Bernie, but all he saw were the jittery tree branches writhing and contorting in the wind.

His heart was hammering against his chest as he stood up and worked his way toward the area where Lenny had disappeared. He was still dizzy and stumbled as he walked. It had happened so quickly. The speed and ease with which Lenny had vanished was incomprehensible to Jermaine. Lenny was as strong as an ox. It couldn't be real.

"Lenny, where are you?" Jermaine yelled out feebly, holding onto a tree to stop himself from wobbling. His head was throbbing, and he guessed he must have hit it on something on the way down. Just then he heard the crashing of branches above him. His adrenaline and reflexes on high alert, he spun around in anticipation of an attack. He then saw Pudgy and Bernie about fifty feet away heading directly toward him. They stopped when they noticed him.

"JP?" Pudgy called out. "Where's Lenny?"

Chapter Ten

The three boys were in full-on panic mode. They had spent the better part of three hours searching the woods along the precarious slope where Jermaine had last seen Lenny being *sucked into the bushes*, as he had described it. Though Jermaine knew it was a lost cause, they scoured up and down the rugged incline, calling out his name until they were hoarse. At the same time, they needed to be careful that they didn't lose their footing and, more importantly, that they remained close together. It was utterly exhausting, and each of them was verging on tears.

It was nearly dark when Jermaine reluctantly called a halt to the search. They were nowhere near the valley floor, and they were exposed to the elements on the slope. The realization that they might have to spend the night on the mountainside slowly sunk in. Of even more pressing concern was the fact that Lenny's pack had held all their crucial camping supplies. They were wet, cold, and now their only shelter was unavailable. Things could not have been more dire.

Pudgy let his pack fall off his shoulders and he slunk down beside it. He was breathing hard and had deep scratches on both cheeks as well as his chin. Jermaine and Bernie joined him. The three sat in silence in the rain for a few minutes, attempting to come to grips with the situation. The thought of spending the night on a dark mountain in the rain without a tent—*and with that…thing lurking about*—was more than they could handle.

It was Bernie who spoke first. "We need to keep going, Jermaine."

Jermaine turned to his friend. He'd never seen Bernie so forlorn. "What are you talking about? It's practically dark."

"We need to get off this hill. Find shelter. We can take our time."

Jermaine thought about it for a moment, then looked over at Pudgy. "What do you think, Pudgy? Can you make it down in the dark?"

Pudgy considered the options briefly, then decided he'd rather die trying than sit around waiting to get pounced on by an undead, blood-thirsty, shirt-and-tie-wearing deranged kid. "I agree with Bernie. I say we book it."

Jermaine himself was now inclined to agree. They were exposed where they now sat. "Okay then. We stick close—even holding hands if we can—and take it *really* slow. Get your packs back on. The sooner we get going, the better."

❖

It was just past seven o'clock in the evening when Officer Cob Stanton stepped out of the dank Command Center trailer. He had been confined to the area at the base of Birch Street for the entire day and needed a change of scenery. There were four other policemen outside keeping watch on the Command Center, two of whom would be pulling the all-night shift.

Stanton walked past them and then eased himself into the police-issued white jeep parked behind the trailer. As he fired up the engine, he plugged a pinch of tobacco into his mouth and reached for the volume button on the radio. His Kenny Chesney CD was still in the player. He turned the lights and windshield wipers on, then turned up "There Goes My Life." It was a fitting tune on such a dismal night in Middle-of-Nowhere, USA, he thought as he slowly drove up Birch Street.

Stanton was at Langmaid's Grocery in under five minutes. He knew that she closed shop at half-past seven on the weekends, so he was in good time. When he walked inside, he heard the familiar bicycle-bell sound above him, triggered from the spring hinge on the top of the door. Mrs. Langmaid nodded without smiling.

Stanton took a quick look around and noticed there was only one other customer at the back of the store—an older African American woman. She seemed completely out of place in Providence, Washington. On closer inspection, she appeared to be some hippie-dippy-gypsy-type, dressed in a most bizarre array of bright clothing and exotic-looking silver jewelry dangling from her wrists, neck, and earlobes.

Stanton eyed her suspiciously as he worked his way toward the snack rack by the front counter. He surveyed the options for his dinner tonight and settled on a couple of lengths of beef jerky and an apple. *That and a pack of Red Man plug should do it*, he thought.

He nodded at Mrs. Langmaid as he pulled the items from the rack and placed them on the shelf in front of her. "Just charge it to the police account. I'll settle up on Friday," he directed the seemingly ancient lady in front of him. He knew well enough not to engage in conversation with her. He'd already heard through the grapevine that she was a weird one.

"Yep, uh-haa," Mrs. Langmaid replied. He wondered how long she had worked behind that large till, serving the community of Providence. He then gathered his items, stuffed them in a paper bag, and turned to leave.

Before pushing through the door, he chanced one more glance toward the back of the shop. The odd-looking customer seemed to be avoiding him—lingering at the back of the shop until he was gone. *Gonna ask some people about that one*, he thought as he pushed through the door and made his way back to the jeep.

It had finally stopped raining by the time he had returned to his trailer. Above him, he thought he could just make out the orange-wedge of moon attempting to break through the clouds.

❖

Guylaine Cloutier headed to the Truscott home again to see how Archie was doing. She had bought him a comic from Langmaid's Grocery and, even though it was almost eight in the evening, she decided it was important to visit. In her heart she knew that while Archie may have a brief remission, he was destined for a very difficult time ahead. Despite the rain, she took the long route—avoiding Main Street. She knew that it was best for her to keep a low profile.

There was no answer when she rang the bell, and as she turned and walked back down the path, she could see someone approaching. It was Yarl Truscott. He looked bereft and exhausted.

He told her that Archie had been taken to Seattle to be monitored and to get some blood work done. His wife, Tammy, had accompanied him, and he wasn't sure when they would be back.

Guylaine leaned forward and touched his arm. "I'm so sorry."

Yarl looked at his feet and nodded. He stood silently for a moment, the recent rain still beading down his raincoat. He then invited her in for tea. She could tell that he could use the company.

Once inside, Yarl invited her to the kitchen and pointed to a chair at the wooden table as he put the kettle on the gas stove. As he opened the fridge to take the milk out, Guylaine could see Archie's drawings on the door.

"Tell me what you know about what's going on in this town," Yarl said without looking up. He was standing over the kettle and appeared to be resolved to wait there until it came to a boil.

"I don't understand," Guylaine replied weakly. They both knew she did.

"Somethin' brought you here. You knew this would be happening. You've seen this kind of thing before." The steam was beginning to rise out of the metal pot.

"I have."

"So what is it?" Yarl pulled two large mugs down from the cabinet beside the stove. Guylaine could see his hands were shaking.

"Not sure, really. Perhaps a virus, like Dr. Lewis said," she lied. It was too complicated and frightening to even consider mentioning.

"Hmm," Yarl grunted. "You always go to places when there's a virus?" He plopped a teabag into each mug.

After a few moments, the kettle began to whistle, and Yarl quickly removed it from the flame and began pouring. Guylaine could sense the mood in the room shifting. She knew that he was hurting and that she needed to ease the tension. "I go where I think I can be useful."

Yarl nodded. "Sugar?"

"Just milk's fine, thanks."

"Thanks for caring about Archie," Yarl said suddenly. He turned and carried the mugs of tea to the table. His eyes were moist as he sat down across from her. He slid one of the mugs across the table toward her. "I don't know who you are or why you are in Providence, but I can tell you mean well."

Guylaine smiled and took the mug from him. "He's easy to care about. Pure heart. Pure soul."

Yarl nodded again. Guylaine could sense him staring at her. They all did. A dark-skinned stranger with blue tattoos and a myriad of bright scarves dangling from her neck and her many silver earrings and bracelets shimmering in the ambient kitchen light was not exactly the kind of typical look in Providence, Washington. Yarl's stare was the same stare she received most places. But it was who she was, and she would never change.

She fiddled with one of her bracelets. A single long, graying dreadlock fell from her orange headscarf and dangled down her arm. She leaned back and tucked it over her shoulder. "What about you?" Guylaine offered. "Have you always lived in Providence?"

Yarl nodded and smiled. "Born and raised. Tammy too."

The tension gradually left the room, and Guylaine spent the next hour listening as Yarl spoke of his children, his wife, and his work. He needed the company, and she knew it felt good to be heard.

❖

It was now completely dark, and Pudgy, Bernie, and Jermaine took turns leading each other down the steep incline. The three boys each carried a small flashlight, which helped them navigate through the dense undergrowth, but it also made it more difficult to help each other over difficult terrain.

The rain had stopped, and the air seemed to immediately become warmer, which somewhat lifted their spirits.

"How much longer do ya think, JP?" Pudgy asked from in front, moving the beam of his flashlight around, from his feet below him to the thick foliage on either side.

"Not sure," Jermaine replied. "Seems to be less steep now, so hopefully not long." Jermaine knew that they were in a whole heap of trouble without a working compass. Tomorrow was Sunday, and they would be expected home by midafternoon. If they didn't return on time, the alarm bells would be sounding, and the town would be sent into a tizzy. His mom would be sick with worry.

"Can we rest?" Pudgy pleaded.

"Try to hold on a bit longer." Jermaine was just about to turn around to look at Pudgy when the most horrific scream came from behind them. He knew that voice like he knew his own. It was Bernie's.

He was in trouble.

❖

The feed shop in Providence sat on its own half acre just south of town and had the equally vital role of keeping a healthy supply of livestock feed for the region, as well as pet food. Its owner, Tucker Paulson, walked from his house to work and back every day—even on Sundays. Still an eligible bachelor in his late fifties, he'd never been able to find the right woman, try as he might online.

He'd already helped out with the search yesterday and again earlier this morning. The remainder of the afternoon and evening he spent behind the desk in the tiny office at the feed shop, getting his orders ready and answering voice mails. It was just before nine o'clock Saturday night when he decided it was probably time to head home. His belly was growling—nothing a bowl of oatmeal and a cold beer couldn't fix.

He shut off the lights, locked the door, and set the alarm. The rain had stopped, and the air felt warm the way a summer evening should feel. He could see the lights of Providence a quarter of a mile away. He began walking along Highway 9, which turned into Main Street at the "Welcome to Providence" sign fifty feet further down the road.

Tucker was almost at the sign when he first heard the sound of what seemed to be someone following him. He quickly stopped and turned around. He heard a couple more footsteps and then silence. It was dark, but the moon was coming out from behind the clearing clouds and he could see that there was no one behind him. Tucker was a large man and not prone to being scared. He chalked it up to his overly active imagination. The search group he had been assigned to that morning had been particularly antsy, and their anxiety must have rubbed off on him.

Tucker turned again and faced Providence, this time quickening his pace. The clear sound of footsteps started again. This time they seemed to be almost beside him.

❖

Commanding Officer Stanton stood by his desk and looked over at the map on his wall, trying to get his head around what was possibly happening in the woods by Birch Street. He looked back down at his notes on the desk in front of his computer.

He had snuck a six-pack in that he'd bought earlier in the week at Langmaid's Grocery and opened up his second bottle. It was a shitty local label, but it was still beer. He knew it was against protocol, but he didn't care. He'd served his time. Besides, he knew old Mrs. Langmaid wouldn't tell tales.

He moved over toward his chair at the desk and sat down, looking at the names on his list on the paper in front of him. Other than the dentist, Teddy Mitchell, all the "victims" were kids. Becky Green, Pickle Town, Duncan Simpson. Even Archie Truscott was fairly young.

Becky Green had been near the woods just outside his trailer where he now sat. She'd been playing hopscotch. The others all seemed to have been lured to the woods by something or someone. Pickle Town and Duncan Simpson—before he went missing entirely—were found not more than fifty feet away from the foot of Birch Street by some of the local kids.

Stanton then thought of Archie Truscott and Teddy Mitchell. Nobody knew exactly how they became "unwell" and drawn to the woods, but both had definitely been "infected." Stanton remembered Officer Thompson explaining to him that Dr. Lewis, the local doctor, had suggested that it could all be some kind of virus. It still sounded like a load of horse crap to him, but he was open to anything if it allowed him to solve this thing and get the hell out of Dodge.

Stanton leaned back in his chair and tried to understand what kind of virus or mental delusion was infecting residents with this strange desire to enter the woods. What caused perfectly rational people to lose their gourd and hear footsteps all the time?

Damned if I know, Stanton thought, taking a long pull on his bottle of beer. *Maybe one more before bed.*

❖

Guylaine stared at the clock by her bed. It was half-past two in the morning. The light of the moon coming through the window had woken her. From where she lay, she could see the outline of the tops of the trees in the front yard. It appeared still and calm. The return of good weather would lighten people's spirits, she thought. It would also help with the search efforts.

She knew that Jermaine and his friends were gone. She hadn't seen any of them throughout the day. She wanted to believe that their parents had taken them away from here, but she knew in her heart that Jermaine was determined to find out about his friend Duncan. She could see in his eyes that he wanted to put an end to this once and for all, and she felt sick to her stomach that she may have added fuel to his quest.

Guylaine thought about telling the commanding officer as much as she could, but having seen him from a distance, she could tell that Cob Stanton wasn't the kind of man who would understand easily. What would she tell him, anyway? That there was a dead boy named Mordecai who was luring the poor residents of Providence into the woods by Birch Street and killing them? That his activity and desire to kill appeared to be getting stronger? That Jermaine Prescott knew about the deed that needed to be done and was probably on his way to try to figure out how to put an end to things? Oh, and by the way, that the young boy and his buddies may be en route to committing a sacrificial suicide?

No, she couldn't. She wouldn't know where to begin. It was always like this. It would all play out soon—*that* she knew. She had seen it many times before.

Guylaine closed her eyes and concentrated on her breathing. Calming her emotions was something she'd learned to master over time. She'd had many reasons in her life to practice, and the town of Providence was just another situation where she needed to remind herself of her own limitations.

What she understood, and what others failed to understand, was that the more she became personally involved, either in finding the grave or helping with the search, the more distant Mordecai would become. It's just the way it was. She didn't know why; she only knew from experience that increased involvement would mean losing contact. And this would make things a lot worse for everyone. It was almost like an unwritten contract between inbetweeners and her family of spiritualists. Her role must remain as an advisor, a person who would supply information to those seeking it, and offer words of hope and support, however feebly, to whomever might listen.

In times like these, Guylaine often thought of an old friend of hers. Jason had originally come from her own hometown, and after college, he had signed up to work internationally for the American Red Cross. He had been stationed in Rwanda during the horrific genocide in the 1990s. After he returned to Louisiana, he explained to Guylaine that, as sickening as it had been to witness, his inaction had been a matter of duty, not morality. At first, she was confused when he explained that he'd watched, without intervening, the machetes relentlessly slashing down upon men only a few feet away from his compound; and he had witnessed the violent rape of women and the slaughter of children—and he did nothing to stop it.

He couldn't.

It was the vow he'd made. It was the oath every member of the Red Cross had to take, understanding what they were signing up for. While her friend's ultimate purpose was to serve, he could only do so if he was able to maintain the fundamental principle of neutrality. In other words, despite his own convictions and desire to take sides, his neutrality had to be observed, because if it wasn't, the situation would end up being much worse. If the Red Cross had been asked to leave, who would be left to help? To observe?

While nothing near the scale of the Rwandan genocide, Guylaine understood that each individual situation she felt called to had to have a similar response. Her role was to advise, encourage, warn, support, and console the grieving residents of Providence—but never to be actively involved. That would be deemed a power shift by the undead. She would lose her power. She had seen it happen before as a child.

Guylaine took a long, slow breath. She could feel the strength of Mordecai's energy. He was active again.

And he was near.

❖

It was just after three in the morning. On any other night, no one would have noticed Tucker Paulson running down Main Street in his boxers, kicking at the air beside him and hollering at the darkness as he sprinted down the road. But tonight, local welder and "fixer of bicycles," Mr. Bashir Lankarani, just happened to be letting his aging golden retriever out for a pee.

The damn dog had been crying at the door for ages and couldn't be ignored any longer; Bashir had finally dragged himself out of bed to attend to him. His wife's snoring had made it impossible to sleep anyway, so he had forced himself up and stumbled to the front door to unlock it, letting his desperate dog outside to the front lawn.

Despite his frantic desire to get out, Target took forever to pee. He always did. *Probably clogged up with prostate issues*, Bashir thought, leaning against the door and yawning as his dog endlessly sniffed at the wet grass in front of the house. It had finally stopped raining, and Bashir thought the air felt warmer.

At first, he thought it was a deer or an elk that was being chased. It was moving fast and was clearly agitated. Then he recognized it as a human. A half-naked human.

A man.

Then he recognized the figure right away. It was his neighbor from two doors down, Tucker Paulson—his curling partner and the owner of the local feed store. He was screaming like a madman and was in obvious distress.

❖

Four minutes later, Commanding Officer Cob Stanton heard the same thing as someone ran past his trailer at the end of Birch Street. He could hear a man crying, "No, no, no. Go away. No…" as he approached the end of the street and the woods.

The screaming was followed by a loud commotion. Frenetic yelling and an obvious physical altercation were occurring just past his trailer. By the time Stanton had managed to pull himself out of his cot, all he could hear was muffled screams. He knew that the two policemen on nightshift outside had encountered someone.

Stanton quickly pulled on his trousers and moved toward the door of the trailer. He yanked his gun from the holster that was hanging on the hook beside his desk and then pushed through the door.

He could see the two deputies just off the road at the edge of the forest. They appeared to have pinned someone down on the ground. He could hear the person beneath them moaning and weeping. Stanton moved closer and noticed that the man was wearing nothing but his boxers.

"Officers?"

"Sir, we just stopped this man from running into the woods," one of the policemen explained, breathing hard from the sudden adrenaline rush as well as the altercation. He was still struggling to contain the writhing man beneath him.

Stanton took a deep breath. The night air smelled of earth, leaves, and the pungent dampness of summer. Stanton knew that things were about to get crazier before they got better.

❖

They had tried for hours to reach him. They could hear him, but they couldn't see him, despite shining their lights down the deep hole.

It was some kind of sinkhole. The deluge of rain had caused part of the surface to collapse into a deep pit. Bernie must have stumbled into it when they weren't looking.

He was about eight feet down the hole and around a slight corner. Luckily the rain had stopped, but the entire area looked like it could collapse in on itself at any moment. As bad luck would have it, Lenny's pack was the one that had contained the spare ropes.

"Bernie, we're gonna get you out, buddy. I promise." Jermaine's voice cracked from fear and fatigue. It was now nearly dawn, and they had been trying to figure out various ways to get him out ever since they had heard his initial scream.

"I know." Bernie's muffled voice sounded frail. They had tried every possible solution they could think of, but nothing worked. It was horrifying thinking of their friend trapped below them.

Pudgy suddenly looked over at Jermaine. An idea had just come to him. "Hey, JP. What if we tied a bunch of our clothes and belts and stuff together? You think that would be long enough? Kind of like a jail break. You know, like they do in the movies with sheets and stuff?"

Jermaine sat down beside the opening and looked over at Pudgy. He might be on to something. Bernie's pack had somehow stayed above ground, falling from his back when he slid down the hole. They knew he had cooking supplies, but they could look for any of his garments that could be tied together.

The two boys scrambled over to the three backpacks and began pulling everything out, separating and piling up anything that could be knotted together. Once they had emptied all three packs, Jermaine asked Pudgy to hold the flashlights while he frantically began creating a makeshift rope.

The fact that the creepy boy might be close by didn't even cross their minds. It was all about saving Bernie now.

"How ya doing, Bernie?" Pudgy asked for the umpteenth time.

"Cold."

"JP is tying some clothing together. We're gonna try to make you a rope."

"Okay."

When Jermaine had finished knotting pants, sweaters, and shirts together, he figured they were still about ten feet short. "Take off all your clothes."

"What?"

"Everything except your boxers, though we may need those as well." Jermaine was already peeling off his jacket, sweater, and pants and adding them to the line. Pudgy reluctantly followed, and soon they had what they believed to be enough clothing to reach at least to the bottom where the hole began to turn. Lastly, Jermaine fastened his belt to the end of the rope—more precisely, Pudgy's long-sleeved hoodie—and then looped it back into itself, thus providing Bernie with a solid item to grasp.

Jermaine leaned over the hole. "Hey, Bernie, we're gonna lower this thing down now, okay?"

"Okay." Bernie's voice was now noticeably weaker. It was pushing five o'clock in the morning, and it had been an emotionally and physically exhausting few hours.

"You gotta try to get close to where the hole turns. When I tell you to, you gotta reach out with your hand until you feel a belt tied to our rope. I'll let you know when we're finished lowering it." Jermaine couldn't believe how brave his friend had been all this time, trapped in a narrow passageway underground in such a claustrophobic space.

Piece by piece, Pudgy slowly handed the ridiculous-looking rope made of various articles of clothing to Jermaine while he, in turn, carefully lowered it down the narrow shaft. Both boys were covered in mud, and everything they touched became slippery. This was their last chance to save Bernie, and they knew it.

Pudgy handed Jermaine the last bit of rope. "That's all of it."

"Okay, shine the light down, Pudgy."

"Okay. Hold on." Pudgy scrambled to grab one of the flashlights and then aimed its beam down the muddy hole.

"I think the belt's on the bottom now, Bernie. You gotta try to reach your hand out."

Both boys stuck their heads over the narrow opening and looked for any sign of Bernie's hand.

"I'm trying. I can see the light. I can see it, but I keep slipping."

Jermaine took a deep breath to steady his nerves. He had to remain as calm as he could for Bernie's sake. "Listen, buddy. You gotta give it everything you got. You hear me? Everything. You can do it, Bernie. I know you can."

Silence.

"Do it, Bernie." Jermaine could feel the opening of the hole begin to give way a bit, and a clump of mud fell down toward Bernie.

"Jesus," Pudgy said, keeping the light steady on the belt—the last item on the rope. Then both boys saw it at the same time. First, some fingers. White against the dark background. And then a small hand followed, reaching out to grab the belt. They both felt the makeshift rope tighten. "Pudgy, you keep holding the light and let me know when he's got it with both hands." Jermaine then grabbed the rope and leaned back in anticipation of Bernie pulling at it.

"He's only got it by one hand."

"Pull me a little bit," they heard from deep below.

"Pull, JP. Carefully," Pudgy urged.

Jermaine felt the rope get taut, and he began to pull it toward him, praying the myriad of knots would hold. He could feel Bernie's dead weight now.

"Slowly," Pudgy directed. "Okay, I see his other hand. He now…he now has it with both hands, JP. Pull!" Pudgy yelled, dropping the flashlight and moving behind Jermaine and also grabbing the rope.

"Okay, one hand after another, nice and slow. On my count. Ready?" Jermaine said.

"Ready."

"One…two, pull. One…two, pull…one—" They could feel the knots slipping, then tightening and shifting—but still holding. So far, so good. "One…two, pull. You okay, Bernie?" Jermaine hollered at the opening between pulls.

"Yep," Bernie yelled, managing to somehow hold onto the muddy belt. "Hurry," he pleaded.

"Faster, Pudgy. One, two, pull. One, two, pull. One, two, pull…" After what seemed like eternity, the top of the belt eventually appeared at the edge of the hole, followed by two muddy hands clenching it. "Hold it tight, Pudgy," Jermaine screamed. Once he felt Pudgy had it secured, he leaped forward to the opening and grabbed both of Bernie's slick hands. "Okay, Pudgy. Help me haul him out."

Pudgy dropped the rope and joined Jermaine, grabbing Bernie's arms and helping to haul him away from the mouth of the hole. The three boys collapsed backward onto the ground in a thick, tangled mess of limbs, clothing, skin, and mud.

❖

It never took long for news to spread across the town of Providence. Even in the early hours of Sunday morning, everyone seemed to be simultaneously aware of Tucker Paulson's late-night episode. By eight o'clock, many residents had already made their way down to Birch Street to find some answers. They were told an information session would be arranged outside of Commanding Officer Stanton's trailer at nine. Most folks milled about, holding their coffees and gossiping quietly while they waited.

Cob Stanton had called Officer Thompson at five thirty and woken him up. He updated him and told Thompson he was to address the crowd this morning. He hated dealing with the public—truth be told, he hated dealing with most life-forms, but it came with the territory.

He directed Thompson to let everyone know that Tucker Paulson had been discovered last night in a state of "acute anxiety" and that he'd been taken to Pulltown, where he would be treated for his abrasions and assessed by a psychologist. Stanton suggested that Thompson remind the locals to stay away from any wooded areas until they could figure out what was going on.

Stanton waited in his trailer until Thompson and Plant arrived. Once they did, he took the opportunity to leave, quickly moving behind the trailer to his jeep. He began driving toward Main Street. There was somebody he needed to talk to.

Chapter Eleven

The initial jubilation they felt after finally freeing Bernie from certain death gradually gave way to silence. The realization of what had recently happened to Lenny and of what lay ahead soon consumed each of them.

The boys painstakingly untied the rope. Each wet knot demanded an enormous effort to undo. Most of their muddy shirts, pants, and sweaters were stretched into ridiculous shapes. Nonetheless, they gathered their belongings and stuffed everything back into the packs. Pudgy and Jermaine got dressed again. Bernie was completely covered in mud from head to toe, but he was relatively unscathed.

The sun began to rise over the treetops, and its warm rays breathed energy back into their aching bodies. It was now Sunday morning. They knew that by two o'clock, or three at the latest, their parents would begin to get worried. The boys had told everyone that Daryl Tanner's mother would be dropping them back from their "camping trip" just after lunchtime on Sunday. If they didn't show, phone calls would be made, and questions would be asked. Once it was discovered that they had lied and that they had instead gone to meet some girls, things would kick into another gear. And finally, when the parents ultimately realized it was all just smoke and mirrors and their boys were missing with no explanation, they would be totally distraught, and the police would become involved.

It was inevitable that they would be deemed missing. They had all signed up for it and understood the consequences. But they had assumed that by this time on Sunday, they would have already found the cabin. Now they were only partway down a mountain, their compass was broken, the boy had attacked and taken Lenny, and they had almost lost Bernie. The bottom line was that they needed to find that grave *before* the search teams and the police helicopters found them.

Once they had their packs back on, Bernie asked to take the lead as they worked their way toward the valley floor.

❖

He was about to call on her at the Breaches' house when he noticed her crossing the street and heading down the road behind Langmaid's Grocery. He turned to follow her and eventually pulled over on the opposite side of the road beside her and rolled down his window. She looked up and smiled.

"Stanton, isn't it?"

Cob Stanton nodded slightly. He wasn't smiling.

"I was wondering when you'd be comin' to find me."

Stanton felt slightly off kilter. It wasn't the response he'd expected. He eyed the strange-looking woman in the outlandish attire with distrust. Like him, she was an outsider, but he had a purpose here in Providence. He was curious to hear what her business was in town. From what he'd heard from Officer Thompson, she was a Southerner. Louisiana, Thompson had thought.

"Need to have a chat," he said.

"Of course. I'm not getting in that police vehicle with you, though. Where I come from, that can be bad news. If you want to talk, come out here and we can walk."

Stanton again felt slightly outmaneuvered. Something he rarely experienced—and he hated it. Nonetheless, he turned his car off, pulled the keys out, and opened his door. Both his knees ached from years of overuse, and he struggled a bit exiting, which made his mood even more foul. He knew he had to get them looked at eventually. It made him appear weak; and worse, he also knew that she'd seen it.

"Great to have the sun back, isn't it," Guylaine observed.

Stanton half hobbled and half strutted across the street toward her. When he finally stopped in front of her, he tucked his thumbs beneath his belt, pushed his shoulders back, and took a deep breath. "Ma'am, I'm not much for small talk. I'm not much for walking either, but I guess I'm stuck doing both, now, aren't I."

Guylaine continued to smile.

"I'm Cob Stanton. I'm the guy in charge of finding out what the hell is going on around here." He didn't extend a hand to greet her. Instead, he pulled out a pack of chewing tobacco and stuffed a dab deep inside his cheek and closed his mouth, enjoying the much-needed rush of nicotine.

"I know who you are."

Her confident demeanor continued to befuddle him. He attempted to recalibrate, taking his time to continue, moving the tobacco against his cheek with this tongue. "You mentioned you were expecting me to find you. You guilty of something?"

"Shall we walk? Standing here at the side of the road feels awkward." She didn't wait for an answer and began to walk away from him.

Stanton had no choice but to move to catch up with her. Her pace was faster than he liked. "You didn't tell me your name."

"No, I didn't. You didn't ask. Where I come from, we don't tell the cops much."

"Louisiana, right?"

"Is it the accent or the word on the street that gave me away?"

"Small town. Hard to remain anonymous here." Stanton was already out of breath. "It's Ms. Cloutier, isn't it?"

"It is. You can call me Guylaine as long as you don't arrest me."

"You're a long way from Louisiana."

"Impressive. A policeman *and* a geography scholar. *Très bien, mon ami.*"

"You always this sarcastic?" Stanton knew he had to turn the tables on her and gain the upper hand, so he stopped walking. "Ms. Cloutier, hold on a sec. I need to speak to you about these disappearances. I think you know something about them, and, in some circles, that could mean you're either a witness or a suspect."

Guylaine also stopped and turned to look back at Stanton. She again broke into a wide smile. "It's because I'm black, isn't it?"

Stanton was gobsmacked. "What? No, it's not—"

"I'm just shittin' you, officer. I do know something about all of this. I'm happy to tell you what I know. But only if you keep walking. I need to get my morning exercise."

Stanton stood with his mouth agape, thin traces of Red Man plug hanging off his lower lip.

❖

An hour after Officer Thompson had updated the anxious locals about Tucker Paulson, search parties had again been organized to go look for Teddy Mitchell. It didn't take long to do; it was becoming a daily ritual. They were geared up and ready to be deployed within thirty minutes. With Stanton's blessing, the drone team had decided to expand their search further afield and had already disappeared into the woods two miles south of Providence.

In Providence itself, there was a seemingly endless stream of media trucks and vans, volunteers eager to support the search, and the usual gaggle of curious onlookers. Most eventually made their way to the top of Birch Street, and Stanton had to have more officers brought in to keep them away from the area surrounding the trailer.

Already teams of psychologists, grief counsellors, and therapy dogs had flocked to the homes of all the victims and anyone else that was in need of support. Health professionals, keen to better understand what was happening, had all descended upon Providence to test their theories and offer their conclusions. The entire town seemed to be saturated by the explosion in its population, which, in turn, seemed to cause even more tension in the air.

The locals themselves had become hypersensitive to anything out of the ordinary. If they thought their neighbor walked a little differently—perhaps more quickly than usual—they called Officer Thompson. If someone seemed agitated or overly distressed, people would begin to gossip and a stealth twenty-four-hour watch would be organized. "Better keep your eye on Farley. He's been acting weird lately."

The entire population was on the verge of combusting—the temperature was high, and the boiling point had been reached.

That's why when Yarl Truscott suddenly announced that his son Archie would be returning home, it felt like a miraculous gift from above.

❖

"Pudgy, what's that?"

Pudgy looked over to where Bernie was pointing. Eventually he saw it under a thick cedar limb. He knew immediately what it was.

Lenny's backpack.

"Don't go over there, Pudgy. Stay here," Jermaine warned. The three boys instinctively huddled together.

"Lenny," Bernie yelled. "Lenny, you there?" he called louder.

Silence.

"Let's move closer," Pudgy suggested. "Together."

"Okay, but let's hold hands," Jermaine said. They all kept their eyes trained on the thick brush around them as they inched closer to the pack.

"Lenny! It's us," Pudgy yelled.

The dappled light of the sun on the forest floor made Lenny's pack seem camouflaged. When they got closer, they realized it wasn't the light. It was blood. Large crimson blotches covered the yellow pack. "Lenny?" Pudgy called out.

"Holy moly." Bernie's eyes began to water. He dropped his hand from the others and ran toward the pack, then fell to his knees.

Lenny's pack seemed to be intact despite the obvious violence that had transpired. When the others joined him, Bernie was crying fully.

Pudgy wrapped his arms around Bernie's shoulders and began bawling along with him. Jermaine soon followed. It was all too much.

❖

Tucker Paulson had stopped screaming and crying. He sat in silence on his bed at the Pulltown Regional Clinic. Because of her recent experience in cases like this one, Dr. Patricia Lewis had been called in to work alongside the local psychiatrist, Dr. Penn, a wily veteran who looked at the young doctor with suspicion when she walked into his office.

They had met once before, but only briefly—at a regional medical conference. He regarded her as the new kid on the block—a rookie, and probably wondering what the hell she'd gotten herself into. "Dr. Lewis, I understand you've seen a couple of cases like this before. I've heard there are some strange things occurring out in Providence."

"To be honest, doctor—it's the craziest thing I've ever seen."

Dr. Penn smiled. To him, she looked to be about twelve years old; he wasn't sure how much she could have seen in her young life. Penn was a year away from retirement. There wasn't much he hadn't seen or dealt with.

"We can talk as we walk," he said, rising from his desk. "I spent an hour with Mr. Paulson this morning. He is sedated now. Let's head over there, and you can fill me in along the way."

Tucker Paulson was on the second floor. They walked down the hall and took the stairs. Dr. Lewis explained to Dr. Penn how it had all started with young Becky Green. Then she told him about Pickle Town, Duncan Simpson, Archie Truscott, and the dentist, Teddy Mitchell. She said that while much of the evidence was circumstantial, it appeared that the presentation of their symptoms all seemed similar. Hearing sounds—usually footsteps, like they were being followed; feeling lured into the woods beyond Birch Street; being hounded by incessant, unimaginably terrifying thoughts. How they all appeared to be incapable of dealing with the intensity of their urges. How there seemed to be no way to comfort them.

Dr. Penn listened in silence as they neared the top of the stairs. He stopped on the landing and looked at Dr. Lewis. There was a slight smile on his face. "The toxicology was negative in all the cases?"

"Yes."

"Yet one of your theories is it could be viral."

"I don't know, doctor. I can't think of anything that would satisfactorily explain the trauma, not to mention the fever, the sweating, the imagined threats, the anxiety and racing heart rate, the fear and panic, and, in some cases, death. It's all as if they had been taken over by something. A virus, or some kind of fever, is my only rational explanation. In truth, I have no idea."

Dr. Penn's face now became serious. "In Seattle, the girl, Becky Green."

Lewis nodded.

"The report said they'd observed her for days; they concluded that she'd experienced a delusional episode. Her heart gave out because of the stress."

Dr. Lewis nodded again. "One case with which I would have to agree. But the list is growing, doctor. Something is 'going viral' in Providence, whether or not it is a virus."

❖

Over the last hour, it had flattened out considerably. Jermaine reckoned they were close to finding Skagit Creek. The sun was high above him, so it was difficult to gauge his bearings; he decided to check the prominence of moss on the sides of the trees, roughly determined north, and told Bernie and Pudgy to begin veering left. They would angle their way down the rest of the slope until they were well and truly in the heart of the valley. They would then make a hard right, and if both his memory and gut were correct, they would eventually bump into the elusive creek. Once there, they would follow it east until they found the cabin. He realized how unlikely it was that they would be successful in finding such a needle in a haystack. But it was all they had.

As emotionally difficult as it was, the three boys had divided the contents of Lenny's pack between them. Jermaine had strapped the tent on top of his own pack. Bernie took the rope, lighters, and extra water bottles. Pudgy carried the first aid kit and both of the hunting knives he'd found in the pack. It had been hard leaving Lenny's pack with all of his clothing behind. It just didn't seem right. But it was necessary.

By early afternoon they had reached the valley floor. They all walked in silence. Pudgy checked his watch. "It's two o'clock." He understood, like they all did, that anytime soon, their parents would be sounding the alarm. They should have been back by now.

"You guys as thirsty as I am? Let's take a break." Jermaine dropped his pack and sat down on top of it. Bernie did the same, and Pudgy soon followed. They were all beyond exhausted, having had no sleep last night.

"Only a bit left," Pudgy said, holding his water bottle in front of him. "We better find that creek soon."

Bernie looked at Pudgy and then at Jermaine. He was soon overcome with the emotion of having been trapped underground, and his love for them could not have been more. He began to tear up again.

"You okay, Bernie?" Jermaine asked.

Bernie nodded.

"Been a long day," Pudgy added. He was about to say more when he noticed the boy standing about twenty feet from them. He appeared to be soaking wet.

And he was smiling at Pudgy again.

Chapter Twelve

She hadn't told him much. But she did tell him enough to entice him to request another meeting with her later that day. Something about Guylaine Cloutier intrigued Stanton. He'd never met anyone like her. She was obviously confident, aloof, and mysterious; but he also sensed that she was perceptive and wise. And, more importantly, she was probably the only person in the entire state that knew what the hell was happening around here.

They had agreed to meet at Patty's Five and Dime Café—the only coffee shop on the stretch of highway outside of town on the way to Pulltown. It was a pit stop ten miles outside of town, popular with loggers and truckers. She had agreed to ride with him only if he promised not to kill her. He didn't smile when she'd said it. But she did. He thought she was incorrigible.

It was agreed that Cob Stanton would pick her up from the Breaches' house at two thirty. When he pulled up in the police jeep, she was already waiting for him outside. Stanton noticed her wide smile and immediately felt defenseless.

Come on, Stanton. Get a grip, he thought, cruising to a stop beside her. "Sorry I'm late," he growled.

"No, you're not." Guylaine opened the door and plopped herself down beside Stanton. "Usually I ride in the back with cuffs."

Stanton turned away and launched a wad of chew out the open window. "Too funny."

"That stuff will kill you, you know."

"That and bullets. I'll take my chances."

"You married?"

Incorrigible.

❖

It was Pudgy's mom who first called the Cartwrights. It was just past two o'clock when Charmaine Cartwright grabbed the phone and answered it on the first ring. "Have you heard anything, Barb?"

"Nothing. I was hoping you had." The Cartwrights were not prone to worrying about their son. But Lenny had never changed plans without speaking to them first. *Ever.* And he certainly had never broken a promise, or worse, lied to them.

"I spoke with Pat. Nothing from Jermaine either. Same with the Maclarens. Hannah told me her folks had already been calling around Pulltown. Nobody's seen any sign of them. Did Lenny leave his cell phone behind?"

"Yes, I tried to text him."

"Same with Pudgy and Jermaine. Both phones in their rooms. Charmaine, I'm so worried."

Simon Cartwright felt all sorts of guilt for having been the one who gave the boys a lift to Pulltown in the first place, dropping them off at Daryl Tanner's house. It had all seemed so innocent and legitimate.

"I'm going down to Birch Street," Barb Murtland said. "We have to tell Officer Thompson, or that Commander Stanton. They need to know."

"I'm coming with you," Charmaine said. "Simon can stay here and man the phone."

❖

Jermaine and Bernie saw the boy as soon as they heard Pudgy scream. He was about a hundred feet from them in a clearing. He was standing still, smiling.

The boys all shifted closer together until they were touching shoulders. None of them moved. He continued to stare at them, his wet clothes glistening in the dappled light.

"Holy moly," Bernie whispered.

"Quiet. Don't move," Jermaine commanded.

The boy continued to stare at them; his cold, hollow eyes seemed to peer right through them.

"Mordecai?" Jermaine addressed the boy.

Mordecai's smile seemed to stretch, and he giggled mischievously. Then as quickly as he had appeared, the boy vanished. Melting back into the forest, like he hadn't been there at all.

"What the heck," Pudgy said, letting out the breath he'd been holding in.

"Come on, let's follow him," Jermaine said.

"What? Are you crazy?" It was clear Pudgy had had enough terror-inducing activities for the day. The last thing he wanted to do was to chase after ghosts.

"I think he wants us to follow him."

"What do you mean, Jermaine?" Bernie asked. His deep voice was hoarse. "He may want to lead us into a trap. He's already killed Duncan and Lenny."

Jermaine didn't respond at first. Bernie was right. There was no rational reason to follow him.

"Yeah, maybe." Jermaine looked up at the sky. It would most likely get dark by dinnertime, as they were within the valley and the sun would disappear behind the trees and hills very early. They were exhausted, and there was little point of continuing to push on. They were still a long way from the cabin. "Maybe we should just set up camp here. Get a real early start tomorrow."

"With that creep hanging around in the woods? Are you nuts?" Pudgy was beginning to question Jermaine's sanity.

"Pudgy, he's always been in the woods around us. It doesn't matter where we are. Besides, as long as we're together, we should be all right." Jermaine glanced around. "Here is as good a place as any. Lots of deadfall for firewood. Agreed?"

Bernie nodded. "Agreed."

Pudgy begrudgingly nodded as well. A fire and a solid sleep were exactly what they all needed.

"We'll need to find water in the morning. Don't have enough to cook with tonight. Looks like raw macaroni or spaghetti is on the menu," Jermaine said.

❖

Patty's Five and Dime Café was empty. Most of the usual local clientele were either in Providence helping with the search or at work. The owner, Patty Lowry, eyed the cop and his peculiar friend. Stanton guessed she was wondering why he wasn't doing his job down on Birch Street finding the missing people.

"Let's sit over here." Stanton pointed to the table at the rear of the shop.

Guylaine Cloutier followed his lead. She pulled off her lengthy yellow woolen cardigan. Stanton noticed the silver jewelry cascading from her ears, neck, and wrists. He also noticed the strange tattoos on her arms and the many scarves that had been tucked beneath the cardigan.

When they sat down, Stanton turned and raised his arm, spreading two fingers. He mouthed, "Two coffees" to Patty, who was still glaring at them from behind the counter at the front of the shop.

"You didn't ask if I wanted coffee." Guylaine leaned back and adjusted her bracelets.

"Everyone wants coffee. Now tell me everything you know."

"You must have a lot of time on your hands."

Stanton ignored her sarcasm. "What do you know about these missing people? We don't have time for games, Ms. Cloutier."

Guylaine nodded and let out a long breath. "I understand. I'll tell you what you need to hear. But it may not be what you want to hear."

"Meaning?"

Guylaine crossed her arms as Patty arrived with a tray holding the two coffees. She placed the mugs in front of them along with a large jar of sugar cubes and a tiny porcelain pitcher of milk. "Anything else?" she asked, a touch of disdain in her voice.

Stanton shook his head and remained quiet until she'd gone. Then: "I'm waiting."

"Meaning I've seen these kinds of things before. These occurrences. That's why I'm here. It will sound like hocus-pocus to you. I can guarantee that. It always does. But it is what it is, so take it or leave it."

Stanton studied the woman in front of him. He had never seen or met anyone like her before. "What do you do? You know, for a living, I mean."

Guylaine grinned, then offered him her trademark response. "I'm a harbinger, soothsayer, fortune teller, clairvoyant, and psychic. I read tarot, palms, horoscopes, and tea leaves. I can be contracted for séance and spirit board services. Some call me a witch doctor, but I prefer healer, and I'm at your service!"

Stanton hinted at a smile. "So, you're a crackpot, then," he said, picking up his coffee and taking a sip.

"You can say that. Or you can learn from me and try to stop more deaths from occurring in Providence."

"I'm listening."

"I come from a long line of people who have followed events such as these. Almost a familial calling, if you will. My people have a certain understanding of things like what is transpiring around Providence. It isn't the first place it's happened."

Stanton could see the sincerity in her eyes and sensed that she'd had similar conversations in the past—perhaps too many times. She was confident, but he could tell she was also honest. "Go on."

"Inbetweeners is what we call them."

"Excuse me?"

"I believe this particular one is named Mordecai. Least that's how it appears in my mind when I try to focus on him; it's not communication per se, but I get vibes from him. Another family skill."

Stanton almost choked on his coffee. He wasn't sure he'd heard her correctly. "Morde-what?"

"Mordecai. He's the one responsible for all the missing people."

Stanton's mouth dropped open. He didn't know whether to break out laughing or simply get up and walk out. "You're shittin' me, right?"

"Mordecai's his name. The boy. It's always a boy. Don't ask me why, as nobody knows."

Stanton glared at Guylaine and took another sip of his coffee and decided to wait for her to continue. This was getting ripe.

"Certainly, for as long as we've recorded the history, we have evidence of these kinds of events. Again, don't ask me why."

Stanton complied. He said nothing.

"As I said, Mordecai is what we refer to as an inbetweener. Dead—but not fully dead. He seeks to lie in peace but will cause death and destruction until he's buried properly. That's the kicker—unless certain rituals are performed, it will not end."

Stanton leaned back in the booth, looking around to make sure nobody else could hear this malarkey. He began to smile. "So, you're telling me that some dead boy is kidnapping and killing people, and until somebody helps him die properly, it will continue."

"Precisely."

Stanton crossed his arms and chuckled. "I suppose I'm not the first person who believes you were dropped on your head too many times as a baby."

"You have no idea," Guylaine responded, smiling back at Stanton.

"Okay, I'll play along." He motioned for her to continue.

"It starts slowly. For years and even decades, inbetweeners are more confused and sleepier. In a daze. Lost. But eventually they begin to get an appetite. They start to forage and kill—little things at first, like rodents and birds. They feed off the land. The more blood, the stronger and more determined they become."

Stanton tried desperately to take in what she was telling him. It sounded so outlandish and preposterous that he was wondering if he was actually hearing her correctly.

"Inbetweeners are rogue spirits, vengeful and without remorse." As Guylaine leaned forward, her many scarves followed, floating down around her toward the table. "But they also want it to end. They want to be reburied properly."

"Reburied?" Stanton asked.

"Only two ways to stop it. Rebury him properly. Or…" Guylaine paused.

"Or what?"

"Sacrifice."

"Pardon?"

"A human sacrifice on top of the grave. It must be on the grave. The ancients did this without question; they knew this was essential. Usually a child was selected. Not so anymore."

"Jesus H. Christ."

"Yes, he was, in a way, sacrificed too," she said with a grin.

"Too funny. Go on."

"Either way, we need to find the grave."

Stanton closed his eyes and rubbed his temples. "You're kidding, right?"

"Or do nothing, and it will continue. Your choice."

Stanton rested his head in his hands. "Shit."

"Yup."

"A grave."

"Yup."

"Where?"

"That's the thing. There will be a grave somewhere. One in which he'd originally been buried, but it could be anywhere."

"And for some reason you're saying that he suddenly got up out of his grave like some raving-mad zombie?"

Guylaine nodded. She wasn't going to take the bait.

Stanton reached for his mug again and lifted it to his lips. "So ultimately you're saying that there's a grave somewhere we have to find?"

Guylaine nodded once more and sighed. "Unfortunately, it's most likely impossible to find. He could have died years ago. It may have been decades since the boy became an inbetweener. Judging by the scarcity of wildlife around here, he's been wandering this area for a long time."

Stanton put his mug down and pulled a toothpick from the small jar in the center of the table and put it in his mouth, rolling it from side to side with his tongue. He remembered the drone reports and what the old hunter, Buck Bridges, had told him in his trailer. The entire area was void of life. He wasn't sure what to say next. It was Guylaine who spoke again.

"There's not a lot you can do while this plays out." She leaned back again before continuing. "Not unless someone around here knows something we don't."

❖

Thirty minutes later, Stanton dropped Guylaine off at the Breaches' house and then returned to his trailer at the bottom of Birch Street. It was four thirty, and the search parties were beginning to return from the surrounding woods. His radio had been silent most of the time he was away, so he knew they'd had no success again.

Officer Thompson knocked on his door as Stanton was about to sit down at his desk. "Come in."

"Sir, just reporting that we've not been able to find any trace of anyone again. Also—" Thompson moved in and closed the door behind him. "Some of the parents of some local boys came down here a while ago looking for you. Seems four boys have gone missing from out Pulltown way. Same boys that found Pickle Town. Also, Duncan Simpson was their best friend."

Stanton pulled some tobacco out of his pouch and tucked it between his lower lip and gum, slowly working it toward his cheek so he could talk. "Don't say."

"Been gone since Friday. Their folks thought they'd gone camping."

"Why were they out that way?"

"No one's sure. But they were due back a few hours ago. Like I said, nobody's seen them since Friday."

It was all blowing up in his face. He could see it but couldn't prevent it. He could visualize the proverbial avalanche approaching but couldn't for the life of him do anything about it. This had turned into an all-out unmitigated disaster, and he had no idea how to proceed.

What nonsense he had heard from Ms. Cloutier didn't help him feel any better. If he were to believe her (which he didn't), there was some random dead boy kidnapping and killing the good residents of Providence; and if they didn't find his grave and do some hoodoo-voodoo, black magic crap on it, this could continue for a while. And just how would he explain that doozy of a tale to his superiors?

"Okay, call it in and keep me posted. Get the support needed in Pulltown. Tell the locals we're on it."

Thompson nodded and retreated back out the door. When it closed, Stanton leaned forward and rested his head in his hands on the desk in front of him. He toyed with the idea of opening a beer, but he was still technically on duty. *What a goddamned shit show.*

❖

It was barely light out by the time they had set up the tent, laid out their sleeping bags, and collected enough wood to last until bedtime. While Bernie worked on getting the fire lit, Pudgy and Jermaine spread the map out flat on the ground and attempted to figure out their exact location. Just in case it was working again, Jermaine pulled out the compass and laid it on top of the map while Pudgy pointed his flashlight at it. The needle began to spin wildly in a circle, so he quickly tucked it back in his pocket.

Pointing at the map, Jermaine did his best to determine their location. "We came down this mountain and began to veer this way. I bet we walked two miles. So my best guess is we are somewhere around here," Jermaine said, moving his finger in a small circle on the map.

"So not that far from the creek, then." Pudgy pointed at the thin blue line of water two inches away from where Jermaine was indicating.

"Hopefully. Maybe a few miles. But it looks fairly flat, and if we start early and keep the morning sun to our left, we're bound to run into it."

The three boys eventually gathered around the small fire. Pudgy pulled out the pasta packages and began passing them around. "On the menu we have the chef's special, raw maca-ghetti," Pudgy explained. They stuffed bits of dried pasta into their mouths.

"I got a surprise for dessert," Pudgy added. "A Snickers bar and some licorice."

"Awesome, Pudgy." Bernie's voice was almost totally gone. He was still caked in mud, and it had hardened over his body.

"You look like a guy from one of those Vietnam movies, Big Balls!" Pudgy said.

Bernie was quiet for a minute. "I miss Lenny calling me Big Balls," he croaked. "I miss Dunc and Lenny so much."

The boys finished eating in silence. As darkness enveloped their campsite, the surrounding forest seemed to lean in on them. They unconsciously moved closer to the fire and to each other.

❖

Yarl Truscott ran out the front door of the house to greet his son. Tammy was crying and Archie was smiling. Yarl grabbed Archie in both arms and hugged him tightly to his chest. He looked over at his wife, and tears started forming in his own eyes.

Archie was home.

After an early dinner, they both walked Archie to bed and sat with him until he was finally asleep. When they returned to the kitchen, Tammy told her husband everything. How initially the doctors had said they had no idea what was happening with Archie. How they thought he'd lost his mind and that his body was reacting to something in his system. His stress levels had been so high that they'd worried he might even have a heart attack.

And then she explained how yesterday, out of the blue, Archie was found sitting up in bed in his hospital room, smiling as if nothing had ever happened. He said he was hungry and asked if he could go home. After a thorough examination, the doctors and medical staff observing him all agreed he was clear to return home. His mother could sign him out that afternoon. Tammy was certain it was a miracle.

Neighbors and friends began arriving by the dozens that evening. News of Archie surviving this craziness had brought hope to the entire town. Dr. Lewis herself drove in to visit the Truscotts, wanting to see for herself that Archie had pulled through and see firsthand such a promising prognosis. She knew that if there was hope for Archie, there was hope for Tucker Paulson, who was still under sedation in Pulltown.

At the same time as the Truscotts were being overwhelmed by the warmth and support of the community, the Murtland, Prescott, Cartwright, and Maclaren families were trying to come to terms with the possibility that their missing sons were somehow caught up in all of this madness.

The police had told them that they'd heard nothing else about the boys ever since they'd walked off the Tanner property in Pulltown last Friday. No one had seen them since, and from what authorities could gather, the boys had never been camping at Lake Teshko, nor had they gone to visit the girls like they'd told Daryl Tanner. They had simply vanished.

Cob Stanton sat alone in the trailer—something he'd done a lot of over the years. Married life had never appealed to him. Having kids even less so. His job was his life and always had been; and lately, he hated his job. The ridiculous turn of events here in Providence wasn't helping the prospects of him changing his mind on that front either.

While the news of Archie Truscott's return was promising, he knew they were still in a heap of trouble here. He again went through all the wild and fanciful things the very strange Ms. Cloutier had relayed to him earlier in the day. It all sounded like complete lunacy.

He then remembered what she had said about the kid, Jermaine Prescott. She claimed to have spoken to him in depth about these strange things on a couple of occasions. She believed he seemed to know more than he let on. Like Stanton, she had no idea that when she had been telling him about everything at Patty's Five and Dime, Jermaine and his buddies had also gone missing. So maybe there was something to look into after all. *Time to visit the Prescotts in the morning*, he thought.

He'd have to tread carefully, as they would be emotional wrecks. But if they had any information that would be useful, he needed to dig in.

Stanton picked up his second Pabst Blue Ribbon of the evening and used his pocketknife to pop the cap off. *Thank God for beer*, he thought as he made his way over to the poor excuse of a bed at the far side of the trailer.

Part Three

The Cabin

Chapter Thirteen

By the time they were five years old, Jermaine and Bernie had already become the best of buddies. Both of their moms had spent all of their time together, so it was natural that they followed suit. They were as close as any two boys could possibly be—for all intents and purposes, they were brothers.

Bernie loved the confusion and energy at the Prescott household—where they usually hung out. At the Maclaren home, his sister was morose and disinterested, but Jermaine's older brothers were playful and loving. Jermaine was the quiet one; his brothers were not. They were rambunctious and havoc-causing. Jermaine's father was a serious, hardworking man and was rarely at home. Like Bernie's own father, when he was home, however, he had clear expectations of behavior for Jermaine and set down the law when he needed to. The difference was, Jermaine's father expressed his affection for Jermaine. It wasn't overt, but it was obvious. Bernie couldn't remember ever experiencing a hug or an encouraging word from his father.

In those early days, Jermaine's mom was fun as well, often laughing along with the boys and teasing her husband if he got too serious. For Bernie, it was a happy home and a refuge from his own. While his mom was amazingly supportive and loving, his father was relentless in his demands. From a young age, Bernie knew he would never be able to live up to the expectations placed on him.

Duncan Simpson was the next to join their alliance.

Duncan was the tall, skinny boy with an inexplicably large amount of curly hair on his head who always sat at the back of the class and made faces at the teacher. He made people laugh, and he always seemed to be in a great mood. One day, he actually asked the teacher out on a date in front of the entire class. Everyone giggled and turned red with embarrassment. Not Duncan, though—he was beaming from ear to ear, attempting to charm Ms. Adair with his charisma. He had to serve detention that day, but from that point on, he was a legend at school. Duncan Simpson was crazy, and everyone who knew him loved him.

One day, in the middle of fifth grade, Duncan randomly asked if Bernie and Jermaine wanted to hang out at his house after school. They were flattered and readily agreed. When they got there, Duncan's older brother, Kevin, and his parents were chatting at the dining room table. Duncan had waved at them, then signaled for Jermaine and Bernie to follow him upstairs.

Outside the first bedroom, Duncan leaned over and mouthed, "Shhh, follow me."

Jermaine and Bernie felt an odd rush of excitement. What could be so secretive?

Duncan moved into the room and turned on the light. They could see by the pictures on the shelves and the posters on the wall that it was Kevin's room. Kevin was a few years older than Duncan, and it felt odd that they were standing in the middle of his domain.

Duncan then walked over to his brother's desk and quickly logged on to his computer. Bernie and Jermaine crowded on either side of him and watched as he moved the cursor and hovered over a file entitled "Homework Assignments."

They both looked at Duncan and then at each other. They were confused, as they had no idea why this would at all be interesting to them. "Whatcha looking for?" Bernie had asked.

Duncan then clicked on the folder. It seemed to be a list of videos. All with *XXX* written in their titles.

"What're those?" Jermaine asked.

Duncan clicked on the first one. It didn't take long until they began to realize what they were watching.

"Holy moly," Bernie had exclaimed. It was the first rebellious thing he and Jermaine had ever been involved in. Duncan *had* to be in the clan.

Soon after, the three of them became inseparable.

Lenny and Pudgy joined the clan later that year. It happened by accident. Pudgy was being teased by some Pulltown boys during a field trip to their library. The two older boys had him pinned down behind the building and were attempting to force candy from his front pocket. Bernie and Jermaine had watched it unfold and were about to intervene, when suddenly Lenny Cartwright had jumped on top of the two larger boys and started punching them. It was just about the bravest thing the boys had ever seen.

Their teacher broke it up as soon as she heard the kerfuffle and sent the older boys scurrying. Pudgy had a bit of blood on his nose, but he thanked Lenny profusely as Lenny helped pull him to his feet. Jermaine offered a hand too, and the five of them sat together until Pudgy felt better.

Jermaine and Bernie nodded knowingly at each other, then Bernie asked Pudgy and Lenny if they wanted to join their clan.

"What's a clan?" Pudgy had asked innocently.

"We hang out. Do stuff together. 'All for one, and one for all' is our motto," Jermaine offered.

Bernie added, "And 'so shall it ever be' is the response we say." The boys all thought it sounded exciting and cool.

Pudgy immediately said, "I'll join."

Lenny was impressed. He liked the idea of having a secret club. "What do we gotta do to join?" The boys knew he was hoping for some kind of physical challenge.

"Nothing," Jermaine replied. "We just always gotta have each other's backs. That's the rule."

"Yeah, that's the rule. Everyone's gotta promise," Bernie added with an air of importance.

So that was that. The beginning of the clan. Jermaine's mom called them "the five little monkeys," like the nursery rhyme they'd all heard as kids. "No more monkeys jumping on the bed!" she used to holler whenever they got too rambunctious.

They knew they needed a fort—a base for their clan. The shed came shortly after. Pudgy had remembered Farmer Granger's decrepit structure at the far end of his cornfield. No one seemed to be using it anymore, so they gradually took it over.

"Should call it Base Camp, like Mount Etna," Lenny offered.

"Everest," Jermaine corrected. He always seemed to know more than the rest of them.

"Whatever. It's a cool name."

The boys all agreed it was cool, and Base Camp was born. As the months went by, its importance only grew. It was more than just a place to plan adventures and to dream; it represented freedom, independence, and a bond that would never die.

❖

Cob Stanton lowered himself into his chair and leaned toward the computer screen as it came to life on his desk. His back, like his knees, had seen much better days, and he was in a foul mood. He checked his watch—it was almost midnight. He hadn't been able to sleep, so he'd grabbed a beer and decided on doing a little digging—just to kill some time.

He couldn't get his bizarre meeting with Guylaine out of his head. Her phantasmagorical tales of a half-dead boy feeding on the living was beyond ridiculous. *What was it she called them? Inbetweeners? What a load of shit*, he thought, opening up his browser.

As crazy as it all sounded, for some reason he couldn't shake the niggly-nagging feeling in his gut. Try as he might to set it adrift, it remained with him.

Since sleep would obviously be an absent friend tonight, he thought he might as well poke a few holes in her story—if only to pass the time. Stanton took a swig from his bottle as he tried to remember every detail that she'd told him about the boy she had called Mordecai. A boy who potentially died (and was buried) a long time ago. And, to top it off, someone who was currently creeping around the woods somewhere beyond Birch Street—luring unsuspecting people into his lair.

A load of shit, he again thought as he typed "Mordecai" into the search engine, then opened Wikipedia. He scanned through the history of the name. It appeared that Mordecai was most likely of Persian or Hebrew origin. He did notice that one of the original Persian meanings of the name could be interpreted as "little boy." In Hebrew, the most common meaning was "warrior." Some of the many other meanings that stood out to him were "bitter" and "bruising." *Fitting*, he thought, typing in a new search: "Mordecai, Providence, Washington."

As he expected, nothing of substance emerged.

Stanton then did the same thing with the communities of Musgrove, Chandler, and Pulltown.

Still nothing.

He briefly considered checking the police database for all the people named Mordecai who had ever gone missing over the years in the region, but then he remembered Guylaine had said that he'd been buried. *Until, of course, he took it upon himself to rise up and begin running around in the woods.*

If such a person actually existed, and if he'd been buried, in all likelihood, he was not considered missing. Stanton decided to focus on people—a boy in particular—named Mordecai who had died and been buried in the area.

Stanton recalled something else Guylaine had said: *He could have died years ago.*

He then decided to look up some statistics on Whatcom County itself to get a sense of the scope of the area. Seeing that it had become a

Territorial Legislature in 1854, he set that as his marker—any information before that year would probably be too difficult to find. With a current population in Whatcom County of just over two hundred thousand people—most of whom lived in and around Bellingham—he estimated that he had a pretty good shot at finding any information about all the boys named Mordecai who had died in the region.

He could have died years ago.

He would start in the present and work backward toward the year 1854. Stanton figured a good place to begin would be to create a list of all the newspapers and local county rags that had serviced the northern Washington State area over the years. From there he could do some basic searches. As he soon discovered, the list was extensive, but not prohibitive.

By three thirty in the morning, Stanton had finished compiling his list. He would try to grab some shut-eye before dawn. Today would most likely be another crazy one.

❖

Bernie had to relieve himself. It was still dark, and he needed someone to go with him.

"Hey, Pudgy, wake up." He pushed his friend until he stirred.

"Whaaa…"

"I gotta crap somethin' chronic."

"Not now, Bern…"

"No, seriously, I gotta take a dump. Come with me."

"Can't you wait until morning?" Pudgy said groggily.

"No. I've been holdin' it all day. Come with me…please."

Pudgy slowly sat up and rubbed his eyes. Bernie pointed his flashlight at him and watched him reluctantly unzip his sleeping bag. "Okay, hurry up."

Both boys stepped outside into the damp, cool night air. Bernie did a quick scan of the surrounding forest with his flashlight, its beam barely penetrating the thick foliage around the tent. "Okay, this way. Over here." He shone his light toward the forest.

"I'm not going to watch you crap, Bernie."

"Just hold the light beside me. You don't have to watch."

"Gross. Okay, but hurry." Pudgy held the light so it shone in the trees just above Bernie as he walked further into the undergrowth. "Hey, Bernie?"

"Yeah."

"We left JP alone in the tent. Think he's okay?"

"Hold on…I'm almost done."

"Hey, Jermaine, you up?" Pudgy called out. Their cardinal rule was that they would never leave someone alone. Ever.

"I'm awake, Pudgy," Jermaine called from within the tent. "Here, I'll put my light on."

"Almost done," Bernie groaned, straining to finish.

Just then, Pudgy's flashlight beam abruptly swung away from Bernie, leaving him in complete darkness

"Bernie!"

"What?"

"Something's in the trees just past you." Both boys could make out the branches quivering as if something had brushed against them.

They could hear Jermaine unzipping his sleeping bag and then stepping out of tent. "What is it, Pudgy?" Jermaine shone his flashlight toward Bernie, who was still squatting in the bushes.

"Over there." Pudgy waved his light into the trees beyond Bernie.

"I don't see any—" Jermaine started to say, then they all saw some branches moving rapidly back and forth.

"What is it, Jermaine?" Bernie asked nervously. He felt as defenseless as he'd ever felt with his pants below his knees, attending to his business.

"Not sure." Jermaine crept closer with Pudgy beside him. "Don't see anything, but something was there."

Bernie grabbed some fern leaves from beside him and quickly performed an ablution, instantly hauled up his pants, and stumbled and crawled his way back to Jermaine and Pudgy. When he reached them, they all shone their lights into the woods that surrounded them. All was still again.

"Let's get back to the tent." Jermaine didn't have to say it twice.

❖

It was only eight in the morning when Cob Stanton knocked on the Prescotts' front door. The mysterious Ms. Cloutier had said she'd spoken with Jermaine in some detail about the current situation, so he decided he needed to dig deeper.

From behind the door, he heard Mr. Prescott say, "I'll get it." A second later, it opened.

Jermaine's father was a tall, fit-looking man. Stanton had been told that he was a welder for True North Pipelines and that he worked most of the week in Chandler.

"Morning." Stanton avoided an introduction. The uniform would suffice.

"Heard anything?" Tal Prescott asked quietly. Stanton could sense the anxiety in his voice despite his demeanor.

"Nope. Nothing yet. Sorry."

Stanton watched as Tal's shoulders dropped slightly. Mrs. Prescott appeared behind him. She looked like she hadn't slept well in a long time. "Officer?"

"Ma'am. Was hoping to speak to you both a bit, if I may."

"About?" Tal asked defensively.

Stanton knew he had to tread carefully. "Not sure yet. Need to connect some dots. Thought you might help me figure some things out."

"What things?"

It was clear to Stanton that Tal was not one for guessing games. He understood he needed to take his foot off the gas and ease the tension. "Possible to get a coffee around here?" Stanton looked beyond Tal to his wife, Pat.

"Certainly. Come on in," Pat offered. Stanton noticed she was in her housecoat and her pink slippers were worn and dirty. She appeared to Stanton to be someone who'd spent a lot of time dressed like that.

Tal Prescott reluctantly moved to the side so Stanton could step in. Stanton sensed he was protecting something. Was it her?

❖

He was sitting up and smiling in bed when Yarl and Tammy went to check on him in the morning. Archie even asked what was for breakfast. After two days at home, he seemed to be completely back to his old self.

The Truscotts were all at once completely elated, relieved—and confused. No one in their neighborhood had mentioned it, but they all were wondering the exact same thing: Why was Archie spared while so many others had suffered? Nonetheless, with all the tragedy and the pall of sadness that had pressed down hard upon Providence, the news of Archie and his seeming resurrection was the good news everyone needed. It was no less than a miracle. It gave everyone hope.

The Truscotts were careful not to be overtly vocal in their joy; their thoughts were still with a community that was reeling from recent events. One by one they quietly greeted the visitors at the front door, thanking them for their support and accepting their gifts of food, wine, and flowers. By the afternoon, Yarl Truscott had headed to Pulltown to help with the search for the four missing boys. If Archie could make it through this hellish experience, he was positive they could as well.

❖

The boys were keen to get an early start and were packed up and walking before eight o'clock in the morning. It was hard slogging through the thick underbrush of the dense cedar forest, and there was a chilling dampness in the air. By Jermaine's rough calculations, they had a couple of hours before they would eventually run into the open area that he'd seen on Google Earth called Mossy Gulch. Once there, they should easily be able to locate Skagit

Creek. They would need a lot of luck, as without a compass, it was pretty much a guessing game.

None of them spoke about the previous night's incident. It had freaked them all out, and sleep was hard to come by for most of the night. Bernie in particular was quiet and chose to bring up the rear and walk behind them. The sinkhole episode and then last night had obviously taken its toll.

By nine thirty, the sun had managed to begin poking its way between the trees. Mist rose lazily in the long beams of light breaking through the darkness. Other than the sound of their own heavy breathing and the snapping of branches beneath them as they walked on the treacherous forest floor, it was eerily quiet—as if the entire forest was watching them in anticipation.

When they reached a particularly sunny patch, Jermaine stopped and dropped his pack. It would be a good place to eat a bit of raw pasta and have a rest. Pudgy and Bernie likewise released their packs from their backs and sat beside him.

"Whatcha think, JP? Much longer?" Pudgy asked.

Jermaine pulled out his map. It was virtually impossible to tell where they were. It was hard enough to focus on keeping a relatively straight line in a vague interpretation of where the creek might be in relation to where they left this morning. Nonetheless, he was fairly confident they had reached Mossy Gulch, as it had flattened out considerably. He was sure that they would hit the creek eventually. They had to; they had no other choice. "Should be soon, Pudgy," he replied, sounding more confident than he actually was. "How're you, Bernie?"

Bernie looked over at his friends. "I'm beat."

Pudgy dug into his pack and pulled out some macaroni noodles. "Here, suck on a few of these."

"Gee, thanks," Bernie replied sarcastically but took the handful of dried pasta from Pudgy.

The three boys were exhausted from being in a constant state of high alert, continually looking all around them for possible movement. Their nerves were frayed, and none of them were sure how much more tension they could take without snapping. Jermaine could tell they were running out of time. The creek would go a long way to help buoy their spirits. "Let's eat up. I can't wait to take a drink out of that cool creek."

❖

Guylaine Cloutier sat down in her usual place in the grass, halfway down Birch Street. While the scene near Stanton's trailer was still chaotic, it had calmed down somewhat once the most recent search for the boys had moved toward the Pulltown area.

She knew there was no sense in her heading that way, though the media didn't know that. They were like fish after chum, and the majority of them had headed to Pulltown. Guylaine knew it was better to stay here. This was the area that Mordecai had been hunting. Inbetweeners expand their territory, but they never simply up and leave to find another area.

Ever.

The news of Archie's miraculous cure meant everything. She'd seen such a thing in the past. She could sense that things were changing rapidly. Mordecai was letting go at the extremities of his terrain and centering himself. *Near the grave*, Guylaine thought.

Her guess was that the boys were heading into the woods by Pulltown because they knew of a route—or perhaps they were simply setting some bait to buy time for their ruse. Whatever their reason, if they were on to Mordecai—which she was sure they were—they would eventually end up in the area directly in front of where she was looking right now—in the woods behind Birch Street. It might be many, many miles away from where she now sat, but, from Pulltown, they would have had to make their way back into his territory.

Guylaine closed her eyes to try to sense Mordecai. To feel him. To let his energy approach her. She breathed in deeply, slowly exhaling through her nose. She then opened her eyes and stared intently at the woods, blocking everything else from her mind. She fell into a sort of meditative state, letting her unconscious open up to him. She reached out to him—beckoning him to respond to her signals.

She waited in silence, oblivious to the myriad of people below her on Birch Street. At first it was a pulse. A murmur.

Then it became clearer.

She latched onto him. While his presence felt powerful, he felt distant now. She could sense he was still in his territory, but not nearby. He also felt less angry—almost pleased.

Guylaine closed her eyes and slowly brought herself out of her lucid trance. As she became fully conscious, she felt a powerful shiver pass through her. She was accustomed to the sensation and waited until it subsided.

Guylaine then stood up and took another deep breath—letting it out slowly and deliberately. One thing was becoming abundantly clear to her.

The boys are getting closer to Mordecai's grave.

❖

Cob Stanton could sense from his brief visit with Pat and Tal Prescott that there was more to the story than they were letting on. More specifically, something told him that Jermaine's mom knew something. He could sense it in the way she averted her eyes when she answered his questions; or how her nervous, shaking fingers fidgeted with the thread dangling from the sleeve of her robe; or the way she always looked up at her husband each time before she spoke, as if she didn't want to alarm him—or reveal too much to him; or the rapid and frequent sips she took from her coffee mug, leading Stanton to suspect that there was more than just cream in her coffee. Stanton had been a cop long enough; he could tell when someone was fighting their own inner demons.

He again thought of Guylaine Cloutier's prediction about the likelihood of him stopping these bizarre events in Providence.

Not unless someone around here knows something we don't…

He knew he needed to find time to visit Mrs. Prescott without her husband present. When she was alone and vulnerable. When he saw Tal in Pulltown signing up for another search party, he knew he'd found his chance. He told Officer Thompson that he had some business to attend to back in Providence and slipped away to his police jeep unnoticed.

A few minutes later he knocked on her door. Pat Prescott opened it slowly. She looked anxious when she saw him. "Any news?" Her voice was weak, and he noticed she was still dressed in her pink slippers and housecoat. Her eyes were red, and she was swaying slightly as she stood.

"Nothing yet. I'm sorry."

"I don't understand…why are you here? I'm so worried." She didn't invite him in.

"Mrs. Prescott, I believe you know a little bit more than you were letting on yesterday."

"Huh? I don't understand." She shifted her gaze away from Stanton. She appeared to be embarrassed and nervous.

"Part of me believes your son might be looking for something. Or someone. Maybe the boys heard a crazy rumor or something. Maybe they just wanted to hunt for their missing friend. But all I know is that there is some crazy shit going on around here, and if you or your husband have anything, *I mean anything*, that you think might help me figure out where they might have gone, it would be best if you gave it to me straight up." Stanton knew he'd come on strong, but it was necessary. He had no other choice.

Pat Prescott backed up slightly and then slowly straightened her back and lifted her eyes to meet his. "Like I said, I don't understand what you're talking about. I think you are wasting your time. Perhaps you'd be better off looking for my son than standing here accusing me of hiding things—"

"Nobody is accusing anyone of anything," Stanton interrupted. "I'm just pretty sure I could use any lead possible—no matter how crazy it is. If you have any suspicion that your son believes he knows something that will lead him to his lost friend, I suggest you let me know. If you don't share it and something happens to him, then you can live with the consequences. If you don't know anything, then so be it. I won't waste any more of your time."

Pat slowly shook her head. Stanton thought she looked more sad than mad. "You're wasting both of our time. Goodbye, officer." With that, she quickly closed the door. From the other side, Stanton could hear her locking it.

Stanton made his way back to his car. He was certain of one thing: his gut instinct had been correct about Pat Prescott. She knew something.

❖

Officer Thompson navigated his cruiser out of Pulltown and onto the main road. He'd been relocated to the area to oversee the investigation ever since they caught wind that the boys had last been seen there. His partner, Officer Ian Plant, sat beside him in the front seat munching on a stale donut. *So cliché*, Thompson thought.

They would be at Lake Teshko for the umpteenth time in the last twenty-four hours in just under thirty minutes. The search effort thus far had turned up absolutely nothing. It seemed increasingly unlikely the boys had been there at all. Thompson felt fairly confident that whatever scam the boys had laid on their parents about going fishing, swimming, and camping at Lake Teshko to get their mind off things was hogwash. So too was the yarn they gave poor old Daryl Tanner about meeting some girls in Musgrove. No, Thompson felt there were only two feasible possibilities: either the boys left on foot from Daryl's house and disappeared into the woods somewhere, or they hitched a ride down the main road toward Chandler and out to Highway 542. From there, they could end up anywhere in America.

Thompson picked up his radio to call Cob Stanton back in Providence. Stanton had been out to Pulltown already today, but he felt more comfortable at the foot of Birch Street. To Stanton, it was still the epicenter. Thompson was inclined to agree.

After a brief conversation, it was agreed that dispatch would release a BOLO. The "Be on the Lookout," or ATL (Attempt to Locate), bulletin would be effective immediately. The boys could be in a whole heap of trouble, and because they had been gone since before the weekend, time was working against them.

❖

Commanding Officer Cob Stanton heard the APB on his radio. All law enforcement agencies across Washington State were now on high alert, and considering the recent inexplicable events in Whatcom County, news of the missing boys would be garnering national interest by nightfall. Meanwhile, in both Providence and in Pulltown, speculation was running rampant about the whereabouts of the four boys. Everyone had a theory about where they might be or what might have happened to them. Stanton liked to deal with facts and tried to avoid engaging with the conspiracy theorists.

Like Officer Thompson, Stanton felt a little sorry for Daryl Tanner. He had been relentlessly questioned by all levels of authorities. It appeared the boy really had no idea of the whereabouts of Jermaine Prescott, Pudgy Murtland, Lenny Cartwright, and Bernie Maclaren. Apparently, the boys had told Daryl that they weren't actually going camping and fishing at all; they were in fact going to see some girls in Musgrove. At the time, Daryl had thought that it was the coolest, bravest maneuver *ever.*

Until now. As that too seemed to be fiction.

If the boys did go to Musgrove, nobody had seen them. To top it off, the entire Lake Teshko area had been searched multiple times, with no evidence the boys had ever camped there. In fact, other than Daryl's brief encounter with them, no one had seen hide nor hair of them since they'd left Providence.

In the afternoon, while he waited for any news out of Pulltown, Lake Teshko, and the Musgrove area, Stanton spent a couple of hours on his computer perusing the list of newspapers he'd compiled earlier, searching for the name Mordecai. At the very least, it helped him kill the time, as waiting for news was the hardest part.

He finished siphoning through some of the traditional, long-standing newspapers servicing northern Washington State, well as the various local rags. There were only a few mentions of anyone named Mordecai. None of them were boys who had been reported as dead and buried.

He was about to move to his next option when there was a knock at his trailer door. He didn't bother standing up. It was probably one of his knucklehead security bozos again. They were always hassling him for trivial things. "Boss, have you seen the key to the Porta Potty?" or "Excuse me, sir, do you know what time the sandwich truck is coming?" or "Didn't mean to bother you, boss, but I can't find my hat."

Bozos, all of them.

"It's open," he hollered, without looking up. He heard the door open and then gently close. Stanton could sense someone was standing there.

"I need to talk to you." It was a woman's voice.

Stanton looked up and saw Pat Prescott in a long jacket and sunglasses, cowering by the door. He stood up and pointed toward the single wooden chair by his desk.

"I'm glad you're here. Have a seat. Tea? Coffee?"

Pat shook her head and whispered, "No, thanks."

Stanton waited until she sat down, then did likewise behind his desk. She was anxious and visibly shaking. She kept her jacket and her sunglasses on. He waited for her to speak.

When she did begin to talk, she was very quiet. She didn't look up at Stanton; instead, she kept her head down and her arms tightly wrapped around her body. "I may have an idea of where Jermaine and the boys have gone," she whispered. "It's only a hunch, but I'd never forgive myself if I didn't mention it."

"All right," Stanton said, leaning back in his chair. He didn't want to pressure her.

"A while ago, I told Jermaine a story. An old story. About a boyfriend I had in high school. It may be of interest, it may not, but Jermaine seemed overly keen to learn about it all."

Intrigued, Stanton remained silent. He could sense she wanted to tell him everything.

"It was so long ago, but it may be important."

"Go on."

Thirty minutes later, Stanton walked Mrs. Prescott to the door. By the time he sat back down behind his desk, he had never been so confused in his entire life.

❖

The terrain had definitely flattened out, and the trees had also become less dense. Jermaine felt they were well within Mossy Gulch. Soon they found themselves in a clearing, and it was Bernie who saw it first. "There it is," he said with excitement. He was pointing to his right.

Pudgy saw it next. "Skagit Creek! Yes! We did it, boys!"

The three boys ran through the thick grass, ferns, and undergrowth toward the shimmering water. It looked much wider than any of them had imagined, almost as wide as a small river, but it was clearly shallow enough to traverse. They knew from their search on Google Earth that to reach the cabin, they would eventually need to get to the other side of the creek. This was looking hopeful now.

When they finally reached the edge, they dropped their packs; Pudgy and Jermaine began hastily filling up their water bottles. Not only were they thirsty, they were tired of raw pasta.

Bernie kept walking into the water until he was waist deep in the middle of the creek. He eventually submerged himself directly into the fast-moving, cold water—covering his entire body. Once he resurfaced, he immediately began to scrub off the thick, dried mud. He had been covered in the crusty mud ever since the sinkhole. Now dark, muddy water swirled around him. For the first time in a while, he was smiling.

Pudgy looked at him and laughed out loud. "I bet that feels good, Bernie," he yelled.

"You have no idea," Bernie yelled back. His deep, hoarse voice was full of joy.

Pudgy turned to Jermaine. "Hey, JP, let's join him. How about a swim?" He was already peeling off his clothes.

Jermaine smiled. "You got it. Give me a second and I'll race you in!"

A half hour later they had crossed over and begun walking upstream through the shallowest part of the creek. It was now late afternoon, and Jermaine suggested they find a place to dry off and, more importantly, to spend the night. The last thing any of them wanted was to stumble upon the cabin just as it was getting dark.

After another twenty minutes, Bernie noticed a clearing beside the creek. Jermaine and Pudgy agreed it would make a fine spot. An hour later, they had set up a tent, got a large fire going, and washed out all of their dirty clothes and laid them out to dry on the warm rocks beside the creek. A pot of water was boiling for their pasta, and their spirits, while heavy with the thought of what they were about to undertake, were somewhat lifted.

By eight o'clock, they were exhausted and ready for bed. Jermaine put another couple of large branches on the fire before heading into the tent. The flickering light outside would be comforting.

Chapter Fourteen

The next morning, they were packed up before the sun had risen above the tree line. The three of them had spent the night squished together as close to the middle of the tent as they could manage. They had been exhausted, and sleep had come quickly. More importantly, the entire night had remained uneventful.

After some more hot pasta for breakfast, they packed up, loaded their packs onto their backs, and headed down to the edge of Skagit Creek. They walked upstream for close to an hour, hugging close to the shore in ankle-deep water. The wide creek narrowed, then became deeper, and then widened again; Jermaine had checked his map frequently along the way and surmised that they were in the center of the area the map referred to as Mossy Gulch. They should now be only a few miles from the structure he had seen on Google Earth. They had crossed the stream early on, and the warm sun reflecting off the water felt invigorating, despite the chilly temperature of the water.

Bernie seemed like a new person. He was reenergized and now walked with purpose directly behind Jermaine. Pudgy brought up the rear. He was full of questions the closer they got.

"Whaddya think we'll find there, JP?"

"Not sure, Pudgy."

"Do you think he'll be waiting for us there?"

"Dunno. Hope not."

"Where do you think the grave is?"

"Probably somewhere behind the cabin."

"Do you think we'll find his bones, JP?"

"Hard to say, Pudgy."

"I'm scared. You scared?"

"Yeah, I'm scared."

"How about you, Bernie. You scared?"

"All for one, and one for all, Pudgy."

"You got that right. So shall it ever be. How much longer do you think?"

"Hard to say. According to the map, we should almost be—" Jermaine suddenly stopped walking and held up both hands. Seeing Jermaine suddenly freeze, Bernie stopped as well. Pudgy saw both boys in front of him stop and did likewise; he leaned to his side to see what they were both looking at. His heart was pounding.

Then he also saw it.

About fifty feet from them. On a small knoll that rose up beside the creek.

A tiny cabin.

❖

Officers Douglas Thompson and Ian Plant were surprised when they'd been asked to aid with the release of Tucker Paulson from the Pulltown Regional Clinic. As Tucker had no immediate relatives in the area, Cob Stanton had suggested that the two officers should drive him back to Providence.

Stanton had received the call from Dr. Patricia Lewis early that morning. According to her, the lead psychiatrist on Paulson's case, Dr. Penn, had said it was a "bloody miracle." He had no idea how Tucker could have snapped out of such an intense psychosis. But he did. And yesterday, as instantly as a light switch clicking on, Tucker had suddenly sat up in bed and asked to go home.

Dr. Lewis would join them in transporting Tucker back to Providence; she wanted to keep an eye on him as well as have some extra support in case the wheels came off again. By the time Thompson and Plant pulled up to the clinic, Tucker Paulson and Dr. Lewis were already waiting outside, chatting away happily.

During the ride home, it became apparent that Tucker had no recollection of what had transpired last Saturday night. He vaguely remembered leaving work and locking up the feed shop. He had a shadowy memory of hearing some noises behind him. But after that, it was all a blur. The next thing he remembered, he was sitting up in bed at the clinic in Pulltown, feeling hungry and confused—and wanting to go home.

Stanton felt a guarded wave of relief when he'd first received the call that they were releasing Paulson. That made two miracles now: first Archie, and now Tucker. There might be a light at the end of the tunnel after all.

But why now?

As he stepped out of his trailer to meet another group of volunteers, he wondered if it had anything to do with the missing boys.

❖

Jermaine exited the creek first, dropping his pack on the muddy bank and scouring the area. He pointed to his pack and signaled for Pudgy and Bernie to do likewise, waiting for them to join him. Pudgy pulled his pack off, reached into it, then took out both of Lenny's hunting knives. He offered one of them to Jermaine. "Want this, JP?"

Jermaine shook his head. "Let Bernie have it. Let's move slowly, and keep your eyes peeled."

Pudgy handed a knife to Bernie. He reluctantly took the large weapon and held it awkwardly at his side.

The terrain ahead of them was open, so visibility was not an issue. They could see the cabin clearly now and began climbing the slight incline toward it. It was immediately apparent that, after so many years exposed to the elements, the abandoned cabin was in a desperate state of disrepair—leaning slightly to one side and barely held together by its rusty nails and the thick vines climbing around it. The musty smell of the damp, rotten wood permeated the air.

As they got closer, they could see that the old porch, which at one time had been attached to the front, had long since slipped away from the cabin and had fallen forward. What was left of the door, precariously clinging to the doorframe only by the top hinge, was bent inward, and they could make out ferns and other vegetation growing on the floor inside. The roof itself seemed to still be intact, though heavily laden with moss, tree branches, and other debris. From their angle, they could see that there were two windows. A larger one at the front beside the door and one on the side. The glass had long since disappeared from both.

The three boys cautiously continued approaching the front of the house, scanning the area as they went. The cabin sat atop a small rise, and the forest immediately behind it looked thick and foreboding. Finally, they reached the remains of the front porch and stopped.

"What now, JP?" Pudgy whispered. He held his knife with both hands in front of him. His arms were shaking, and his breathing was shallow and quick.

"I think we should check inside, just in case."

"In case of what?" Bernie asked.

Jermaine looked at his buddy. "Bones. In case his are in there."

Bernie and Pudgy glanced at each other, then back at Jermaine. "The three of us?" Pudgy asked, looking at the ramshackle remains of the porch in front of him.

"No, just me. Let me take a quick look." Jermaine pulled the small flashlight from his front pocket. "You both keep an eye out. Holler if you see anything at all." Jermaine was already moving toward the front of the porch.

"Be careful, Jermaine," Bernie said. "We got yer back."

Jermaine maneuvered himself up the slippery, tilted porch, careful to avoid the various rusty nails poking through the surface. Once he reached the entryway, he leaned forward and grabbed the doorframe on either side and awkwardly stepped over the two-foot gap between the porch and the door.

Before entering, he paused briefly to allow his eyes to adjust to the dim interior. He then turned on his flashlight and stepped in.

The dank smell of rot was overpowering. The air suddenly became chilly and damp. Jermaine took a step inside. He could feel the wooden floorboard, swollen with moisture, bend beneath his feet.

Shining his flashlight to his left, he could see the remnants of a small kitchen. A porcelain sink was cracked in half and full of sediment and weeds. The wooden counter was cluttered with blackened pots, plates, and more debris. On the floor—intermittent tufts of ferns and other vegetation. In front of him was a small rusty wood stove, and beside it, a doorframe that Jermaine surmised led to a small bedroom at the rear of the cabin. To his right, a single cot—its thin mattress torn and stained, most of the stuffing lying all around it from burrowing rodents that had obviously infested the abandoned structure.

Jermaine shone his light ahead to the bedroom door. The actual door was still on its hinges and appeared to be fully closed.

"You okay, JP?" It was Pudgy.

Jermaine took another step inside. "Yeah. Just gonna check out the bedroom at the back," he replied over his shoulder.

"See anything yet?" This time it was Bernie. His voice was full of fear.

"Not yet." Jermaine took another step closer to the bedroom door, sweeping his flashlight back and forth in front of him, then back toward the floor—careful to walk along the floorboards that would most likely still be able to take his weight.

Jermaine moved his flashlight to the left and then slowly to the right. Then he stopped. There was something on the floor between the thick weeds. It was large and metallic.

Jermaine carefully walked over to it and bent down. It was some kind of phone. A strange, large antenna sticking out the side. He could see the word *Motorola* written on the front.

Jermaine's heart quickened. He knew exactly what it was. *The satellite phone Mom talked about*, he thought. *The one her boyfriend called her on.*

Jermaine moved his light back up toward the door and took another step. He heard a sudden, loud *crack* and could feel the wooden plank beneath him giving way. To avoid falling through, he reacted by diving forward—somersaulting toward the door and landing hard on his back.

"What was that?" He could hear Bernie's muffled voice from outside.

Jermaine reached for the doorframe to help pull himself up. "I'm okay. Almost fell through the floor. It's all rotten."

He took a deep breath to steady his nerves, then directed his flashlight to the rusty doorknob in front of him. He grabbed it with one hand and tried to push it open. It moved an inch and then stopped. He shone his light down to the floor again and could see that dirt and weeds had piled up in front of the door. He assumed it was the same on the other side.

Jermaine leaned down and put his shoulder against the door. He gave it a solid nudge, and it moved another few inches. He shone his flashlight through the crack. He could see nothing but dark shadows.

He could hear his friends murmuring outside and knew they were getting anxious. He leaned down again and, this time, gave the door a heavy push. He heard the hinges give way, and the entire door fell inward with Jermaine on top of it. His flashlight fell from his hand and rolled along the floor beside him.

"You okay?" Bernie yelled.

Jermaine then heard someone stumbling around the side of the cabin.

"JP?" It was Pudgy. He was outside, below the bedroom window.

"I'm fine. Just knocked the door in."

Still lying on top of the door, Jermaine reached for his flashlight and quickly shone it around the tiny room. Tattered garments were scattered everywhere. He could see a broken chair and a small chest of drawers kneeling to one side, an old hurricane lamp on the bedside table, and a shattered mirror frame still hanging on the wall above the bed.

The bed itself, like the cot in the main room, had been pulled apart by mice. But he could see there was something very different about this one. Scattered on top and beside the bed were the obvious skeletal remains of a large human. Jermaine pointed his light at the large femur closest to him. He immediately felt sick to his stomach.

Jermaine gagged and quickly rolled over and jumped up to his feet. He then slowly maneuvered his way back into the main room, carefully choosing where to place each step. As fast as he could manage, he retreated toward the bright light coming from the front doorway. He was pretty sure he had just found his mom's boyfriend.

❖

With Tucker Paulson and Archie Truscott back in Providence and fully recovered from their inexplicable episodes, the general hue and cry around town was that it might have been a virus after all. Perhaps everyone was getting all bent out of shape over a silly bug. Furthermore, maybe the disappearance of Jermaine Prescott, Lenny Cartwright, Bernie Maclaren, and Pudgy Murtland was not related at all.

Maybe they were just lost. An adventure gone awry.

Regardless, the crowds continued to pour into Providence, and the police presence at either end of the main road was now significant. Officers Thompson and Plant had recently been assigned the task of coordinating the fortification of Providence and Pulltown, and it had become a full-time commitment.

During his afternoon break, Thompson drove down to the Command Center trailer at the end of Birch Street. When he arrived, Cob Stanton was standing outside of the trailer looking at the woods directly in front of him. Thompson got out of the vehicle and slowly walked over to where Stanton stood.

"Afternoon, sir." Thompson smiled at Stanton. He didn't expect a similar gesture.

Stanton briefly glanced at the handsome young cop, then looked back at the woods.

"Getting crazy up on Main Street. Lots of folks wanting to have a look-see down here," Thompson said.

Stanton nodded without looking at him, continuing to stare into the wall of tall cedars in front of him.

"Anything new down this way, sir?"

Stanton slowly turned and looked directly at Thompson. "You ever heard of a place called Mossy Gulch?"

"Mossy Gulch? No, sir. Why?"

"Me neither. We may want to find out about it."

"Mossy Gulch? Why?"

Stanton feigned a smile, then pushed some chew into the side of his mouth. He turned again to face the trees. "Do me a favor and ask the locals what they know about it." Stanton then turned, spit a gob of tobacco on the ground in front of him, and walked back toward the trailer.

Officer Thompson watched him leave and then turned to look at the forest. *What the hell is Mossy Gulch?* he thought as he watched the breeze blow through the thick boughs above him. *Sounds like a disease.*

❖

After Jermaine emerged from the cabin and they had digested what he told them he'd found, the boys decided to have a cursory look in the woods behind the cabin. It was now midafternoon, and they knew they wanted to get the tent set up and some firewood collected before it became dark. They were in the valley now, and nightfall would descend early and swiftly.

Directly behind the cabin, the woods immediately became thick and almost impenetrable; the gnarly undergrowth was particularly difficult to walk through. All three boys already had countless scratches and cuts beneath their torn and ripped pants and shirts from the arduous journey.

They stayed as close together as they could, hyperaware of any signs of movement. For over an hour they moved through the eerily quiet forest surrounding the cabin. If there was a grave anywhere in the vicinity, it wasn't directly behind the cabin.

"What now, Jermaine?" Bernie asked, exhausted, as both the emotional roller coaster of the last few days and the exertion of clambering through the forest had taken their tolls.

It was Pudgy who answered instead. "I think we should get set up for tonight. Tomorrow we can find the grave. We need to get the camp going."

Jermaine looked over at his friend. "You okay, Pudgy?"

"I'm just saying we need to get a campsite set," Pudgy replied curtly. He looked unusually anxious and preoccupied.

"Okay, buddy. We can do that." Jermaine led the way back out toward the front of the cabin. After the brooding darkness of the forest, the dappled light of the afternoon sun seemed inviting. They could see the bright sunshine shimmering off the surface of the creek below them and eagerly moved toward it.

❖

Cob Stanton flung his hat on the chair beside his desk and pulled off his jacket—hanging it on the hook beside the door. It had been another spectacularly unspectacular day. Lots of activity with nothing concrete to show for it.

Nada.

The plethora of law enforcement personnel, drone and tracking teams, and dozens of volunteers in and around the area where the boys had last been spotted, was both impressive and entirely overwhelming. The looks of despair, confusion, and sadness on each and every face was palpable. To top it off, the crush of media reps, concerned locals, and curious gawkers all pushing closer to the investigation areas was becoming almost unmanageable, and Stanton had been forced to ask for an upgrade of peripheral support around both Pulltown and Providence to keep the wolves at bay.

Stanton poured the last remnants of the morning's coffee into his "I'd Rather Be in Iraq" mug and moved toward his desk. He was exhausted and at his limit with dealing with the constant noise of the incessant crowds. He needed some downtime. A quiet space to reflect and get his bearings—while the news of Tucker Paulson's release was promising, what Mrs. Prescott had shared with him had unnerved him.

He plopped himself in his chair, then grabbed the computer mouse and wiggled it, bringing his monitor to life. He looked at the list of newspapers and media outlets that he'd compiled on Monday night. He thought it should be relatively simple work to search online for any dead boys named Mordecai who'd been buried in the area over the years. Even archived data from the pre-internet era that had, at one time, been stored on dusty shelves or on microfiche was now easily accessible. Everything was a click away at his fingertips. Stanton tried to imagine doing his investigative work without the internet. The idea made his head hurt. He had no desire to return to the Stone Age.

He began in broad, sweeping searches on the major search engines. After finding nothing of substance, he then decided he would have to go into each outlet individually and drill down. He started with the biggest one, *The Bellingham Herald*, and began to work his way through their historical records. By six o'clock in the evening, he still had come up with nothing.

He decided to head to Langmaid's Grocery to grab something for supper. As he pulled up in front, he saw Archie Truscott and his mother sitting on the bench outside. Stanton immediately noticed the spectacular woman standing beside them chatting. It was Guylaine Cloutier.

"Evening, folks," Stanton said as he climbed the steps in front of the store.

"Evening," they replied in unison.

"Archie, good to see you. How're you feeling, son?"

"I'm good," Archie replied without looking up. He was already walking down the steps past Stanton to admire the lights on the roof of the police jeep.

"You must be relieved, Mrs. Truscott," Stanton said, standing in front of her and nodding his head toward Archie.

"You have no idea. It's a miracle."

Stanton eyed Guylaine and smiled. He decided to pretend they'd little knowledge of each other. "Well, best be getting inside to pick up some supplies. The trailer's getting a little scarce on food these days. You two have a great evening."

"You as well, officer—and thanks for working so hard on our behalf. We really appreciate it," Mrs. Truscott said.

Stanton smiled and pushed through the screen door, hearing the bell on the door ring above him. The look on Guylaine's face as he walked past had said it all. She followed him with her eyes as if she were trying to tell him something—or perhaps as if she were pleading with him.

To do what? he thought as he picked up a bag of mixed nuts and a large package of beef jerky. He walked toward Mrs. Langmaid, deciding to grab a bag of salt-and-vinegar chips from the shelf in front of the counter. As he reached over and handed her a ten-dollar bill, he all at once understood what Guylaine's look was about. She was attempting to communicate something to him.

Things were happening. He needed to find out about Mordecai.

❖

As expected, the sun had well and truly disappeared behind the thick forest wall by six o'clock, and darkness was descending quickly in the valley. They'd found a relatively flat area for their tent, a few feet from Skagit Creek. It was far enough from the cabin to allow them to at least try to ignore it for a while.

They searched for chunks of driftwood and deadfall and gradually made a substantial pile beside the makeshift fire pit, outlined by a circle of rocks that Bernie had found in the shallow of the creek. Before long, a large flame took the chill out of the evening air.

Jermaine noticed that Pudgy continued to appear agitated and quiet—almost morose. Jermaine emptied the last portion of pasta they had left, dividing it up equally into their bowls. "How you guys doing?"

"Okay," Bernie mumbled in between mouthfuls. "That was pretty freaky today."

Jermaine nodded and looked at Pudgy. Pudgy shrugged his shoulders and stared at the fire. He wasn't eating, and Jermaine wondered if it had all become a bit much for him. He decided to discuss what he'd seen earlier in the day in the cabin. "I'm pretty sure that the bones in the bedroom weren't Mordecai's. Too big. The leg bone beside me was definitely from a tall man. I bet the bones were Bobby's—my mom's high school boyfriend. It makes sense that nobody found him. I mean, who the heck would know this old place existed?"

Bernie nodded. "Yeah, this place is crazy far. Who'd have wanted to live out here, anyway?"

"I'm heading to bed," Pudgy announced suddenly.

Jermaine looked at him with concern. "But it's only—"

Pudgy stood up. "I'm not feeling great. I'm heading in."

"Okay. Let me know if you need anythi—"

"Night, boys."

After Pudgy had entered the tent, Bernie looked over at his friend and whispered, "What do ya think's up with him, Jermaine?"

"Not sure. Let's keep an eye on him tonight."

❖

Guylaine Cloutier lay in bed and looked out her window, watching the clouds moving lazily across the moonlit sky. She knew something was about to happen. She could feel it in her core. It was hard to determine what was about to transpire—but something was brewing. Mordecai was hyperactive.

Even excited.

She knew full well that inevitably, inbetweeners sought peace. They desired closure. But at the same time, over the years, they acquired a taste for killing, so they became conflicted.

The energy Guylaine had been feeling over the last couple of days was growing, and it was one she'd experienced before. Something significant was about to occur, and the proverbial fan was about to be hit.

And there is absolutely nothing I can do about it.

Cob Stanton, the man in charge of the investigation, could go either way. He could tap into his curiosity and do some digging, or he could do what most people did: blow her off as some kind of lunatic. It wouldn't be the first time—indeed, it was the norm. She knew he was suspicious of her and was potentially obstinate, but she might have made him curious enough to have a little look.

Jermaine and the boys were really the only hope, and this gave Guylaine some reason to be optimistic. She saw something in Jermaine's determination and maturity that made her believe he might have a chance at solving the riddle. She also understood too well that there could be sacrifice and a great deal of sorrow still to come if he did. That was always the cost of doing business with inbetweeners.

Guylaine thought back to the first time her mother had let her in on the family secret. She had been eight or nine, living in a small house in the southern Louisiana delta with her mother and her *mawmaw*. For no apparent reason, a man had begun visiting the house each day. He'd come at the oddest hours and always appeared frightened, and the house immediately filled with tension when he arrived.

He would sit with them in chairs in the tiny living room and would speak in anxious, hurried whispers to her mother and grandmother. Guylaine learned that he came from another town miles away.

One evening he had arrived after her bedtime. When she heard him come in, she snuck out of her bedroom and listened to their conversation from the doorway of their tiny kitchen. The strange tales she heard about a wandering, murderous boy and the need for finding a grave terrified her. At one point she had gasped after hearing a particularly graphic description of a killing. Her mother looked up and had come running into the kitchen to find her, then quickly escorted her back to bed.

Later that night, her mother lay with Guylaine, stroking her arm. She slowly began to pass down the history of Guylaine's strange family gifts. Before falling asleep, her fears had mysteriously subsided and she'd become resolute in the desire to embrace her inheritance. She was desperate to understand more.

For the next few years, she immersed herself in honing the skills needed to sense the inbetweeners. And eventually, like generations of her family before her, she dedicated her life to providing a service to those who could not understand.

It had been a long, lonely journey, and there had been a great deal of persecution and suffering along the way. But it was her vocation and she wore it with honor, despite spending most of her life being alone and ostracized by the civilized world.

Guylaine rolled over and closed her eyes. The next few days were going to be critical.

❖

As was becoming the norm, Cob Stanton found sleep impossible to come by, so he stumbled from his cot and made his way to the main room and to his desk. He logged on to his computer, and the warm light of the monitor lit the entire room. He again began to drill down his list of all the newspapers and media outlets that he could find online, ones that would have had any influence in the northwestern part of the state over the years. He could see that he'd almost reached the end of his list, and it wasn't looking promising.

He made his way through two more digital newspaper sites: *The Columbian*, and its reinvention a few years later, *The Olympian*. Neither paper had many references to anyone named Mordecai. "The Daily O," as some people still referred to *The Olympian*, spoke at some length about a Mordecai who "lived out Pulltown way," but he was a farmer in his fifties who claimed to raise "the fastest cows in the West." Unsure why that was a good thing, Stanton moved on to the next paper, a defunct publication called *The Washington Standard* that he found on a general site dedicated to historic American newspapers.

The Washington Standard predated *The Olympian.* A quick search informed him it had only been published twice a week, from 1860 until 1921, and it mostly served the city of Olympia and the surrounding area.

A shot in the dark, for sure, but what the hell, he thought.

He typed in the name Mordecai, and, as usual, he received a few random hits. On the seventh of April in the year 1897, there was mention of a horse named Mordecai that had won the half mile in fifty-one seconds. On January fifth, 1861, there was mention of "Mordecai & Company," for those interested in "fine harnesses and carriage trimming." On and on it went. Each search was becoming more tedious, as the system was designed in such a way that he had to manually type in the individual years rather than being allowed to search through a period of time.

It was when he had just started searching through the individual publications in the year 1876 that his blood felt like it froze in his veins. On the second of four pages, in the June twelfth, 1876 edition, halfway down the page and hidden within a typical list of community announcement items, he saw it.

Tucked between a notification of a landslide on the Northern Pacific Railroad "being removed before train time" and directly above a short piece about $16,000 being "the amount expended for schoolteachers in Walla Walla County during the year 1875," he read:

> Died. Mordecai Leeuwen (10), only son of Ezekiel and Mary Leeuwen. By drowning, on their homestead at Mossy Gulch in Whatcom County.

Stanton stared at his screen without moving. He'd been searching through so many publications with no luck that it took a moment for this discovery to sink in.

He looked at it again. *A dead boy…named Mordecai…at Mossy Gulch…in Whatcom County.*

Heart racing, he looked again at the date of the publication. 1876. He then leaned forward and searched for any mention of Ezekiel and Mary Leeuwen beginning in 1876, then searched backward, a year at a time. Then forward.

It was a painstakingly slow process, but he was on a mission now. Two hours later he had kneaded together the various snippets of information he could find. It was obvious that the Leeuwens were religious folks—zealots, some might say—who had ventured into the wilds to live a utopian life.

When their only son, Mordecai, died, they buried him, packed up, and abandoned their homestead. It was back to the city for the young couple.

Stanton found information about them again in Seattle—helping to form a religious movement called Divine Glossolalia, and later in San Francisco. No mention of either of them could again be found until the announcement of Mary Leeuwen's death of encephalitis in 1886.

Stanton's head was spinning. He looked at his watch. It was three in the morning. He half wished he'd not found anything. He didn't want to give any credence to Guylaine's ridiculous assertions. If he'd found nothing, he could have found other explanations—*eventually*.

But now…it was another ballgame.

Like Guylaine had claimed, a boy named Mordecai had died in the area. He drowned in a place called Mossy Gulch. As much as he didn't want to admit it, Stanton knew in his heart of hearts that he now needed to find the damn grave.

Stanton leaned back in his chair and imagined telling his colleagues about why he wanted to expand his search to include an abandoned cabin in an area called Mossy Gulch. *"Change of plan, boys. We gotta go find a grave in the woods because some dead boy is eating up the locals."*

Oh, this is gonna be ripe.

❖

It was dark. Very dark.

The fire had long since died out, and try as they might, both Bernie and Jermaine failed to stay awake long enough to keep an eye on their friend. Sleep had eventually taken over the exhausted boys.

It was the scream that woke them. It took them both a split second to get their bearings.

An empty sleeping bag. An open tent zipper.

Water splashing.

Someone calling for help.

It was Pudgy's voice.

More water splashing.

"No!"

Horrific screams of pain.

Jermaine grabbed his flashlight and bolted from the tent, stumbling in the direction of Pudgy's screams. He was in the creek.

Bernie followed close behind, watching as Jermaine shone his flashlight toward the commotion. They both saw it at the same time—Pudgy being pulled into the middle of the creek by something just beneath the surface. Only Pudgy's head was still above water, and he looked back at Bernie and Jermaine with terror in his eyes.

The water around Pudgy was frothing. Then, in an instant, he was pulled below the surface. Something then began dragging him at an impossible speed against the current, away from Jermaine and Bernie. A bulge of water moved rapidly upstream, like something being pulled underwater behind a ski boat. After nearly twenty feet, it rounded a natural turn in the creek and disappeared into the night.

Silence.

"Pudgy!" Jermaine and Bernie both screamed, jumping into the water and attempting to follow.

Bernie tried to keep up, but after a few steps, he tripped and fell facedown in the water. By the time he managed to get back to his feet and steady himself against the swift current, Jermaine was already twenty-five feet ahead of him and awkwardly propelling himself forward in the waist-deep water. Bernie could see his friend's flashlight beam moving side to side as he worked his way upstream in the middle of the creek. "Jermaine, wait up!" Bernie screamed.

Chapter Fifteen

At first light, Cob Stanton put his coffeepot on, got dressed, then carried a steaming mug out the front door of his trailer. It was a misty morning, and it looked like it could rain. He offered a cursory wave to the two security men standing beside the trailer.

"Quiet night?"

One of the men gave a thumbs-up. The other one said, "Not a peep, sir."

Stanton nodded and walked down to the edge of the forest where the pavement ended. He took a long, deep breath, inhaling the damp air, then sipped his coffee. Stanton was trying to strategize his next move. Whatever actions he undertook over the next few hours would have serious consequences on many levels. Not the least of which was his future as an officer of the law.

Behind him, he heard a car pull up and stop. He turned and saw it was Officers Thompson and Plant. Only Thompson got out and walked over toward him.

"Morning," Thompson said. He smiled and looked out to the woods where Stanton was staring. "Up early," he observed. "Whatcha doing?"

"Just thinking," Stanton replied. "What brings you down here so early?"

"Mossy Gulch."

Stanton didn't respond, but he felt his heart skip a beat in his chest. He looked over at the handsome young man, waiting for him to continue.

"Found it pretty easily on Google. It's a valley about twenty or thirty miles from here. Not much there but a big creek. Also asked a few of the locals; they couldn't tell me much."

"I see."

"One of them said he thought there might be an old hunter's cabin out that way or something, but he'd never been."

Stanton turned and looked back at the woods. His next move could be his last. After a moment, he started walking to his trailer, leaving Thompson standing on his own.

Time to throw some rocks at the hornets' nest.

❖

Jermaine and Bernie had spent most of the night searching for Pudgy in and around the creek. By morning they had returned to their tent, exhausted and despondent. Neither of them had any more tears to shed. The sadness they felt was profound.

Both boys carried a tremendous amount of guilt. They deduced that when Jermaine had pushed down the bedroom door in the cabin, Pudgy had been so worried that he'd run to the side of the cabin to try to look through the window. Even though he had only been alone for a brief moment, that was obviously all that was needed. They both agreed that Pudgy had been acting differently from that point on. The boys figured he must have encountered the Follower.

Mordecai.

It was impossibly hard for either of them to even think about heading back to the cabin, but they also knew they had no other choice. They had no more food and they were at the end of their physical and mental tethers. They had to find the grave today.

They didn't bother packing anything up.

❖

Guylaine was just leaving for a morning walk when she saw his police jeep parked across the street. She could see Cob Stanton sitting in the driver's seat with his sunglasses on and sucking on the wad of chewing tobacco packed against his cheek. He was looking her way. It was obvious he was waiting for her.

She walked across the street to the vehicle and smiled. "Good morning, officer. What brings you to this fine part of town?"

Stanton didn't return the smile. "Looks like it may rain today. You need a ride anywhere?"

Guylaine shook her head. "Sounds like you need to talk."

"Yup."

"Well, maybe you want to walk with me a bit."

"Nope, tried that before. Not my thing."

Guylaine moved closer until she was standing directly beside the jeep. "I can see you know something, *mon ami*," she stated emphatically.

Stanton nodded and looked away from Guylaine and out the front windshield. "Found some stuff out that…shall I say, might corroborate your crazy story."

"I see."

"Think I know where the cabin is. If those boys had it in their minds to go after him, it's probably there."

Guylaine crossed her arms in front of her. "I'm impressed."

"You know how bloody ridiculous this all sounds?"

"I do. I've been down this road before, remember?" She could tell he wanted validation before he made his difficult decision. "How far away is this place?"

"It's far enough and isolated enough that it means bringing in air support."

"What are you going to tell them?"

"As little as possible," Stanton replied, looking back up at Guylaine. "Anyway, thought you should know. That's all."

Guylaine slowly reached out and touched his shoulder. "Good luck. Acting quickly is important. Mordecai is extremely agitated."

Stanton moved his chewing tobacco to the other side of his mouth and nodded. He started his car, and Guylaine backed away. It was time to radio in a new lead.

❖

The cabin appeared as they had left it the day before—a small, dilapidated structure on the edge of a thick cedar forest. By the time they reached it, the first few raindrops had begun to fall.

"We should head this way first," Jermaine said, pointing to his right. He was now holding Pudgy's hunting knife. "This is the only area we didn't cover yesterday."

Bernie nodded, holding his own knife in a tight fist.

After five minutes, Jermaine suddenly stopped and again pointed. "Hey, look." He was staring at a small structure to his right.

Bernie quickly moved beside him and saw what appeared to be the remnants of an old well. The handle was long gone, but the pulley system still seemed to be intact, and a thick rope was attached to it and descended into the hole. Bernie looked back at the cabin; it was still visible through the clearing. He guessed they were standing on the remains of a path through the forest. He looked beyond the well, and the path appeared to continue. "Let's keep going that way," he suggested.

Jermaine nodded. As he turned and began to walk, something on the ground caught his eye. "Bernie," Jermaine whispered.

"What?"

"Look."

Bernie looked to the forest floor. He could see something white gleaming from the otherwise dark shadows of the forest floor. It was a necklace.

A puka shell necklace.

Duncan's puka shell necklace.

Both boys looked at each other, then instantly scanned the forest on either side of them. Jermaine picked up the necklace and tucked it into his front pocket. Bernie's eyes quickly filled with tears, so Jermaine put his arm around him and hugged him close. He could feel his own warm tears streaming down his cheeks. "It's okay, buddy. It's okay."

Gradually they both agreed that it was best to continue. A few minutes later, they came upon a small opening. The rain was falling harder now, and the noise of it hitting the vegetation on the forest floor was loud and unnerving. They moved slowly into the clearing and simultaneously stopped. They both saw it at the same time.

❖

Cob Stanton stood outside the trailer. He held his radio in one hand and rested the other on his hip holster. The sheriff's office would coordinate the search and rescue operation. The local SAR team was being assembled and, weather permitting, would be airborne in twenty minutes. Coordinates had been relayed along with a detailed plan of where the team would be dropped from the helicopter.

The sheriff didn't question Stanton's lead. Everyone knew he was a no-nonsense man who wouldn't make such a request if he wasn't positive that the boys were in the area known as Mossy Gulch. But it did catch him off guard when Stanton had then requested armed escort to head in first.

"Excuse me?"

"A possible abduction. Most likely armed and dangerous," Stanton had lied. Dangerous, yes, but *armed* was a stretch—unless a human-eating zombie-boy was technically considered armed.

Like a wildfire burning out of control, the news of a change of location of the search soon whipped through the streets of Providence. Apparently new evidence had been found that suggested the missing boys were miles away from where everyone had previously been looking. The Maclarens, Prescotts, Cartwrights, and Murtlands were all asked to stay close to home and wait for news. Officer Thompson had promised to let them know as soon as he heard anything. Nerves were frayed, and everyone's patience had reached a boiling point.

Stanton looked down at the pavement below him. He could see the outline of the hopscotch court where this entire nightmare had begun. *Well, Becky, hopefully justice is coming your way.*

He then glanced up Birch Street and noticed someone sitting in the rain in a patch of grass halfway up on the right. It was Guylaine Cloutier. Stanton nodded knowingly, then headed toward his trailer.

❖

The wooden cross was tipped to one side but still intact. It had been nailed together in the middle with three large rusty nails. The words that once had been written on the wood had faded to the point that they were illegible.

Below it, freshly disturbed black soil.

"The grave," Bernie whispered, his words almost lost in the din of rain pounding down around them.

Bernie and Jermaine inched closer. They both held their knives out in front of them.

Surrounding the grave on either side and glaring against the dark green forest were what appeared to be piles of white bones. Looking beyond the grave, as far as they could see, they could make out similar white bones scattered throughout the woods. They were mostly animal bones, but it was clear that bits of human bones were also among the skeletal remains—including not a few skulls.

Neither boy had to say it, but they were both thinking the exact same thing. Some of the bones surrounding them most likely belonged to Duncan, Lenny, and even Pudgy. Jermaine unconsciously reached down and felt for Duncan's puka necklace in his front pocket.

Bernie began to slowly lean forward. At first, he began to heave, and then without warning, he purged himself violently, spraying the ferns beside him. Jermaine felt like doing likewise—until he thought he heard a faint, haunting giggle. It seemed to be very close. He lifted his head toward the cross. Mordecai was standing five feet behind it in the pouring rain, staring at him.

He was smiling.

"Bernie, look up," Jermaine whispered.

"Huh?"

"Look up," he repeated louder.

Bernie wiped his mouth with his wrist and looked up toward the grave. The heavy droplets of water bounced off Mordecai's head. His unblinking eyes were focused in on them, and his smile appeared to be growing wider.

"What do we do?" Bernie asked meekly without taking his eyes off the boy. He raised his knife in front of him again, pointing it in Mordecai's direction.

Jermaine put his arm around Bernie's shoulder and squeezed him close, raising his own knife in the air. He was unsure of their next move.

Then, as suddenly as he had appeared, Mordecai vanished into the surrounding foliage. The only movement they could see was from the rain hitting and bouncing off the dense vegetation where he'd been standing.

"Holy moly!" Bernie exclaimed, slowly exhaling.

"We need to find his bones." Jermaine had already determined they needed to work quickly.

Bernie inspected the area around the grave. Finding the boy's bones seemed an impossible task. "But look at all of them. How do we know which ones are his?"

Jermaine examined the dark soil. The freshly turned earth was muddy from the heavy rain. "Let's start there," he said softly, pointing in front of him. "Find something to help us dig."

Bernie didn't move at first. He was frozen with fear and shaken to his core. The thought of digging up the grave of a boy who had just been standing there and looking at them was almost too much to comprehend.

"Hurry up, Bernie." Jermaine was already scouring the area for a suitable implement. He suddenly paused over a femur of an elk or large deer. He picked it up and returned to the grave and immediately began using it to claw away at the earth. Large chunks of mud began to fly in the air.

Jermaine's determination woke something up in Bernie. He hurried to Jermaine's side, threw his knife to the ground, dropped on all fours, and began frantically pulling the dank, heavy dirt back behind him. All the while, both of them scanned the surrounding woods for any sign of Mordecai.

After forty minutes of exhausting digging and probing for bones beneath them, Jermaine decided it was time for a rest. They were both panting heavily from the exertion. Jermaine peered into the hole. He estimated it was close to four feet deep, and there was no sign of any bones. They had now begun to hit more roots, solid clay, and bedrock.

Jermaine took a deep breath and looked at Bernie. Then he slowly stood up. "I think we need to go back to the creek."

"The creek? Why?" Bernie could hardly stand; his knees were shaking wildly. He picked up his knife from beside the grave and steadied himself by leaning on Jermaine's shoulder.

"I've been thinking about this for a while. Remember how every time we've seen him, he was soaking wet? Today doesn't count because it's raining. But even my mom had said that her hunter boyfriend had described the boy being soaking wet. Like he'd been swimming or in the water or something."

Bernie nodded. It was true—Mordecai had always appeared wet every time they'd seen him.

"My bet is the kid drowned in the creek. If he did, maybe that's the clue."

Bernie thought it was a reasonable argument. Besides, he was more than happy to leave the area. "Okay."

Jermaine turned and began walking. Bernie was about to follow but paused. "Hold on."

Jermaine halted in his tracks and looked back at Bernie, who was pointing further down the path. "What?"

"It could also be the water well. The path goes right past it; he could have drowned there. We could look there first."

Jermaine nodded. It was worth checking it out on the way to the creek. "Good idea," Jermaine agreed.

A few minutes later, they were standing by the old well. The opening was no more than three and a half feet wide. Jermaine thought that a child could certainly have fallen in and drowned. He also noticed another thing: only one of them could possibly fit inside that well. After Bernie's sinkhole experience, there was no way he was going to let his friend go down.

As if reading his mind, Bernie leaned over to peer down the narrow opening. “It’s gotta be me that goes down there. You’re too fat.”

Jermaine moved beside him. “No way, Bernie. You’ve had enough of holes lately.”

“No other choice. Besides, I can climb down and up this rope on my own as long as it’s secured.”

The rope was thick, but it was obviously old and weathered. There was no telling how reliable it was. “Let’s check out how long it is first,” Jermaine offered. “We can pull it up and see what we’re dealing with.”

Bernie nodded, and together they began pulling the rope through the pulley. There was a loop at the end with a rusted metal hook; originally a bucket would have been attached to it for drawing water.

They both looked at the length of rope and determined it to be about thirty feet long. “Plenty long enough,” Bernie guessed. Neither of them knew how deep the well was. He seemed buoyed by the opportunity—taking control of the situation. He tied the other end of the rope around a sturdy sapling directly beside the well. He then placed the rope back through the pulley and lowered it into the darkness.

"Give me your flashlight," Bernie demanded. Jermaine knew too well that when Bernie had something on his mind that he wanted to accomplish, there was little chance of convincing him otherwise. Much like when his father told him he hadn't earned the right to have a new bicycle. Within a few weeks he had created his own. His agency and stubborn determination were unrivaled.

Jermaine handed him his small flashlight and watched Bernie click it on, put it into his mouth, then hoist himself up onto the stone edge of the well. Without hesitating, he reached over and grabbed the rope and gave it a couple of hefty yanks to test the soundness of his knot and to ensure it was taut enough to hold him.

They both took one last look around to confirm they were alone. "I won't be long," Bernie said. Jermaine was about to ask him to rethink his plan when Bernie disappeared over the edge and began descending, hand over hand, until Jermaine could see nothing but the beam of the light moving further down the shaft, illuminating the dark wall as he went.

Jermaine took another brief glance around him. The rain was not letting up, and it was impossible to see anything beyond a few feet. He knew he was vulnerable to Mordecai now that he was alone. "Whatcha see?" he hollered down the well.

"Almost at the bottom. Water below me," Bernie replied. His voice sounded distant.

Jermaine looked at the rope tied around the sapling. The tree shimmied each time Bernie shifted his body further down the rope.

It seemed like an eternity, but finally Bernie called out. "At the bottom. About two feet of water down here. Muddy as all get-out," he yelled from below.

The rope slackened, and Jermaine peered down the shaft. He could see the light moving and reflecting off water. Bernie was searching the bottom of the well. "What do you see?"

"Just feeling around in the water and muck. Don't see anything."

Jermaine never ceased to be amazed at the courage of his friend. *As if looking for bones in a dark well was something he did every day.*

"Nothing here."

"Okay, hurry up and get outta there."

"Hey, Jermaine?"

Jermaine recognized the tone, and despite their dire situation, he smiled. "Let me guess, you gotta crap something chronic?"

"You got it! On my way up."

Jermaine could see the beam of the flashlight facing sideways again and assumed it was back in Bernie's mouth. Much to Jermaine's relief, it only took a minute before Bernie surfaced over the edge of the well. His muddy, wet clothes clung to his body. Bernie handed Jermaine the flashlight and stood up. "We better check the creek."

Both boys quickly turned and ran back down the path, past the cabin and to the creek's edge. The rain was coming down even harder now, and when they arrived, the surface of the water was dancing with the heavy droplets.

❖

Stanton turned up his radio so he could hear it over the rain pounding on the roof of his trailer. The last report he'd had was that despite the weather, the first of three teams was preparing to depart the Pulltown area and make its way by helicopter to an area called Mossy Gulch. The first two helicopters were each holding six Special Weapons and Tactics members. If there was an armed kidnapper, they would take him out first. The five-member team inside the third helicopter was part of the SAR unit and would only take off after being informed it was safe to do so.

He looked at his watch. It was almost noon. The first two SWAT helicopters would be taking off in five minutes. Just under thirty minutes later, they would begin their descent into Mossy Gulch—landing beside each other on the shore of the shallow creek, a hundred feet from the hunter's cabin.

Stanton had a knot in his stomach. If they failed to find anyone or any evidence that the boys had been there, he would have a whole heap of explaining to do. This was not a cheap operation, and it demanded a whole series of permissions from many levels above him. Contrarily, if they did find the boys, and if they did actually encounter Mordecai, he may have even more to deal with. Either way, there would be hard questions to answer—not the least of which was why he ended up following the advice of a crazy woman dressed like a hippie.

Stanton tucked some Red Man into his mouth, sank into his chair, and tried to fight back the indigestion. It was going to be a bitch of a day.

❖

By the time they had searched two hundred feet of shoreline on both sides of Skagit Creek heading east, the rain had eased off. It was hard going, as they wanted to check each nook and cranny along the shore—basically any place where a body might have washed up, particularly if the water had been running high during flood season or winter.

Jermaine suggested that they cross the creek again and work their way west, past the cabin. After twenty minutes, they had passed their campsite. They were exhausted, and Jermaine announced that they should sit for a minute on a log that was sticking out toward the creek.

Neither boy said a word. They knew how hopeless it was attempting to find the remnants of somebody's bones near a riverbed that experienced floods almost annually. They also knew that without finding Mordecai's bones, they had no choice but to make a very tough decision. Bernie leaned forward and rested his hands on his knees. He was breathing heavily and close to tears. He looked over at his friend. A wave of emotion immediately rolled over him as he realized that it was only him and Jermaine left. The others in the clan were gone now—Duncan, Lenny, and Pudgy. Jermaine Prescott was the only friend he had left in the entire world.

It was unimaginable.

Jermaine's eyes were brimming with tears as well. Bernie could see he was almost done; there was barely anything left in the tank. The rain had let up, but the air was cool, and they were soaking wet and shivering. Bernie understood that it was now or never. It was the defining moment.

"Life can be tough, but you have to be stronger," Bernie's father always said. He understood that it was his dad's way of making sure that nobody would get the better of him. Everything about the way his father dealt with him seemed designed to make Bernie capable of handling life's disappointments. "Chin up. Don't be a cry baby, kid," he'd say if Bernie ever fell or bumped his head. "Suck it up, princess," was his response to any disappointment. "Stiff upper lip, boy," if he ever felt sad.

Preparing Bernie for life's pitfalls seemed to have been his father's entire modus operandi. Out of all of life's lessons, being strong and brave were the only ones that mattered. It was how you faced these pitfalls that declared your worth as a human. "Are you a man or a mouse?" he'd yell if Bernie ever gave up at something. "How do you expect to have any success in life if you can't handle the tough things? Go big or go home, son."

Jermaine got up from the log. "Come on, Bernie. Let's get going. We can go another few hundred feet, then cross over and make our way back," Jermaine said, looking at his friend. "Follow close behind me, okay?"

Bernie nodded vacantly and watched as Jermaine turned and continued walking west in the shallow part of the creek adjacent to the shoreline.

But Bernie didn't follow. He knew what he had to do.

Bernie waited until Jermaine was ten feet away; then, slowly at first, he began to trot in the opposite direction. After taking a quick look over his shoulder to ensure Jermaine hadn't noticed, he began to sprint as fast as he could back in the direction of the cabin. He knew it was a gamble, as either of them could be taken at any moment by Mordecai.

But he also knew there was no other option.

❖

The knock on the door startled him. "Who is it?"

"Officer Thompson, sir."

Stanton had been so focused on the updates, he hadn't even noticed the rain had stopped pounding on the roof of the trailer. "It's open."

Thompson looked anxious. So many people had invested so much in this operation, he could tell Thompson simply wanted to know if there was any news. "Choppers should be landing in about ten minutes. Weather looks good," Stanton offered.

Douglas Thompson looked relieved. "Do you mind if I wait here with you?"

Stanton pointed to the chair by the desk. As Thompson was about to sit down, there was another knock on the door. "Is this a goddamn party I'm hosting? It's open," Stanton hollered at the door.

This time it was Thompson's partner, Ian Plant. "Just want to know if there's been—"

"Jesus. Come in and park it."

The radio crackled to life again. "Zulu Victor Lima One. Eight minutes until descent. Altitude six hundred fifty. Copy, over."

"Roger that, Zulu Victor Lima Two. Over." It was the second helicopter replying.

Officer Plant stepped into the room, closed the door behind him, and walked over to the chair beside his partner and sat down. The tension in the air was thick. Even Stanton looked stressed—something neither of them had seen previously. Stubborn—yes. Obstinate and rude—absolutely. But never stressed.

"Zulu Victor Lima One. Seven minutes until descent. Altitude five hundred and twenty. Copy, over."

Stanton opened up his pouch of chewing tobacco and grabbed a wad, packing it deep into the side of his mouth. He leaned forward on his desk, closed his eyes, and began rubbing his temples. He thought of Guylaine Cloutier sitting halfway up Birch Street and tried to work out how he'd gotten himself into this mess in the first place.

❖

By the time he had passed by the front of the cabin, he was sucking for air so hard that he was dizzy and almost near the point of passing out. The adrenaline kept him moving—but the terror and anticipation of what was coming next caused his mind to swirl. His head was pounding, but he forced himself to keep pushing forward—urging his legs to keep going, drawing on every ounce of energy he had left.

As he ran through the thick forest, he thought he could hear some of the voices of his fallen friends urging him on through the gnarly undergrowth. *Go on, Bernie. You can do it!* Was it Lenny? Duncan, maybe?

Bernie. You can do it. Pudgy, perhaps?

He pushed on, and after a few feet he found the old well and briefly stopped to glance back to make sure Jermaine hadn't followed him.

He was alone. But he knew it wouldn't be long before Jermaine would come looking for him. Ahead he could see the opening in the forest.

When he finally reached the grave, he noticed the hole he had dug with Jermaine had disappeared. Once again there was a mound of fresh dirt. He immediately collapsed on top of the pungent, muddy soil. He gasped for air, and at the same time, he began to cry. Lying on top of the grave, his chest heaving, he then began wailing like he had never done before.

You can do it, Bernie. The voices of his friends called to him.

When he finally caught his breath, he slowly opened his eyes and gradually got to his knees.

Go on, Bernie.

He stared at the lopsided cross in front of him.

You can do it, Bernie.

He then took the hunting knife that he'd been carrying and, with both hands, pressed it against his throat—feeling its cold metal on his skin.

Go on, Bernie.

Bernie noticed a slight movement behind the cross. Mordecai slowly emerged from the forest and began walking toward him. Bernie watched as he moved closer. His smile appeared wider than before, his hollow eyes anticipatory. Bernie closed his eyes again.

"Bernie! Bernie!" It was Jermaine, screaming from somewhere behind him. He was closing in on him fast. "No, Bernie!"

Bernie squeezed his hands tighter around the handle of the knife.

Go on, Bernie.

A stream of tears worked its way through the mud on his cheeks.

Do it now, Bernie.

He could feel the pulse in his neck pounding against the cold blade of the hunting knife. He pressed it harder against his throat.

We love you, Bernie.

Epilogue

He met her on the front steps of Patty's Five and Dime Café. Her bus would be arriving in ten minutes. Her single green suitcase rested beside her, and she watched as he pulled up in front of the steps. He turned off the jeep and got out. He paused to stretch his back before speaking.

"Time for a coffee?"

"I don't drink coffee, remember?"

"Everyone drinks coffee." Stanton smiled. "How about a soda?"

"I'm good. No time. We can chat here." She smiled warmly. "Nice of you to drive out this way. How'd you find me?"

"The Breaches said you caught a cab to the bus stop. I used my detective skills to find the only bus stop in the vicinity. That's what cops do." Stanton shrugged and moved toward the steps where she was standing. "Anyway, I came here to thank you."

"Thank me for what?" Guylaine replied. "There have been too many deaths here. There's so much grieving. I only wish I could have done more."

Stanton nodded and looked at the woman standing on the steps. The hem of her cardigan and the many colorful scarves that encircled her neck fluttered in the slight breeze. *She was right all along*, he thought. "There could have been more."

"What did they find there?"

Stanton looked around. They were alone. "One of the boys, Bernie Maclaren, was found lying dead on an overgrown grave. Looked as if he took his own life. And, like you predicted, it seems the sacrifice worked. They found Jermaine by the creek in front of the cabin. He was inconsolable. He kept mentioning Bernie and all the bones all over the place. His friends' bones."

"But you found nothing." It wasn't a question. She knew they wouldn't have found a thing.

Stanton shook his head.

"It's always that way. Everything returns to dust. Like it should. Balance is restored."

"Doesn't much help to bring closure to families."

"Never does."

Stanton rubbed his chin, looking out at the field across the road. Guylaine Cloutier was perhaps the most intriguing woman he'd ever met. "Don't you ever get tired of this? I mean, seeing all the death and sadness?"

Guylaine smiled. "I'm always tired of it. But I have no choice. As I told you. It's in my blood—it's my calling."

Stanton chuckled. "That and all that voodoo witchy crap," he teased.

"I'm a harbinger, soothsayer, fortune teller, clairvoyant, and psychic. I read tarot, palms, horoscopes, and tea leaves. I can be contracted for séance and spirit board services. Some call me a witch doctor, but I prefer healer, and I'm at your service!"

Stanton smiled. "You may be crazy, but you're pretty darn good at being nuts."

"Why, thank you, officer. I've never met a cop that gave me a compliment before."

The bus approached. It was early. Guylaine watched a plume of dust rise up behind it as it pulled off the paved road. "So, when are you heading out? I expect you've had it with small-town life."

"Soon as we tie things up here. There'll be lots of explaining to do about how I knew about Mossy Gulch. I'll just pretend that I'm that good at what I do." Stanton reached down to pick up Guylaine's suitcase. "You heading to Louisiana?"

Guylaine followed him down the steps. "Eventually. There's been some chatter in Wisconsin that I'm keeping tabs on. Might be some activity there."

The bus pulled up in front of the coffee shop, and the loud sound of the air brakes releasing announced its arrival. The driver got out and nodded at both of them. He took the luggage from Stanton and opened the cargo door beneath the windows, shoving the suitcase in alongside the others.

Stanton watched him head back to the entrance of the bus and then turned again to Guylaine. "Don't suppose you'll be keeping in touch. Though it might be nice…you know, be good to hear how you're doing," he said awkwardly, reaching into his pocket and pulling out a pack of Red Man.

Guylaine smiled and followed the driver up the steps of the bus, then stopped and turned around to face Stanton. "Who knows, I just might do that," she said, winking cheekily. "Besides, I've always had a thing for cops." She then blew him a dramatic kiss and turned and boarded the bus.

Stanton backed away as the bus pulled onto the highway. He waited, watching it disappear down the only road leading to Pulltown. He then looked at the bag of chewing tobacco in his hand, and as he walked by Patty's Five and Dime Café, he tossed it into the garbage container beside the steps and ambled toward his jeep.

❖

Six Months Later

Jermaine paused at the top of Birch Street and carefully dismounted his bike. It was the first time that he'd looked down the cul-de-sac since his return to Providence so many months ago. Everything appeared as it had been before the craziness had begun—before so many lives had been shattered.

All the equipment and fencing were now gone, as was the trailer, and the throngs of people and vehicles that had once crammed into the dead-end street. Now all was quiet and empty. Once again—it was simply an unused street surrounded by trees.

The weather was cold now, and thick, dark clouds hung just above the tree line. The winter months in the Pacific Northwest were always damp and gray. Today was no exception. Jermaine reluctantly walked his bike down the middle of the street toward the bottom where the forest met the road. He quickly glanced at the grass to his left where Guylaine Cloutier had first told him about Mordecai and the grave.

At the end of Birch Street, Jermaine could just make out the faint outline of the hopscotch court; he gently lay his bike down on top of it and walked toward the edge of the road. It seemed another lifetime ago that he and the clan had been in this exact spot, beginning their search for Pickle Town.

Jermaine glanced up at the trees as they swayed in the breeze and, for a moment, thought—perhaps hoped—that it all was simply a dream. Maybe his friends were back in their homes waiting for him—ready for him to plan a meeting at Base Camp.

He breathed in deeply and listened—half expecting to hear his absent friends' voices echoing from within the deep forest. But all he heard was the whisper of the cedar boughs brushing against each other, and the wind whooshing down from the dark canopy above and from within the thick forest in front of him.

Jermaine shivered, then slowly turned and again mounted his bike. He paused briefly for one last look at the foreboding trees. Then he heard something that he'd not heard since he was much younger. A couple of ravens were calling to each other from the treetops high above him. Life had returned to the forest surrounding Birch Street.

He quickly pedaled back up the hill toward the main road and away from the forest and all its memories. A few minutes later, he was crossing Farmer Granger's empty cornfield. The cold wind whipped across the barren landscape and met him head on. He leaned into the stiff breeze and navigated the bumps across the muddy field. Base Camp sat like a welcoming beacon at the far side of the desolate field. As he pedaled, Jermaine was immediately overcome with emotion, and he fought hard to suppress the tears.

Once he reached Base Camp, Jermaine slowly dismounted his bike, leaned it against the old wooden wall of the shed, and pushed through the front door—the wind slammed it shut behind him, startling him.

It was dark and even colder inside—but he was home.

Instinctively, Jermaine walked over to the desk, pulled out one of the rusted lighters from the desk drawer, and, after a few tries, lit the single candle still standing like a sentry in the middle. He then looked back in the drawer and pulled out four more candles and lit them all, lining them up in a row in front of his candle.

Jermaine then looked around the old shed. The five milk crates on the floor sat where they had left them after their final meeting. Pudgy's Ouija board was still leaning up against the wall—its planchette beside it. Jermaine slowly dragged his milk crate up near the desk and sat down.

Outside he could hear the wind picking up, and it was now howling over the roof of the shed and whistling through the many cracks and holes of the wooden walls. Jermaine wrapped his coat tightly around him and moved closer to the five candles.

The five little monkeys, as his mother called them.

The best friends he would ever have.

Jermaine closed his eyes. He wanted to spend some time imagining each of his friends sitting there with him. When he was ready, he opened his eyes, still concentrating on feeling their presence, and again stared at the flickering flames of the five candles. Gradually the sound of the wind around him seemed to fade away, and he could almost believe they were there with him.

One by one, he attempted to feel their presence.

He stared at the first candle in the row. He could clearly envisage Lenny Cartwright's face. Handsome and carefree—thick hair blowing in the breeze as he dismounted his bike, laughing happily as he watched it careen away from him. Jermaine had always envied Lenny. He was a wild one, yet deeply compassionate and loyal beyond belief.

Jermaine could still see him teasing the others in the clan. He could hear him telling Pudgy to hurry up and finish his stupid stories and to stop being so dramatic. Jermaine missed his strength and his confidence. He missed how the clan felt protected whenever Lenny was with them. He remembered the horror he felt as he watched him being dragged into the trees by Mordecai—never to be seen again.

Jermaine then reached into his front pocket and pulled out Duncan's puka shell necklace that he'd found near the water well behind the hunter's cabin. He laid it on the desk in front of him. The white shells glistened in the candlelight.

Jermaine waited until he could feel Duncan Simpson's presence. He smiled as he envisaged Duncan's large head on his tall, skinny body. He could just make out his goofy voice and wacky sense of humor as he told yet another dumb joke. Jermaine then grinned, imagining Duncan betting the others that he could explode a firecracker from any part of his body. "Just pick one," he would yell. "Your butt," Pudgy would holler back at him.

Challenge accepted.

Then there was Pudgy Murtland. Jermaine stared at the third candle until he could see and feel Pudgy sitting right there beside him in Base Camp—bits of licorice sticking out of the front pocket of his silver basketball shorts hiked up high on his waist and his face stuck in a Cosmic Ghost Rider comic. He was so old-school.

Jermaine recalled the sheer panic and fear in Pudgy's eyes as he disappeared down the creek. Pudgy was the most loyal, joyous, and empathetic member of the clan. There wasn't a thing he wouldn't have done for his four best friends. In many ways, Pudgy had been the glue that held them all together.

Jermaine slowly moved his eyes to the last candle in the row. He thought of his oldest and dearest friend, Bernie "Big Balls" Maclaren. He'd first met Bernie when he was a baby, or so he was told by his mom, and until now, he had never known life without him. He could still hear Bernie's deep voice calling him by his real name: Jermaine. He loved it when Bernie was excited, and his voice would crackle and slide between octaves. How he yelled, "Holy moly" whenever he was gobsmacked by something.

He then thought of the supreme sacrifice Bernie had made at Mossy Gulch just before he could reach him. How the policemen had called it a tragic suicide. Jermaine knew that no one would ever know that Bernie Maclaren was a hero. The bravest and truest of them all.

Jermaine remembered how he'd been relentlessly questioned by the police about why Bernie had killed himself and what he knew about the disappearances of Pudgy Murtland and Lenny Cartwright. Jermaine had been silent. They got nothing from him. They would call it Post-Traumatic Stress Disorder. They would realize that the incomprehensible trauma Jermaine had experienced would most likely never allow them to know the entire truth.

Jermaine knew they would never know. They couldn't.

Bernie was as honest as the day was long. He remembered Bernie's resolute, unwavering loyalty, and, with his green helmet sitting atop his head, coming up with silly lines like: "I gotta crap somethin' chronic!" But most of all, Jermaine remembered Bernie's unceasing desire to win his father's approval, though never receiving it. *Ever.*

Bernie would have been dumbfounded to have witnessed his father at the funeral held to celebrate his life. A shell of a man, bent over in a ball, wailing inconsolably—utterly overcome by grief. It was as clear as day to

Jermaine that, at that moment, Bernie's dad must have terribly regretted having never told his boy that he loved him and that he was proud of him.

Jermaine wanted to believe that Bernie had somehow looked down at the service and had smiled.

Jermaine watched as the shadows of the flickering flames danced along the shed walls. He knew he would never again return to Base Camp. *All for one, and one for all*, he thought as he stood up. He could still hear the gusty wind humming through the cedar trees high above him. He leaned over and blew out the candles and turned to leave.

So shall it ever be.

Acknowledgements

To my daughter Emily for coaxing me to the finish line. To my beta readers Rick Rodrigues and Brian Carr, and to my editor, Kate Schomaker—much appreciation for your feedback, insight, and honesty. To that glorious well-worn length of comfort where *Five Little Monkeys* began and ended: my couch. What started out as a short story gradually inched itself into a novel. *Five Little Monkeys,* like my couch, was a welcome escape from the bizarre *'truth-is-stranger-than-fiction'* world of 2020. Finally, a shout-out to my 90-year old, Auntie Louis in Ohio who told me that there was too much cursing in my first book. I hope this one meets with her approval.

ABOUT THE AUTHOR

C.W. Johnston resides on Vancouver Island in British Columbia, Canada. He has a BA (McMaster University), and a B.Ed. and M.Div. (University of Toronto) and has worked in education most of his life. He blogs and posts updates on his website **www.cwjohnston.com**. You can find him tweeting as **@Real_CWJohnston** or taking pictures on Instagram at **c.w.johnston**. You can also visit his official Facebook page at **@cwjohnston60**

Also by C. W. JOHNSTON

FIGMENT (2020)

He loves getting away from civilization. Now he might be the only person who can save it…

Professor Tyler Stevens believes there's nothing like fresh mountain air to clear the mind. But on a weekend trip in the rugged Montana countryside with zero cell phone service, he's shocked then terrified by a cascade of ominous texts. Struggling to comprehend the surreal messages, he stumbles into a world where delusion and horrific realities swirl.

Fearing he may have lost his sanity, he ventures deeper into the dark futurescape and makes a shocking discovery. To prevent the apocalypse, he must commit cold-blooded murder…

Has the professor's isolation driven him crazy, or is he destined to rescue humanity?

Figment is a pulse-pounding psychological thriller. If you like edge-of-your-seat action, determined heroes, and harrowing twists and turns, then you'll love C. W. Johnston's mind-bending novel.

Buy *Figment* to piece together the truth today! Available on Amazon and Kindle.

Made in the USA
Monee, IL
28 November 2020

49941308R00223